CW00498909

To Liz,
for her unwavering support

Imagine having all the peace you could dream of,
but no freedom of choice

Visit the Unity website: **www.unitystory.com**

UNITY

By
Mike Bodnar

Original characters and original storyline © Mike Bodnar, 2023
Cover design by Mike Bodnar

ISBN: 9798387556555
Imprint: Independently published

DISCLAIMER

Unity is a work of 'fan fiction' written by Mike Bodnar.

While most of the characters and the majority of the storyline have been originated by me, I do not claim ownership of the plot of *The Prisoner* (on which this work is based) nor any of the television episodes referred to in this work.

The Prisoner himself, the various characters who play the role of 'Number Two,' and most of the action that takes place in 'The Village' are characters and plots created by Patrick McGoohan, George Markstein, and various other scriptwriters. I do not claim ownership over their creations, nor any of the original material now owned by ITV.

My part of the story is made up and is therefore not part of the original property. Some of the characters are real; the others are purely fictional. Any resemblance of the fictional characters to persons living or dead is purely coincidental.

The partial lyrics to the song 'Dry Bones' is in reference to the musical work of songwriter James Weldon Johnson and his brother, J. Rosamond Johnson.

As a work of fan fiction, *Unity* is intended only for entertainment, and outside of the original canon. I do not make any profit from sales of this work. The price of the book is to cover production and publishing costs. Any inadvertent profit will be donated to the Royal National Lifeboat Institution.

ACKNOWLEDGEMENTS

I have numerous people to thank for their – sometimes unknowing – help in writing this book. Here they are in no particular order:

Alex Cox for his very useful reference work *I Am (Not) a Number*, which contains episodic breakdowns and analysis of all seventeen episodes of *The Prisoner* television series.

The First Draft Review Group, who took the time to read *Unity* in its 'raw state' prior to publication and to give me excellent feedback on the story, the zeitgeist of 1967, and all the typos. Your help was invaluable. They are: Janine Andrews, David Austin, Shaun Cooper, Rick Davy, Brian Formby, Ian French, Barry Manson, Ceri Margerison, Gary Murfin, Ross Pearce, Liz Prendergast, and Craig Walter.

Appreciation also to Robert Fairclough, Roger Langley, Dean Motter, and David Stimpson, for their replies to my random emails seeking advice on how to get *Unity* 'officially' published and not end up in court.

Thanks also to the Six of One Prisoner Appreciation Society for their support in launching *Unity*, and to the Unmutual website for their coverage and encouragement.

I have been entertained over the years by many writers but would like to single out some here who have in part influenced the way I have written *Unity*: Michael Connelly, Robert Crais, Jeffery Deaver, Ken Follett, Adam Hall (Elleston Trevor), Robert Harris, and Stephen Hunter. This is in no way saying that I'm an equal or that I even come close to any of them!

And finally, special thanks to Patrick McGoohan for creating such an enigmatic and enduring work. I can only hope he would have approved of *Unity*.

A NOTE FOR FANS OF *THE PRISONER*

The *Unity* story parallels what are regarded by many as the seven 'essential' episodes of the original ITC television series *The Prisoner*, as follows:

> Arrival
> Free For All
> Dance of the Dead
> Checkmate
> The Chimes of Big Ben
> Once Upon a Time
> Fall Out

But you don't need to have seen any of the episodes!

Mike Bodnar
Sunbury-on-Thames
March 2023

1967

Central London

The thunderclap came out of nowhere. It shook windows in office buildings. Shoppers and tourists stopped in their tracks and looked to the sky which was bright and hazy. Confusing; no sign of rain. A second equally loud thunderclap shook the air, rolled on for a moment, and then – at least for those in Westminster – morphed into the thunderous roar of a small sports car speeding through the streets.

The driver didn't react to the thunder, didn't slow down, actually didn't care about the weather. He had more urgent things on his mind. He swung round a corner, chopped from second to third and put his foot down.

Virgil Street Garage, London

Charles wound down the last of the windows of the gleaming black vehicle halfway and began the almost ceremonial wiping of the tops of each door glass with his chamois cloth. Not many people know to do this final thing after washing a motor car, he thought. It's the attention to detail that counts. Anyone sees these windows open won't see any dried droplets along the top, or streaks. It's what sets a professional apart, he smiled to himself.

'There Tommy,' he said to his mechanic who was at the workbench. 'That's how to properly clean a motor car. Spick and span, ready for inspection.'

Tommy turned and shook his head. He'd heard this many times before.

The phone at the back of the garage rang, and Charles wrung his chamois cloth out as he headed for the office door. 'I'll get it,' he said.

It was the red phone, Charles noted. His heart rate increased, and he cleared his throat, picked up the receiver.

'Yes?'

'I understand you can supply half a dozen red roses on the 27th,' a woman's voice said clearly, then paused.

'A dozen for anyone called Moira,' Charles replied.

'Right. Charles, job for you, priority one.' The caller, satisfied that the counter-response was correct, now talked hurriedly.

'No problem ma'am, where and when?'

'Now actually – we might already be too late. One male. We're confident he'll be leaving the underground car park any moment. Green and yellow Lotus sports car.' She gave him the registration number: Kilo Alpha Romeo, one-two-zero Charlie.

'He'll likely go home, Buckingham Place, SW1, but we're not certain. Head there if you lose him. If he doesn't turn up immediately, wait. He'll arrive eventually. Be careful, he's angry. Make sure the subject is compliant before entry. You know where to take him, the ambulance will be on stand-by.'

'Of course ma'am. Leave it to me.' The anonymous caller cut the connection and Charles put the phone down.

'Tom! We're on!' he called. Tommy wiped his hands on a cloth and pressed the control that opened the garage door, then climbed out of his overalls and grabbed his black suit coat. Charles peeled off his own overalls to reveal his formal clothing underneath. He grabbed his own black coat and two spotless top hats off a shelf and ran to the hearse, throwing the hats and coat into the middle of the front seat.

Tommy climbed in the passenger's side and the gleaming Austin Princess eased out onto the street, the garage door closing automatically behind.

Charles picked up the radio handset from under the dashboard. 'Mobile Black, Mobile Black to Mobile Control, receiving, over?'

The radio speaker crackled and a female voice answered immediately. 'Mobile Control, Mobile Black, receiving. You have your instructions?'

'Yes, en route now. Traffic seems good, ETA five minutes.'

'Make it three. Out.'

'What's the job?' asked Tommy, checking his tie in the vanity mirror on the sun visor. He combed his red hair with his fingers.

'Extraction,' said Charles. 'Just the one. Male. We'll use the gas, through the keyhole.'

'Then what?' asked Tommy.

'Then I drop you back at the garage and you go about your business, as usual. I'll take care of the funeral.'

Century House,
100 Westminster Bridge Road, London

Riley put the telephone handset back in the cradle and blew his cheeks out.

'What's the matter old boy?' asked Symes, turning from the window and breaking his gaze from the river which he'd been watching between the office buildings and the hospital.

'He's resigned. As we expected. Seems he was rather angry.'

'Jeepers. Do we know why?'

Riley picked up the phone again, pressed one of the buttons on the console, covered the mouthpiece and replied, 'No. He submitted his resignation letter but there was nothing much more in the envelope, just something about it being a matter of principle. Hello? Director, Strategic here. Get me Anastasia, quickly,' he said into the phone.

Symes sat at his own desk and gripped the arms of his chair. 'And this was just now?'

'Just now, in the last ten min... ah, Anastasia? Have you heard? Yes resigned. Mmm, well yes, our top man, as you say.... I know... and, no clear explanation. He's furious apparently. Should we... you know… take action? Really? The undertakers are on the job already? I say, that was quick… well yes, I suppose so.'

Symes noted Riley ran a finger under his collar as he listened. 'Of course. Of course Anastasia, absolute top secret, I'm sure we both recognise that.' He shook his head at Symes in despair at being told the obvious. 'All right, see you there shortly.'

Riley stood and grabbed his suit jacket from the coat stand. Symes rose too, the colour draining from his face. 'The funeral director's involved? So this is it?'

'Yes, this is it. Not a drill, not a rehearsal. Call the undertakers on the radio and keep tabs on the extraction. They're mobile now and tailing him, to his place we think. Let me know if anything goes wrong. I'll be in a meeting in Sub-3 for a while, but brief me when you can. D-Ops is alerting the facility.'

He paused momentarily, looked through the windows at the city and rubbed his face. 'I'm not sure this is a good idea. Not at all.'

4

Sub-basement 3, Century House

The lift doors opened and Riley stepped out, almost colliding with Anastasia Walker.

'Ah, Anastasia.' He fell in step with her and they headed quickly down the quiet dimly-lit corridor.

'Riley.' Anastasia acknowledged him with a nod, but kept walking purposefully.

'You know we haven't had anyone of his calibre in the facility before,' Riley said.

'And your point is?'

'Well, he's our number one operative. And he is our number one because he's so very damned good at what he does. Plus, he's not retired, he's resigned.'

Anastasia Walker suddenly stopped. 'Exactly. Which is why we absolutely cannot let him out of our sight. He's far too valuable to be on the loose, especially the mood he's in, and *especially* given the nature of the project.' She set off, and Riley hurried to keep up.

'Yes, I suppose you're right. But...'

'But nothing. Think about the information he's got in his head. Along with information we probably don't even know about.'

They reached the black door at the end of the corridor. Walker punched the access code into the buttons on the lock and the door swung open automatically with a hum. They entered a dark cavernous space, almost black, except for a large structure in the centre, raised about three feet off the floor. It was a windowless room, isolated from its surroundings and lit from beneath. It seemed to almost float in mid-air. There were no windows. Access steps led to a steel door in the front of the structure, with another keypad beside it which Riley unlocked this time. The door swung open, again automatically.

After Riley and Walker had stepped inside, those already there, seated around a large oval conference table, turned to face them.

'Ah, Walker, Riley, please, take a seat,' said the bald man with glasses at the head of the table. He had a voice like syrup.

'I think you know everybody,' said the man, whose name was Stone. If he had a first name nobody knew it.

Walker and Riley took the only remaining seats and sat down, nodding to those present. The table was bare save for some water jugs and glasses. Nobody had any notebooks or jotters, or even pencils. No record-taking was ever allowed within this secure room.

Stone looked at each person in turn, as though summing up their qualifications to be present, which in fact was exactly what he was doing. The meeting was too important to take any chances. He seemed satisfied.

'Right. Let's begin. The only person in this directors-only meeting you're not likely to know is Miss Wilson here.' Stone gesticulated to an unsmiling woman with a severe haircut to his right. 'Olivia, perhaps you'd like to introduce yourself.'

Olivia Wilson pushed her chair back and stood up with her feet slightly apart and her hands behind her back. She squared her shoulders and raised her chin before speaking. Most in the room immediately recognised the clues: she came from a military background.

'Thank you sir. I am Major Olivia Wilson,' she said to the group. 'I'm a qualified psychiatrist as well as having qualifications and extensive experience in psychology. I was... quietly seconded to this organisation over a year ago. My skills are applied in the field of psychological strategic planning and operations, which, as you probably know, involves interpreting or manipulating the thought processes, emotions and beliefs of a subject or subjects to our advantage.'

She sat down again, and Stone resumed. 'Thank you.' He turned to the group. 'Major Wilson holds the interim role of Director, Psychological Operations. Any questions?'

A man to Stone's left, older, in a pin-striped suit which probably first saw a hanger in 1950, cleared his throat. 'Er, excuse my asking, but what is Miss Wilson's clearance?'

Stone stared at him for a moment before replying, his rimless glasses fully reflecting the light so that the man couldn't see his eyes, only two pale orbs of luminescence. 'Adequate,' he snapped, 'or she wouldn't be here.'

He turned to the rest of the group. 'Now, I've asked Major Wilson to join us today because, although we find ourselves in a somewhat expected situation, we didn't anticipate the timing of it. And it's a situation which, from today, will demand all our initiative, intelligence and indeed cunning. We are dealing with what could be an unhinged mind.' Stone glanced briefly at Wilson. 'Not just any mind either. The mind of this man...'

Stone turned towards the wall behind him and pressed a remote control on the arm of his chair. The image of a good-looking man in his late 30s or early 40s appeared on the wall screen.

Stone turned back. 'As you can see, he has a half-smile on his face. He appears confident, at ease. As indeed he was when this photograph was taken just a year ago. Then he was at the top of his game, operating effectively in the field, and doing our bidding wherever we sent him, which was far and wide.

'He became, as you know, the best operative we have. Or at least had, until today. He has resigned with immediate effect, and on a "matter of principle." Exactly what we're not sure, but we can, I believe, make an intelligent guess. However, we need to ask, what does he know that's tipped him over the edge, and whose side is he on?'

'And how will we find out?' asked a woman to Stone's left.

'A brief stay in the facility should be all that's required. He's already begun his journey there. Major Wilson will explain what will happen upon his arrival.'

Wilson stood once more, clasped her hands behind her back, and faced the room.

5

Virgil Street Garage

Tommy watched the hearse drive regally down the short road under the railway arches and turn the corner, Charles using his indicator even though no other vehicles were in sight. Perfectionist, he thought, always the perfectionist. And then he recited the numbers to himself out loud: 'Two, two, seven, nine, six.' He repeated them, committing them to memory: 'Two, two, seven, nine, six.'

A train rumbled past over the bridge behind him as he turned and unlocked the garage's side door. He stepped inside, switched the lights on, headed for the office and stopped in the doorway. He removed his top hat and placed it on the shelf where it lived, then filled the kettle from the small sink in the corner and put it on the gas burner. He loosened his tie, thought about putting his overalls back on, but instead sat behind Charles's Desk.

He called it Charles's Desk (with a capital 'D') because he wasn't allowed to sit behind it. As with the rest of the garage, it was spotless, immaculate. Topped in green leather, it would have looked more at home in a gentleman's study, but then Tommy didn't know much about Charles's background, or where he lived, nor was he supposed to.

The man carried himself with military bearing, always ramrod straight in his walk, thumbs to the front as his arms swung as though on parade. He was tall and lean, despite the cream buns Tommy had seen him devour for morning tea. He wondered how he stayed so slim, so... lanky.

The whistling kettle brought him out of his reverie, and he made himself a mug of tea. His was the tin mug; Charles had a bone china one. Of course, thought Tommy, he would.

Not that he envied him in any way, well, not much. Charles was a good boss – not many blokes of my age have such interesting jobs, he thought. But then again, just what *is* my job, he wondered. It was obvious on the surface, but his real duties were less clear.

Tommy had not done brilliantly at school. Yes he was bright, always achieving good marks for most subjects, but he was never a team player. His reports frequently noted that, 'Tommy is a loner', 'Tommy doesn't seem to mix well with others,' and so forth, yet his English teacher – who doubled as the school's drama coach – adored him. 'Tommy could play Hamlet!' she wrote once. He was also good with his hands and did well in woodwork and especially metalwork.

He never did play the Prince of Denmark, though uncharacteristically he'd joined an amateur repertory group and had scored some good roles. But his day job had been as an apprentice mechanic. He'd joined a large engineering firm and, after going through all the usual initiations – he was too clever to fall for the 'Go and ask stores for a long weight' ruse – worked hard and diligently. Until he was accused of stealing.

It still riled him of course. He hadn't stolen a thing, it was fit-up, that's what it was. He slurped his tea, and put his mug on the desk, then thought better of it and got a saucer to put it on in case the hot mug marked the leather. Before he swung his feet up onto the desk he placed a cloth on it to avoid scratching. He didn't want to lose this job, because now he worked for 'the government', even though he wasn't quite sure which part of it. Charles was his boss, and the only person he answered to.

He thought about this morning's job. It had gone smoothly. They'd arrived outside the underground car park just in time, then tailed the subject to his flat. The man hadn't once looked back to check if they were there, which made it easy. Very easy. Inside, knock-out gas cylinder and hose ready, into the keyhole, then after a few minutes bring in the casket and off we go. But where, he wondered? Where do they go, the departed?

Thomas Alex Deighton finished his tea, lifted his legs off the desk and wiped it to make sure Charles wouldn't know he'd sat there. He washed and dried his mug and turned to leave the office but then stopped and took his top hat off the shelf and placed it on his head. He looked in the mirror on the wall beside the door, tilted the hat to a jaunty angle and tapped it on top to ensure it stayed in place.

I work for the government, he thought. As a mechanic, and 'an undertaker's assistant.' Sure. Of course that's what I am. But at least my so-called criminal record has been wiped. Now all I've got to do is keep my nose clean and deal with the 'funerals.' His reflection smiled a lop-sided smile back at him and he started singing softly to himself.

'Dem bones, dem bones, dem... dry bones, dem bones, dem bones, dem... dry bones...'

6

RAF Northolt, West London

The hangar doors opened upon Charles beeping the horn and closed again after him as he drove in and parked. He exited the driver's seat and closed the hearse door, the sound echoing in the cavernous interior of the hangar.

In front of him was a military ambulance with blacked-out windows on the sides and rear doors. The ambulance driver walked over to Charles and they shook hands. They'd shared jobs like this a few times.

'You've got the patient then?' asked the driver, in Cockney as thick as butter.

Charles indicated the hearse. 'In the back Don, sleeping like a baby. Mind you, it's your job to keep him that way for a while. Have you got the kit ready?'

Don nodded. 'Yeah, but come and take a butcher's. We've got a bloomin' transfer pod now, no expense spared,' and he led Charles to the open doors at the back of the ambulance. Inside the vehicle, which was lined in gleaming white and stainless steel, Charles saw a large, clear half-tube that fitted perfectly over a custom-made stretcher. He noted there were arm restraints inside it. Various flexible pipes and cables were attached to the tube, while a panel on the side housed a row of lights, and a round green screen showed a long flat line on a grid, waiting for the moment when it would detect a heartbeat.

Charles raised an eyebrow. 'This is fancy. And this can keep him out of it until his arrival?'

Don nodded and looked admiringly at the gleaming equipment. 'Long enough for me to get him to the facility and for the removal blokes to get the furniture from his flat. In fact he'll wake up fresh as a daisy... sometime tomorrow.'

'Impressive,' nodded Charles.

Don looked away from the interior of the ambulance and sighed. 'I dunno why they go to so much trouble and expense, but then ours is not to reason why, is it?'

'No, it's not,' Charles admonished, ignoring the temptation to finish Tennyson's quote. This wasn't a good time to mention death even though he was dressed as an undertaker.

'I'm sure our lords and masters know what they're doing.' He took his pocket watch from his waistcoat and checked the time. 'Anyway,' Charles said, 'you've got a bit of a journey ahead of you so let's get him into this pod thing of yours and you can be on your way.'

'Yeah,' said Don, 'don't want him there dead on time, eh, do we? Dead on time? Geddit?' Charles didn't respond. Don shook his head and sighed; some people had no sense of humour. 'Okay, back up and let's get him in.'

Charles headed back to the hearse and climbed in. As he started the engine and turned the vehicle round, the tyres squealing on the polished concrete floor, he muttered to himself, 'Talks too much that one.'

The hearse reversed quietly to a stop, its back to the ambulance. Charles climbed out and opened the rear door, exposing the polished oak casket inside. There were no flowers, no cards, just the casket.

7

Sub-basement 3

The meeting had gone well. Each of the departmental directors seemed well-organised and responsive to the emerging situation. Stone was cautiously pleased, although he knew there was no time to relax.

He dismissed the meeting, but said, 'Walker and Riley, would you stay for a moment please?'

The others filed out and the door hummed shut. Riley and Walker sat again, this time at opposite sides of the table, and faced Stone. Riley ran his fingers under his collar again, wishing he could loosen his tie which seemed to be strangling him.

'Well, that was most satisfactory overall,' Stone said. 'Don't you think?'

Riley looked at Anastasia, who didn't look back at him. She was facing Stone, and said, 'Absolutely sir, it seems as though everything is in hand. I particularly like the way things are being set up in the village.'

Stone's forehead creased slightly. 'That's not a word we use loosely Anastasia, as I'm sure you know, especially if ears are listening. We don't want to reveal too much – in fact anything – to anyone who might be... interested.'

Riley felt they'd been asked to stay behind to be tested. Anastasia had just failed.

'So, Riley, what about you?'

Riley feigned surprise. 'Me sir? What about me?'

'Your thoughts?'

'Well, I...' Riley searched the table in front of him for inspiration. 'The departments appear to be very well organised, as my colleague here has just said. They are... what do the young people say today? On the ball?'

'Indeed,' Stone nodded. 'And?'

'Well, ahem, the only thing – if this is the appropriate occasion on which to mention it - is, what part I – er, we – might play in this... this "escapade" as it were?' A trickle of sweat made its serpentine way down his temple. But he stopped talking; Riley knew when to shut up.

Stone swivelled in his seat and brought the screen behind him to life once more. This time an aerial view of a pretty Italianate village appeared, built on a leafy hillside facing an estuary. The buildings were quaint, romantic, and painted in various pastel hues. Cobbled roadways and paths wound their way between them, bordered by shrubs, lawns and trees. There were ponds, and a bell tower. It looked idyllic, a hillside paradise, and could be anywhere in the world, or at least Europe.

'The facility,' he said, glancing back at Anastasia briefly and emphasising the word. 'Yes, to all intents and purposes it looks like a village, but you both know what it's for. At least, you think you do.'

Stone had their full attention now. The meeting had confirmed operational matters of how the 'subject' (as he was referred to) would be transferred to the facility, would be managed once there, and how security and surveillance would ensure that he remained 'a guest.' Plans had been discussed as to how the man would be encouraged to cooperate.

Olivia Wilson, the meeting was reminded, had been recruited to oversee the general village psychological operations, along with the administration of drugs and other medications, some of which were new and experimental, but whatever form they took they had one goal in common: compliance. Now she had an extra challenge.

Wilson had been instructed by Stone not to over-stretch her newest resident while attempting to gain what they most needed from him: information. He was to be carefully managed, and drugged only sparingly and when absolutely necessary.

But the meeting had finished, and the attendees had left, apart from Riley and Walker. The atmosphere in the sealed-off room remained electric.

'As you know,' Stone continued, 'this facility has had a rather wider agenda implemented in the past year or so; the trialling of new therapy programmes, drugs and so on. But the outcome has been satisfactory so far: obedience, conformity. The residents are peaceful and lack the will or motivation to question, argue or rebel. But one programme in particular, which is driven by the Ministry of Defence, is being trialled with the intent of it being used much further afield, and in a military capacity: Unity.'

Riley and Walker stole a quick glance at each other before Stone swivelled round from the screen and continued.

'Imagine, for example, a battle scenario, in a foreign land say. We, the British, are defending a position against an invading legion, fully armed, disciplined, well-equipped, and outnumbering us. We would need an advantage. We would need something that could render them harmless, such as some of the drugs and techniques being trialled in the charming community you see here.' He gestured at the screen behind him.

'Imagine further then, an enemy rendered compliant, an enemy that would be peaceful and see no need for violence or aggression. They could be overcome simply by being told to lay down their arms and surrender. It would give us a major strategic advantage. We would win the battle.'

Stone paused for a moment to let them take in what he had just said. 'But now imagine what might happen if the *enemy* had this technology, and was able to use it on us, to *their* advantage. It is *we* who would lose the fight. Which is why we must break our new resident and find out what he knows. If he has found out about Unity, then we should be concerned. What has he done with this information? Has he told anyone? Who is he working for? And of course, why did he resign, which is rather unclear.'

Neither Riley nor Walker was inclined to respond, but they were saved from having to.

There was one telephone in the room, on a side table against the wall near where Stone was sitting. It had no dial – indeed it had no cord or cable and seemed to be a self-contained unit - and was for receiving calls only. It also had no bell, although a light flashed on the front of it now.

Stone tutted at the interruption but picked it up and listened. 'Very good. Thank you,' he said and replaced the handset. He turned his attention back to Riley and Walker.

'That was Monitoring upstairs. The subject is on his way, and the contents of his study are being loaded by Removals.' He checked his watch. 'So, by later this evening our man will be where we want him. His accommodation is being readied and soon his home furniture will be installed. When he wakes up he will think he's back in his flat. At first. Obviously when he opens the door or looks out of the window he'll be in for a shock, and will certainly be in some confusion. Which of course is the point.'

Stone paused and looked at the others at the end of the table. Anastasia Walker squirmed slightly in her seat, while Riley held Stone's gaze and said, 'And then the process begins.'

'Yes, the process begins. This will be ground-breaking for us. We have new technology, enhanced... security, and a smorgasbord of innovative interrogation techniques. In fact, our subject doesn't realise just how important his role is now; he will be our testing ground.

'And, with so much at stake I need someone to oversee the process, from arrival to departure... whatever form that takes.' Stone paused.

'Are you saying you want us to take charge of the operation?' asked Anastasia. She looked uncertainly at Riley, who glanced briefly at her, then back to Stone. 'I thought Major Wilson had the lead...'

'She does, yes, certainly as far as breaking our latest resident is concerned. But one can't be too careful. Does that trouble either of you?'

Walker shook her head. 'Not at all sir, no. It would be an honour.'

She looked across at Riley, who clasped his hands in front of him on the table and said, 'What about that "thing" we've started using? It's not fully tested, and we've had some trouble controlling it. I worry that it sometimes seems to have a mind of its own. I'm not sure I would be comfortable vouchsafing an untried... security... *blob* is the only word I can think of.' He looked back to Stone.

Stone smiled and shook his head. 'You needn't worry, Riley dear chap. The more we use it the better it gets, and the scientists who've nurtured it are confident. It does indeed at times seem to have a mind of its own, but that appears to enable it to learn. The facility controller has nicknamed it "Rover," which I'm told stands for Remotely-Operated Village Enforcement Resource. I rather like that.

'Now, when I say I'm giving you oversight of this particular operation, I mean I want you to both observe and influence the proceedings as necessary. And of course, report to me. You know what's at stake, but few others do. I have people who will continue the important and essential work on the primary project. But for you, it might mean going to the site itself, especially if you need to personally intervene – which I hope you won't – but mostly you'll be able to work from here I should think.

'You'll be given full access to Monitoring in Sub-2; I've already let them know to expect you. In fact this is going to be an intense period, so you'll be better off working there full-time. You can split the shifts between you, starting immediately. That's all for now.'

Anastasia and Riley stood slowly and turned to go, but Stone said, 'Anastasia, might I have a quick word? Thank you Bill,' Stone nodded his dismissal to Riley, who half raised an eyebrow and glanced at Walker, but then turned and left the room. As the door hummed shut, Walker sat down again.

'Anastasia, I want you to keep an eye on Riley for me. It's not that I don't trust him of course – his record is impeccable – but I'm not convinced he's fully committed to what we're doing at the facility, if you get my drift?'

'Of course sir, leave it to me,' Walker said, and smiled.

8

The Facility
Location: Classified

The sun was still high in the sky. Warmth blanketed the pastel-hued buildings of the pretty hillside village. Seagulls wheeled overhead.

An announcement had just been made over the many speakers dotted around the verdant grounds, and marching music now played.

But the seagulls weren't the only ones in motion; throughout the grounds and between the picturesque buildings people were on the move, walking purposefully towards the building with the domed roof. Well, as purposefully as they could – many were elderly, and most were male. But moving they were. They had been summoned. The piped band music helped them on their way, whether they liked it or not.

Crescents of seats had been set up inside the dome, facing a slightly raised dais. In the centre of the platform was a freestanding control panel, but nothing more.

Dim lighting around the curvature of the dome's floor was the only illumination, apart from a spotlight aimed at the centre of the dais.

The villagers filed in and took their places, and when everyone was seated the doors through which they'd entered automatically hummed shut.

Any talking dropped to a murmur, and then faded completely as the audience saw a round panel slide open on the floor of the dais. Up through it, with a slight mechanical whirring, came a round black chair, almost half a globe really, its interior upholstered in blue. It was supported on a pedestal.

Within it sat a man with black Brylcreemed hair and a tanned face. He wore a dark blue jacket and grey flannel trousers. A striped scarf lay casually round his neck, the end thrown over his right shoulder. His garb was at odds with the outfits everyone in the audience wore, which were a variety of bright colours. Some wore straw boaters and capes, some jackets, and many had striped tops. They gave the impression that they were employees of some sort of holiday camp, except there was nothing festive behind why they were there.

'Good day to you,' the man with the scarf said, his voice smooth and cultured. He rose from the chair. 'And welcome. I realise you all know this building of course, but it's always been off-limits. This is probably the one and only time you'll be in here, and after you've left... you will forget, won't you?'

'We will forget,' came the automatic response from the audience, speaking as one. They were conditioned to do this and obeyed without question. Their dilated pupils remained focused on the speaker.

'Good,' he said. 'I am here to brief you on what will be happening in the next few days here in our... community. It's important to know what's going on so that you can happily remain here, enjoying the life you've all become used to, the life which you all appreciate so much.'

There was no response from those in the audience; they merely watched the speaker and listened intently to his every word. If there was any concern or unease it wasn't evident.

'As you know,' the man continued, 'you've all been given numbers, and from now on that is the only way you will refer to each other: by number. I, for example, am Number Two. But we also have a new person joining us. The new resident will be Number Six. He arrives tomorrow, and will possibly want to talk to you, to question you. Do not engage with him, except for pleasantries. By all means discuss the weather, or, for example, how to order a taxi. But be very careful in what you tell him. If in doubt say nothing, or direct him to me.

'Within a short time after his arrival we will be demonstrating our security measures to him. These are, as you're aware, designed to keep you safe, to protect you from... well, uncertainty. So, I'd just like to remind you that when you hear the command "Be still," you should immediately stop whatever you're doing, become motionless, and wait until you are told to resume.'

Number Two looked around at their placid faces, seeing the dull acceptance in their eyes.

'As I say, this situation should last only a few days, maybe two weeks at the most. After that life here will return to… normal.

'In the meantime, *unity* is the key. We will work as one. As *one*,' he emphasised. 'In unity lies strength. However, joining you there will occasionally be new people, sanctioned individuals who will have specific roles to play. They will usually be here for just a short time. Number Six will be here for longer, until such time as we feel it prudent to allow him his freedom. Unless of course he wishes to stay, as you have all decided to do.' Number Two smiled, although no warmth touched his eyes.

'That is all for the moment. Remember what I've told you. But as I said, you were never here. You will forget.'

'We will forget.'

9

Virgil Street Garage

Tommy shrugged back into his overalls and turned his attention to completing the oil change on a Rover 3.5-litre, one of half a dozen government 'pool' cars in the garage. He admired the car, but preferred the Triumph Spitfire in the corner, awaiting a new exhaust system. He liked its sleek styling and low profile. This was the car he always looked forward to testing following a service. The Rover was a bit too 'gentlemanly' for his tastes despite its powerful engine.

He was down in the pit beneath the car when he heard the garage door open. He peered out from underneath the vehicle and watched the hearse drive slowly into the garage. It stopped, and he could see Charles filling in the logbook which he kept in the glove compartment. Or rather, kept *locked* in the glove compartment – Tommy wasn't party to the hearse's paperwork.

Charles climbed out of the Austin, stretched and looked around. 'I'm down here,' shouted Tommy. 'Just draining the oil. How was the traffic?'

Charles bent over to see Tommy in the pit, glimpsing him in the glow of the inspection lamp between the sill of the driver's door and the floor of the workshop.

'Not too bad,' he said. 'Thanks for your help. Went well I thought.'

Tommy carried on loosening the sump nut. 'Did you get caught up in those road works on Victoria Street? Absolute chaos there yesterday.'

Charles grunted. 'It was all right. Helps if you know the short cuts,' he said and headed for the office.

Tommy saw him shut the door and pick up the phone, the red one, and make a call. He couldn't hear what he was saying, but Tommy smiled. Now he knew that Charles had headed north across the river, at least to begin with.

In the office Charles finished giving his report, listened for a moment, and said, 'Of course ma'am. I'll make sure it's done.' He put the phone down and returned to the garage, squatting down beside the Rover.

'Got another job, but this one's for you. Our bosses want us to bring that Lotus we followed back here for keeping in storage. You'll find the keys under the doormat outside the flat; the removal men left them there. Take a cab, then bring the car back here.'

Tommy wiped his hands on an oily cloth. 'Now?'

'No, in three weeks. Yes now,' he barked. 'You can finish the Rover tomorrow. Off you go.'

Tommy came up the steps from the inspection pit and went over to the workbench where the hand cleaning gel was. He watched Charles go back into the office, then, wiping the last of the oil from his hands, Tommy quickly looked into the hearse, and whispered to himself, Two, two, eight, three, zero.'

*

In the back of the cab on the way to Buckingham Place, Tommy congratulated himself on memorising the odometer reading when Charles had dropped him back at the garage. Now he did the mental arithmetic and worked out that Charles had driven thirty-four miles in the hearse. But that was the round trip, which means he went somewhere about seventeen miles away, he thought. But where?

After crossing the Thames Charles could have headed north, west or east, or anywhere in between. It doesn't help that I have no idea where he would have taken the subject, he worried, the only reference he had to the unconscious man. A hospital? A holding cell somewhere? A transfer facility? Did Charles hand him over to someone else or just dump him somewhere? Not likely. If the idea was to get rid of him they'd have used something a lot more permanent than knock-out gas, so Charles's bosses obviously wanted the man alive.

So, reflected Tommy, we've done this before with a few others. In the six months I've worked at the garage there have been three – now four – people we've been required to extract, and each time it's been the same, or at least very similar: drive in the hearse to the appointed address, subdue the subject, load them into the casket and drive off.

Charles would call in the status of the job as soon as they were mobile, and Tommy knew that their visit would be followed up by a team whose job it was to search the now-vacant premises. Or remove evidence. Or, for all he knew, vacuum the carpets, empty the fridge and wash the dishes. He had no real idea what went on, but a so-called 'removals' team always came in once they'd left.

And each time it followed the same pattern; Charles would drop Tommy back at the garage and drive off down the road, only to return within a couple of hours, with the casket now empty again. Any questions on Tommy's part had always been ignored, and after asking a third time what they were really doing Charles had put his hands on Tommy's shoulders, squeezed none-too-gently, and stared at him unblinkingly for a couple of seconds, then his eyes softened.

'Look lad,' he'd said quietly, 'just be thankful you've got a job. You were saved from a very embarrassing situation remember. You could have been fined, or gone to prison. Yes, I know, I know, settle down... you've said you didn't steal anything and I believe you, even if the police didn't. But you're here now, you've got a job – which you do well – and you've got security. We work for the government, that's all you need to know. So, take my advice son,' – and here Charles had squeezed Tommy's shoulders further with a surprisingly strong grip – 'don't ask questions. I've told you before, just do as you're told. I don't need to remind you that your job could end at any time. All right?'

That was all. The subject was dropped and Tommy had never brought it up again, although it hadn't stopped him thinking about it, and wanting to know.

10

Century House

Riley sat heavily in his chair. Symes wasn't at his desk, so he had the office they shared to himself. He gazed out of the window but was snapped out of his tumbling thoughts by the phone ringing.

'Riley,' he answered, distractedly.

'Ah, Bill,' – the familiar syrupy voice on the other end of the line. 'Pleased to have caught you. Just a quick one, shan't bother you for long. Just wanted to say how much I appreciated your and Walker's input today. I'm sure you'll work well together on this.'

Riley loosened his collar. It wasn't often Stone telephoned him directly. And he'd only recently got back from the meeting with him, so this was doubly surprising.

'But one thing,' Stone continued, 'would you keep an eye on Anastasia for me? I'm not entirely sure she's as committed to this project as you are, and I don't want any surprises. Keep me informed would you?'

'Of course sir, of course. No problem,' Riley tried his best to sound confident – and committed.

'Good chap. Call me any time, day or night.'

The line went dead, but Riley was slow to return the handset to the cradle. His mind was racing. What *was* going on? He and Walker had been appointed guardians of the internment and interrogation of the recently resigned operative, and some not-inconsiderable resources were now potentially at their command. In fact, he knew this whole operation must be costing a fortune, and was glad he wasn't the one responsible for explaining the budget to a select committee, although with sensitive operational matters most details were deliberately kept hazy anyway.

And keeping things hazy was part of what this business was about, he thought. To all intents and purposes the facility was a retirement village, and was described as such in those few memoranda and other documents that referred to it. Many in the organisation knew vaguely that such a place existed or was being trialled, but few knew of its exact status, and even fewer of its whereabouts. Riley knew rather more, as did Anastasia Walker. However the facility's recent re-purposing, the investment in technology and enhanced security, and – as he'd discovered at the meeting – the wider purpose of the drug testing programme, and Olivia Wilson's appointment for psychological oversight of the newest resident, were clear indications that things were changing.

His phone rang again. This time it was Walker.

'Do you want first or second shift?' she asked. This took him by surprise.

'Er... well, I haven't really thought about it.' He had, vaguely, but now he wanted to see what her thoughts were first.

'Well I have,' she said curtly. 'I'll go first, starting this evening. They're long shifts, and we'll need some overlap at each shift change too, so we can debrief on handover. You can take over at 0600 tomorrow.'

'How about we go down to Sub-2 together first, just to see where we're up to, introduce ourselves, see where we'll be working, that sort of thing. We don't get to go there much. It'll help put the team at ease,' Riley suggested.

There was a pause as Walker considered this. 'All right. Yes. Meet you outside Sub-2 in fifteen minutes.' She hung up.

When they met outside Monitoring, Walker seemed on-edge, Riley thought. Mind you, he rationalised, aren't we all? They punched the access code and went in.

The large room, split onto distinct sections, was dark, the better to view the rows and rows of television monitors, in front of which sat numerous operators whose job it was to view – and to record and report on – whatever their screens showed. The rows of screens were tiered, and had the monitors not been there it would have looked more like a lecture theatre in a university, or a theatre auditorium.

At the front, much larger - in fact giant - screens displayed in more detail whatever the supervisor wished to see. The room was quiet, apart from the hum of the air conditioning, and occasional whispered words between the operators, most of whom sat with headphones clamped over their ears.

A man talking to one of the operators towards the front looked up at their arrival, broke off and strode up the steps between two of the sections. He was short, tousle-haired, clean-shaven and with piercing blue eyes.

Walker held out her hand as he approached. 'Anastasia Walker,' she announced. 'This is Bill Riley, I believe we're expected.'

'Indeed,' said the supervisor. 'Holland. George Holland,' he said, shaking their hands. 'There are three supervisors sharing shifts in here, I'm on till midnight tonight. I believe you're sharing shifts between you, twelve hours each, is that right?'

'That's right,' Riley said. 'I trust there's a coffee-maker?'

'Oh yes, indeed. I think you'll find everything you need. Are you familiar with what we do here in Monitoring?' They nodded, but Anastasia suggested that he treat them as new interns and said they'd be pleased to know more.

'Right, let me show what's what,' Holland beamed.

He guided them to the left at the top of the rows where there was an observation lounge with double soundproof glass overlooking the whole area. Inside this room they found two cot beds, a desk, telephones, typewriter, stationery stores, filing cabinets and so forth. Built into a long desk there was a bank of multiple small television screens each with its own control panel in front.

'You can pretty much see everything you need to from in here,' Holland explained. 'These monitors can be selected to show anything the operators are looking at on the floor, and you've got headphones to listen in as required. The switches and things are all labelled but shout out if you need any help.'

'And the coffee-maker?' Riley asked. Walker rolled her eyes, which Holland noticed. He smiled. 'There's a kitchen through there with tea, coffee, a fridge – it's all restocked daily.'

'Thank you,' Riley said. 'I don't wish to seem as though refreshments are more important than the work,' – he glanced here at Walker – 'but personally I'm not used to watching more than an hour's television at a time, so...'

'Quite,' Holland nodded. 'The beauty of this of course is there are no commercials,' he laughed.

Walker sighed and looked through the window at the banks of monitors. 'Tell me what we're looking at here.'

Holland joined her at the window, and Riley also looked into the vast room.

'To the left we have current operations where we can tap into existing closed-circuit TV cameras, or where our operators in the field have set up cameras or microphones remotely,' Holland explained.

'To the right the monitoring staff are available to tap into whatever anyone upstairs wishes to see, usually because they're trying to track a vehicle, or a person of interest. This might be to gather evidence for example, or to assist in profiling a subject's behaviour. You'd be surprised how many cameras we can access.'

'And the middle section?' Riley asked.

'Ah well, that's what you'll be most interested in. That whole section at the moment is devoted to activity within and around the retirement facility. We have more cameras concentrated there than anywhere else, partly because of course the organisation runs the place, but also due to the necessity of maintaining security and knowing exactly what's going on at any given moment.

'Some of the cameras are out in the open, partly to act as a deterrent, but most are hidden. Here, let me show you...'

Holland bent down at the array of monitors to one side of the observation room and brought one of them to life. He pressed a few keys on the panel in front of him, and an image of a leafy pathway appeared on the screen. Riley was impressed by the full-colour display.

'This camera for example,' explained Holland, 'is hidden inside the head of one of the many statues in the grounds. Not a real statue of course, completely hollow and full of electronics. We can even...' and here he manipulated a small toggle stick on the control panel, 'rotate the head to follow a subject as they go up or down the path. Quite fun really.'

Walker raised her eyebrows. 'You can control the cameras even from here?'

Holland let go of the toggle stick and stepped back. 'Yes we can, although usually it's Village

Control who do that since they're Johnny-on-the-spot and can react quickly to whatever they see. Orange Alert and all that.'

He gestured to the operators beyond the window. 'I've sent a message to everyone here via their screens to tell them you'll be here and keeping an overwatch – they'll be happy to answer any questions you might have, as will whichever supervisor is on at the time. So, are there in fact any questions?'

Riley looked back from the window. 'Yes, where are we up to with the transfer of our latest subject?'

'I was just getting an update on that when you came in,' Holland said. 'The transfer vehicle – an ambulance, as usual – has left Northolt and is on its way. Removals have been to the subject's flat and have the contents of his study in their van. They've taken photographs of everything so it can be replicated.' He checked his watch. 'They should be finished now and on their way as well. Given the journey times there probably won't be anything to see until around, ooh,' he glanced at his watch again, 'say, 2130? That's when the ambulance should arrive and the subject will then be taken to the community hospital and kept sedated.'

'And then?' asked Walker.

'And then the removal van arrives, the subject's furniture is installed in his new accommodation, and in the early hours of tomorrow morning he will be placed *in situ*, as it were. The fun will begin when he wakes up and discovers he's not at home. In fact, not even himself any more, just a number,' Holland chuckled.

Riley frowned. 'There's nothing funny about this,' he chided. 'This man is one of the best, one of the cleverest, one of the most agile operatives we've ever had. He will not take kindly to being drugged, transferred, duped, cheated or numbered. Mark my

words: he will be the most difficult resident the facility
has seen so far.'

11

Buckingham Place, London

Tommy took the receipt from the cab driver and stuffed it in his jacket pocket.

"'Ere you are mate,' the driver said, handing him a couple more receipts, but blank. 'Fill 'em in and claim a bonus sometime,' he laughed.

'Thanks man,' Tommy said gratefully, and exited the cab. He watched it drive down the road and smiled.

As he'd been trained by Charles, Tommy had asked the cabbie to drop him further back up the road, away from his actual destination. Now he walked along the street in the early evening light towards where the Lotus was parked outside the flat where they'd performed the extraction earlier.

He hummed quietly to himself. This was the sort of job he really enjoyed: driving someone else's car. It certainly beat the Triumph 500 motorcycle that was his own transport, much as he liked the bike.

He checked up and down the road, pretending to look at his watch as though waiting for someone – something else he'd been trained by Charles to do. 'The more you blend in,' Charles had said, 'the less you'll be noticed. Be the grey man,' he said. 'Be nobody.'

Tommy had taken the advice to heart, and his quick mind had not only absorbed the instruction but had come up with various creative ploys which he now used to go unnoticed.

So it was that he strode up to the door of the Buckingham Place flat and knocked. He waited a moment, then knocked again. He knew of course that nobody was home, but he turned, looked up and down the road, and again checked his watch.

He then sat on the top step and waited. To anyone watching, this clean-shaven presentable red-haired young man was supposed to be there and was now waiting for whomever it was he was due to meet.

As he looked back down the road, Tommy slipped one hand under the mat he was sitting on and felt for the car key. Sure enough, it was where Charles said it would be. He palmed it, stood up and looked back at the flat as though perplexed that nobody was home, then went down the steps and stood by the car. Traffic was building now as people began heading home from work, and cars, vans and motorbikes vied for position on the main road to his left.

He saw a large van about to turn into his street, and timed his leap into the Lotus's driver's seat as it slowly passed him, blocking the view of anyone across the road who might be watching. He slid the key in the ignition, started the engine, checked his mirror (Charles had warned him, 'Always drive carefully. Again, don't draw attention to yourself'), and pulled out.

Tommy was in no hurry to get back to the garage. Charles had been about to go home for the day when he'd left, and anyway, how often did he get the chance to drive a sporty Lotus? He sat at traffic lights, and was tempted to go back to Virgil Street via, say, Middlesex, to see how the car performed on some nice country roads, but he also knew he had to 'be invisible' and not draw any attention to himself. Still, he thought, it wouldn't do any harm to take a longer way home, would it?

The traffic started moving and Tommy shifted through the gears as he threaded his way round the back of Buckingham Palace and into Belgravia. The roar of the exhaust echoed off the expensive homes either side of the road, and he quickly got a feel for the car. He could see why the owner liked it – the Cosworth-tuned

1500cc engine was zippy, responsive, and the car was nothing short of, well, maverick.

He weaved his way through Chelsea, and as he drove his mind wandered back to Charles, and where he might have driven the hearse. Seventeen miles, he thought, somewhere in a vast semi-circle north of the river. Charles could have delivered the casket anywhere, but then Tommy realised that if he'd driven about seventeen miles, all he had to do was find a map and draw a radius, with maybe two arcs about a mile or so apart to allow for error. Perhaps then he'd see something within that range that would be a likely destination.

Tommy began looking for a bookshop, and soon saw one that was still open. He pulled over, leaped out of the car and went in, asking an assistant where he would find local maps. She pointed to one of the many shelves and within a minute he found what he was looking for, a detailed roadmap of greater London.

Emerging from the shop he saw a café a few doors down, went in, ordered a coffee, sat down at a table and opened the map. He checked the scale, roughly measured eighteen miles north, then another point about seventeen miles north, and marked them on the map with his pen. He went back to the counter and asked if he could have a saucer. It would do in the absence of a compass, and using the upturned saucer he quickly drew two semi-circles through the points he'd put on the map, using the Virgil Street garage as the centre-point. It was rough, but it would do.

He sat back, took a sip of coffee, and looked at the corridor within the arcs he'd drawn. Somewhere, he thought, somewhere within this rainbow is where you, Charles, took our subject. He began looking for likely locations. He felt sure it would be a government facility of some sort. He was getting closer.

12

Century House

Major Olivia Wilson finished typing, pulled the page up in the roller of the Remington, and scanned what she'd written. She tutted, reached for a small white bottle of correcting fluid, and dabbed a spot of it on an error. She blew on it to help it dry, waited a few seconds, then rolled the page back in again and typed over the mistake. She quickly re-checked it then pulled the page out of the machine, added it to the pile on her desk, picked the whole lot up and placed it in a red folder. It was marked Top Secret.

She picked up what was left of the cigarette that had been burning in an ashtray beside her, took a deep draw, and sat back and stared out of the window. The smoke she blew out merged with the light but overcast sky outside.

She reflected on her presentation at the meeting in Sub-3 earlier. Her briefing on the strategy to manage the new resident had been met largely with silence. Not that it worried her – she knew she had Stone's full support – but she'd hoped for a bit more enthusiasm from the various heads of department around the table. Only Anastasia Walker had seemed overtly supportive, although her colleague Riley had had a furrowed brow throughout.

'Messing with his mind,' is what Riley had called it, her plan for breaking the subject. 'Have you considered the possible consequences?' he'd asked.

She had assured him that she had. 'He's resourceful, resilient. He will be tough to break. In his psych tests he's always scored highly and displayed an even temperament, although sometimes impatient,' she'd said. 'If anything we shouldn't underestimate the consequences for ourselves.'

Riley had nodded at that. 'Exactly! He will likely wear your people down, wear them out. Have you thought about that?'

She had. She went on to explain that the individual in control of the facility would be replaced regularly.

'There will be a new Number Two on at least a weekly basis,' she'd clarified. 'This will mean that we have a fresh new... energy, regularly. It will unnerve him. He will never be sure whether the command has been replaced because he himself has worn them down, or whether we have an unlimited supply of interrogators. The whole point of all the tactics combined is to support the strategy of confusion; he will never be sure of anything.'

'Who is Number One?' one of the other directors had asked.

'There isn't one,' Wilson had explained. 'Again, it's to cause disorientation. Where there's a Number Two we would typically expect there to be a Number One. However, the absence of a leading figure is also designed to be unsettling. That's not to say there won't ever be one, but in the short-term at least the identity, in fact the existence, of a Number One will remain a mystery.'

Stone had interrupted at this point. 'Numbers in place of names will also be unsettling. Identities will be hidden. Our new resident will be Number Six, although we expect him to rebel against that, do we not?' He had turned back to Wilson and gestured for her to continue.

'Exactly sir. Not using names removes the ability of the subject – in this case Number Six – to potentially identify origins. We did consider using a wide variety of international names – Pablo, Gustav, Hans, Signe,

Sandrine and so on – but the danger is it introduces a degree of comfort and familiarity. A number is a cold and impersonal form of identification. It suggests hierarchy, but little else.'

None of the facility's residents, she'd said, nor any of the staff, would be known to Number Six, apart from one, and he would be the only one whose real name would be used: Cobb. She had explained the rationale to the group.

'Cobb is known to the subject. They've worked together in the field, and there's a degree of trust and even friendship. Putting Cobb on site as himself, as someone who – like Six – has been "captured" could, we hope, encourage our man to open up. It might work, it might not, but initially Cobb's will be the only familiar face he will see, and a familiar face in a community of strangers is something most of us would appreciate.'

There had been some comments and discussion, but Stone had wrapped up the meeting saying that time was of the essence and that they needed to get on with their appointed tasks to ensure that everything was in place before the subject woke up in his new 'home.'

'So,' Stone had looked at them around the table, 'any last questions or observations before we disperse?'

Riley had cleared his throat, then asked, almost as though he were thinking out loud, 'What, might I ask, in the end, do we want from this whole... charade?'

Stone's smile was tight, like the slash a scalpel might make in soft flesh.

'Information,' he said smoothly. 'We want information.'

*

And we will get it, Olivia Wilson thought as she stubbed out her cigarette. She picked up the phone and dialled an internal number.

'Yes, it's Major Wilson,' she said when the person at the other end answered. 'I need to talk to you about getting rid of someone. Yes, employee. Can we meet?' She listened for a moment. 'Now, preferably. Good, you know where to find me.'

Wilson took the red file from her desk and locked it in a cabinet, pocketing the keys. She looked out of the window, down at the street below. Traffic was crawling slowly, apart from a small sports car which was moving very fast. She saw it weave in and out of other vehicles, then make a sharp left turn at the traffic lights, which were on red.

A police siren caught her attention and she watched as a blue and white Panda car raced in pursuit, its tyres squealing as it too ran the red light and rounded the corner.

She knew what would be going through the sports car's driver's mind right now: fear, anticipation, maybe joy at the thrill of the chase. Anxiety and adrenalin in equal parts. We all react to danger in different ways, she thought.

That's what makes this job so damned interesting, she said to herself as she sat once again at her desk, reaching for her pack of Cadets and drawing another one out. As she lit it she made a mental note that this was her tenth cigarette of the day, though if there was any guilt it didn't show on her face. Or in her head for that matter; she knew guilt was a wasted emotion, and it played little part in her life. And anyway, she'd successfully given up drinking some years ago, so she knew she could do the same with smoking if she wanted to, any day. But not today.

She took a personnel file from a stack on her desk and glanced at it. The name Cobb, followed by his initials, was on the cover. She opened it and glanced through the contents to refresh her memory of the man's service career.

Placing him in the facility as himself – and as a colleague of the subject Number Six – was a risk, but a minor one given the contingency she had devised.

A knock on her door broke her chain of thought. 'Come,' she barked.

13

The Lonely Pheasant Pub, London

Riley took his half pint of bitter and sat in a booth on his own. He put his hat on the seat beside him, loosened his tie, and – as was his habit – blew out his cheeks. He reached for the glass and took a large gulp.

He looked around the pub with its red velvet banquettes, gleaming mahogany bar, oak panelled walls and a red patterned carpet that had seen better days and in fact probably better decades. People were beginning to come in for an after-work drink, and he was glad to have a booth to himself.

His thoughts returned to the monitoring room, where he'd left Anastasia Walker in the – he thought – not-so-capable hands of George Holland.

'Silly prat,' he muttered out loud. A woman passing his table stopped and glared at him.

'What did you say?' she demanded.

'I, er... well I...' Riley stammered.

'Bloody hell,' the woman said, placing her glass of vermouth on his table. 'Roger me sideways twenty times, if it isn't Bill Riley!' She sat opposite and stared at him, then took hold of his chin and turned his face this way and that. He tried to ease his head away but her grip was fierce.

'Older – the grey at the temples suits you – still with the squinty eyes, that never seem to stay on any one thing for long. But you look tired Bill. Where have you been these last – what is it? – five years, maybe more?'

Riley sighed. He'd hoped to have a quiet drink before heading back to his flat and getting a good night's sleep before his six o'clock start the next morning in Sub-2 – Monitoring – but he feared his plans had just become like the pub carpet: threadbare, stained and needing replacement.

'Miss Tench,' he said, with a weariness bordering on the theatrical. 'What a pleasant surprise. I would take my hat off in respect, but I already have, and I would invite you to join me, but here you are. So let's dispense with the pleasantries. Are you here working or is this a chance encounter? And I wasn't calling you a prat, I was referring to someone else.'

'I'm pleased to hear it. Anyway, I suspect "prat" is a masculine form. And as you know dear Bill, I am far from that.' She smiled, took a sip from her glass and winked at him over the rim.

Riley shuffled in his seat. 'So...?' he asked, shrugging his shoulders.

'Chance encounter old thing, chance encounter. This is my local now, recently moved in round the corner. Lovely place, you must come up and see it some time. Or does that sound like a line from a movie? Anyway, how are you and what's making you look so weary?'

'Judith. You know I can't talk about my work, just as you can't talk about yours, assuming you're still employed across the river. In that we are the same. The only difference between us right now is that you look as fresh as a daisy, and...'

'You look wilted, and in need of watering. Shall I get you the other half?' she asked, nodding to his glass.

'Oh hell, might as well,' Riley said, and downed what was left of his beer. 'Thank you.'

By the time she came back with the fresh half pint Riley had decided he might be able to use this 'chance encounter' to his advantage. She sat down and slid the glass in front of him.

'Awfully kind. My turn next,' he said, and took a sip. 'So, just as a matter of interest, because of course we can't discuss details, are you still gainfully employed?'

'I am. Are you?'

'Well, employed anyway. Gainfully? Not so sure. The next few weeks will tell.'

'Oh? Why?'

'Can't say, sorry. But what about you? What can you tell me about what you're doing now... and who you're doing it with?' he asked, smiling.

'Oh Bill, are we talking about my personal or professional life now?' she smiled back at him.

'Let's stick to professional,' he said. 'Can I ask you a blunt question?'

'Of course, but you might get an even blunter answer.'

'How close are you to the shadow minister?'

She theatrically looked around the bar before leaning towards him. 'Close. Very close,' she breathed. 'Why?'

'Well, there's something in the wind, something going on that he might, as it were, need to know about.'

'Ooh, something secret? Something naughty?' she giggled. 'What level is it?'

'Need-to-know,' Riley said.

'And you think he needs to know, but he probably doesn't at the moment, is that it?'

Riley glanced over her shoulder at the bar and then back to Tench. 'Maybe. I don't know what he knows, do I?'

Judith sat back in her seat and sighed. 'Oh Bill. Let's stop playing games. If you give me a clue I'll see what I can find out. But *I'd* need to know that it wouldn't put him under threat, or in any way compromise his position. As shadow minister with responsibility for state security he absolutely cannot be seen to be involved in anything underhand. You of all people should know that.'

Riley twirled his glass round as he thought. He shrugged, looked like he was about to say something, then twirled some more.

Judith slapped her hand on the table and leaned toward him. 'Oh for God's sake, give me a word, or a phrase, or a hint; something I can work with.'

Riley looked at her, his eyes squinting. 'Unity.'

14

Police Station, Central London

Tommy leaned back against the holding cell wall and stared at the paint peeling on the ceiling. He could hear activity further down the cell block corridor – someone whistling tunelessly, a phone ringing and ignored, a door slamming.

He looked at his watch. Three hours. Three hours he'd been in the cell, and still nothing. An interrogation in the interview room, smirking coppers who were convinced he'd stolen the car, and a sergeant who threatened to beat him up if he didn't 'come clean.'

They'd lost patience with him in the end when he wouldn't tell them anything and had shoved him in the cell. He hoped the phone number he'd given them would be effective, but as the hours passed his optimism drained. Anyway, he knew he was in trouble, serious trouble.

It had just been bad luck, that's all. Not his fault. Well, not really, he tried to tell himself. He hadn't broken any traffic laws, was driving carefully after he'd left the café, but then the police Panda had latched onto him anyway, the two-tone siren wailing and lights flashing as the vehicle followed him.

He should have just calmly pulled over. He knew that now, but instead his reaction was to floor the accelerator and try to get away. Stupid, he realised, as they'd have already clocked his registration plate. Although if he did get away they wouldn't have his name, only that of the owner, and they weren't about to find him at home.

So he'd driven fast, dodged traffic and pedestrians, dashed down side roads, used all his knowledge of central London to the best of his ability, even run a red light, but still had been unable to shake the pursuing Panda. In the end he had made a mistake and driven into a dead end, and that was it. End of the chase, end of his freedom. Charles would be furious.

A key rattled in the lock and the door squeaked open. Tommy stood up, hoping it was a cup of tea and a biscuit. His café visit seemed an age ago.

A man in a tweed coat was ushered in by the police sergeant. The door remained open.

'Here he is,' the sergeant said grumpily. 'The car thief.'

'Alleged car thief,' the man responded in a cultured and confident voice, briefly glancing at the officer, then settling his gaze on Tommy. 'It's all right Sergeant, I'll take it from here.'

The sergeant remained in the doorway. 'This isn't normal,' he grumped. 'This isn't procedure. We caught him in a vehicle that's not his, he tried to evade us, drove dangerously, even went through a red light., and he's got blank taxi receipts obviously for fraudulent purposes... we can't be having his sort out on the roads!'

'That's as maybe,' the man said, 'but he's in our care now Sergeant. You can relax, there's a good fellow. Now then,' he turned back to Tommy, 'You've been a naughty boy. But let's get you out of here.'

The sergeant backed into the corridor as the man led Tommy out by the arm.

'Thank you sergeant. Have a good night.'

They walked down the corridor, and stopped at the main desk where an officer reluctantly gave Tommy back his personal belongings, including the map of greater London. The man in the coat grabbed it before Tommy could.

'I'll take that if you don't mind.'

The desk officer then went to hand Tommy the blank taxi receipts but tore them in half first. 'Oops,' he smirked, letting them flutter to the countertop.

'What about my car?' he asked.

'*Your* car? Oh it's your car now is it?' snarled the policeman. 'It's been impounded. You can collect it tomorrow, since this gentleman here has assured me that – *obviously* – you didn't steal it.'

The officer slammed the car keys on the counter and turned away, shaking his head.

Tommy got into the man's Rover parked outside and the stranger started the engine. 'Right, let's get you somewhere less conspicuous.'

It was a short drive through the now-dark streets, and Tommy was both surprised and worried when they turned into Virgil Street and stopped in front of the garage where he worked. Surprised because he'd never met this man before, and worried because Charles might be there. However, the place was locked up and in darkness, and yet the man had a key. He unlocked the side door and stood back for Tommy to enter.

Tommy switched on the lights, relieved to see that Charles definitely wasn't there. 'So who are you then?'

'Who I am doesn't really matter,' the man said. 'But you can call me Mr. Symes. And well done for remembering the emergency phone number Charles gave you.'

'How did you get me out of the nick?'

'Powers of persuasion,' Symes answered. He looked around the garage at the various vehicles in for servicing or repair, his eyes settling on the hearse. He walked over to it, then around it.

'Why did you have the map?' he asked.

Tommy leaned back against the workbench and stuck his hands in his pockets. 'Find my way around London,' he shrugged.

'What's the significance of the rings drawn on it?'

Tommy shrugged again. 'Thinking of getting a flat further out. Too expensive in the city.'

'Really?' The man opened the driver's door and peered inside the hearse. He stepped back and closed the door again. 'I don't believe you.'

He walked up to Tommy and stopped, staring him in the face. He glanced over Tommy's red hair, his prominent cheekbones, then came back to his eyes.

'You were clearly told when you were given this job that you were to keep quiet, not ask questions, do what you were told and – importantly – stay out of trouble. I believe you've failed on at least two of those. I could arrange for Charles to fire you, like that,' he said, snapping his fingers in front of Tommy's face. Tommy didn't blink.

So the man knew Charles well. Obviously, since he had a key to the garage, but maybe Symes actually employed him.

Symes turned away and walked over to the hearse again. He turned back to Tommy and leaned back against the sweeping front wing.

'What's your job here?'

Tommy tilted his head slightly and smirked. 'I think you know that.'

'Indulge me.'

'I'm a mechanic. I help Charles service and maintain the cars that are brought here. They're government cars I was told.'

'And?'

'Look man, who are you? Yeah, okay, your name's Symes, maybe. But I don't know who you work for, I don't know how well you know Charles, and I don't know that I should be talking to you. I was told to keep quiet, remember?'

'Good man,' said Symes. 'Quite right. But then, I'm the one who just got you out of jail. The charges have been dropped and your record remains clean. Although theft of an automobile and stealing from that engineering firm you worked for previously, well, the charges could of course be renewed at any time. It wouldn't look good for you.'

Tommy's patience was running out now. He was tired, it was late, and he wanted to go home. He pushed himself away from the workbench and squared up to Symes.

'That was a fit-up, and you know it!' he hissed, balling his fists. 'I didn't steal nothing, and I think you know that too!' he shouted.

Symes was unmoved. 'I understand your frustration, despite your double negatives,' he said, picking at a speck of dust that wasn't on his coat, 'and I'm sure you'd rather just go home. But tell me first, what else do you do here, apart from oil changes and cleaning spark plugs? Where do you go in this beast?' he asked, patting the wing of the Austin Princess.

Tommy's shoulders fell slightly. 'You already know that too, man.'

'Indulge me, again.'

'Okay, so Charles gets a phone call occasionally and we have to go out to a location somewhere, sometimes a flat, sometimes a house. There's someone there who needs transporting. We transport them. That's it.'

Symes actually laughed, showing perfect teeth and matching dimples. 'Excellent. Well done.' But the smile dropped quickly. 'However, now you're beginning to question why, aren't you? You've just undertaken – pardon the pun – your latest extraction assignment, and now you're curious as to where your... "clients" shall we call them? are taken. And why. Yes?'

Tommy remained tight-lipped. Symes continued.

'You've somehow worked out that your boss took the hearse north today, and the rings on your map, these arcs...' – he waved the map in his hand – 'are your guess as to where he might have gone.'

Tommy raised his hands in denial and was about to argue, but Symes interrupted him.

'Don't bother. We know what you're thinking. But let me tell you,' he said, pushing himself off the hearse and once again placing himself squarely in front of Tommy, 'you are still in trouble. You might not be in a police cell any more, but you are not out of the woods.'

He glanced at the map. 'Actually, you've been rather clever.' Symes slapped the map onto Tommy's chest, giving it back to him, then abruptly turned and headed for the side door. He stopped when he reached it and looked back.

'Yes, really rather clever. We might have a use for you. Now go home, and try not to get arrested, there's a good chap.'

He stepped through the door into the night and was gone.

15

Century House, Sub-basement 2

Anastasia Walker checked her watch, yawned, and wondered not for the first time why she had volunteered to take the initial shift in the monitoring suite. Nothing had happened. Well, not much.

Holland, the supervisor, had left and been replaced by a taller, balding and bespectacled chap with sloping shoulders. He was as annoying as Holland had been, Walker thought, making little quips and what he thought were *bon mots*. Oh well, I guess if you work in here, permanently underground, permanently in the dark, you would have to find some way of relieving the boredom, she thought.

'Oh it's not all dull!' Quentin McCauley, the replacement supervisor had assured her. 'No, not at all. Many's the time one has witnessed... events, shall we say, that have almost changed the course of history. Yes indeed!'

He leaned towards her conspiratorially and whispered, 'One has seen members of royalty in positions not just of power, as it were!' he chuckled.

'Has one?' Walker had sourly replied, turning her attention back to the monitors showing the facility's lush grounds, and the room the man had been taken to in his still-drugged state. That had been just an hour or so ago, and now she was nearing the end of her shift. She regretted that Riley would be the one to see the action when the subject awakened.

Walker poured herself a final coffee from the pot, put the mug to her lips then changed her mind. All she wanted to do now was go home and sleep, and coffee wouldn't help. She'd seen the articulated removals lorry arrive, watched as the subject's room was furnished according to the photographs of his flat, been impressed with the attention to detail that had been achieved in such a short time, and then, just now, had been slightly concerned for the subject as he was carefully laid fully clothed on the divan.

She worried that he might not wake up, or that he would wake up but be damaged in some way. She didn't like the use of drugs or knock-out gasses, but she recognised their value in this scenario. And anyway, all the residents were medicated in some way, so she wasn't sure what nagged at the back of her mind in this particular case, or why she should be especially concerned. Except what he might know about the project.

The monitoring room door opened and in stepped Riley. Not as fresh as a daisy, Walker thought, not exactly bouncing with energy and ready to go. She was pleased that she wasn't the only one who was tired, but wasn't about to hang around and discuss Riley's sleep pattern for the night.

'Ah, there you are,' she said, getting up from her chair and grabbing her jacket from a hook on the wall. She shrugged into it.

'Not much to tell really. His furniture arrived, he arrived, everything was put in place and now all you have to do is watch him wake up and see what happens.'

'Righty-ho,' Riley responded. He sat down and plonked a paper bag on the console desk. 'Breakfast. I won't be able to operate without it. You could have some if you'd like.' He didn't sound like he meant it.

'No thanks. I'm off. I'm told Olivia Wilson the psych lass will be joining you this morning. Watch what you say, or even think. I get the impression she can read our minds. I don't trust her. Have a lovely morning Riley.' She smiled, though the smile didn't exactly light up her face. She left, and Riley looked out through the double glazed windows into the monitoring room where screens glowed in the darkness, silhouetting the operators who were watching them while controlling their cameras and microphones.

McCauley popped his head round the door and waggled the fingers of his left hand by way of greeting. He stepped into the room and Riley unfolded himself from his chair.

'McCauley, Quentin.' He extended a hand which Riley took.

'Riley... Bill.'

McCauley shook his hand vigorously and grinned. 'Ah! "The Ace of Spies" perchance?'

Riley withdrew from the handshake. It was going to be a long day.

'No. Different spelling. But I did read the book. I don't think I'm as suave or as sophisticated. And hopefully I'm not on the Soviets' target list.'

McCauley's eyes glittered; he felt he might have found a kindred spirit. He was wrong.

Riley decided to take charge. 'Right, Director of Psych Operations Major Olivia Wilson is coming in soon. I'd like you to brief her about what's happened during the night, bring her – and me – up to date. This whole thing...' he gestured towards the central section monitoring the grounds and buildings of the pretty yet sinister village, 'is largely her doing.'

McCauley almost bowed. 'Of course, of course, message received and understood. Admiral on deck, that sort of thing, what?'

'Quite.' Riley said.

The door suddenly flew open and a young woman burst in, flustered.

'Sorry, sorry to interrupt, sirs,' she blustered in a Yorkshire accent that belied her Jamaican origins, looking from one to the other, 'but he's waking up. He's awake!' She looked at McCauley. 'You asked me to let you know sir...'

McCauley put an avuncular hand on her shoulder. 'Quite right Delyse, I did. Thank you. We'll be right there. Put the apartment camera on the main screen.'

Riley reached for the phone. 'I'll let Olivia Wilson know.'

Wilson arrived within minutes. McCauley and Riley were standing in the main theatre watching the action on the largest of the screens as the subject left his accommodation and tried to get his bearings. Wilson joined them.

'What have I missed?' she asked.

'Not much,' Riley responded. 'After pacing around his study he's looked out of the window and realised he's not in Kansas any more. Looked a bit like a caged lion. He left his accommodation and is now exploring the grounds.'

'Normal behaviour,' Wilson nodded. 'In a way, that's exactly what he is, a caged lion.'

'Why, if you don't mind my asking, have we gone to all the trouble of replicating his study when all he had to do was open the blinds and see he's somewhere else?'

Wilson kept her eyes on the screen. 'It's the first stage of disorientation,' she said, closely watching the subject as an external camera captured him climbing the steps up the village's bell tower, still trying to make sense of where he was.

'The whole point of this is to take *away* the familiar,' she continued, somewhat tersely. She disliked having to explain her profession or her strategies, and she felt she'd already done so at the directors' meeting. 'The more confused he is, the more pliable, and the more vulnerable.'

They continued to watch over the next few minutes as the subject tried to engage with various members of the community – café staff, a taxi driver, and the shopkeeper in the general store; the village was extremely well-equipped.

Riley and McCauley didn't need Wilson to explain the rationale behind some of the events. The subject at this point had no idea where he was or even what country he was in. He was told by the taxi driver that she'd expected he might have been Czech or Polish, while the shopkeeper had spoken in what might have been Italian, or Spanish.

'What language *is* that?' Riley asked.

Wilson shrugged. 'Doesn't really matter. What matters is that he's kept in a state of confusion. We're trying not to give anything away.'

Riley's shift was certainly proving more enjoyable than Walker's, and his breakfast went untouched as he became engrossed in the action on the screens. As the morning progressed they witnessed the subject become increasingly agitated. The map he'd got from the store proved useless, as Wilson explained they knew it would, since it showed only the local grounds. Beyond its boundaries on three sides it said simply 'Mountains.' On the fourth was the estuary.

They watched as the man received an invitation to breakfast in the Green Dome. An invitation from Number Two.

Olivia Wilson responded to their unspoken questions as soon as McCauley and Riley turned to her.

'Number Two. The first of a few, as I said in the meeting. I like this chap; he's smooth and self-assured. I chose him to be the first for that very reason. He's the antithesis of the subject at the moment – calm, at home in this environment, in charge. Exactly all the things the subject is not.'

'And the diminutive butler?' Riley asked, gesturing towards the screen as the formally attired servant served breakfast.

'Ah, him,' Wilson smiled briefly. 'He's our little joke.'

McCauley chuckled. 'Ooh, is that a pun? I rather like it ma'am!'

Wilson glared at him. 'It's not. The joke here is that the butler is one of the very few consistent characters in this whole piece of grand theatre.' She waved an arm at the screen. 'He will be there the whole time, he will become a familiar face to the subject, and yet he will tell him nothing because he literally can't. He's mute. But not stupid. He's a qualified helicopter pilot among other things, as you'll likely see at some stage. And it's not ma'am,' she added through gritted teeth. 'I prefer "sir."'

The smile dropped from McCauley's face and he turned back to the screen. They all did, and watched transfixed at how Number Two skilfully managed the upwelling of rage within the new resident.

One of the more unsettling of the morning's events was the security demonstration. Wilson had warned them it was coming, but nothing quite prepared Riley for the eeriness of it.

Number Two demonstrated how he could command all the village residents to remain still with a single order, but one younger resident disobeyed, panicked, and ran in a state of fear and alarm.

Whether he was suffocated to death or merely fainted through a lack of oxygen wasn't clear, and Olivia Wilson didn't elaborate, but the message was clear: the sinister shape-shifting white 'blob' could be engaged at short notice to control errant residents any time it was required. It bounded, rolled and morphed its way around the village, equally nimble on land or water. Its exterior was bare, pure white. There was no face, no features of any kind. What it was remained a mystery, which made it all the more terrifying for the residents, and it could appear seemingly from nowhere at any time.

Riley shuddered and made obvious his distaste to Wilson beside him. 'I don't hold with this,' he said. 'I've made it clear before that there should be limits placed on how far we should go with this... this... so-called security.'

Wilson remained staring at the screen, a slight frown on her face. 'I know you have, and you're not alone.' She turned to him. 'I'm a psychologist remember; I'd much rather mess with his mind as you call it than have this… resource… physically chase and smother him. It's not fully developed yet, still very much experimental I'm told, yet effective enough.'

She turned back to the screen. 'So, see this demonstration as a salutary lesson. Hopefully we won't have to deploy it again and this warning will suffice.' She was wrong, but of course didn't yet know it.

16

The Savoy Grill, London

Stone sat at the table and scribbled notes with his fountain pen in a leather-bound notebook lying between the silver cutlery on the white linen tablecloth. He took a sip of water from the crystal glass beside him and tapped his pen against his chin while he contemplated what he wanted to get from this lunch appointment with the secretary of state and foreign affairs.

'Thank you, thank you young man,' he heard an approaching familiar voice say. He looked up and saw the foreign secretary dismissing the maître d'.

'Ah, you beat me to it,' said the secretary, extending his hand as Stone stood. 'Apologies if I'm late.'

'George. Good to see you. No not late at all. Please, sit...'

The sommelier appeared as if by magic beside them and took their drinks orders.

'The driest sherry you have for me as an aperitif please – chilled of course – followed by... are you having fish or meat?' he asked Stone, who at this stage hadn't really decided, but he knew the wine was more important to his lunch companion than the main course.

'I'll choose according to the wine,' he smiled, and picked up the menu.

The foreign secretary quickly scanned the wine list, though he knew it almost by heart. 'A bottle of the '55 Château Cheval Blanc if you please.'

'A very good vintage sir, thank you. I will decant it personally.' The sommelier disappeared. Stone looked round the room, pleased that their table was in a corner and somewhat distant from the others.

'So,' George Brown said jovially as he sipped the glass of water that a waiter had poured him, 'how're things in "the department within the department"?'

Stone smiled back. 'Fine George, thank you, the department is operating efficiently and effectively, although there is one development I think you should know about...'

Brown too looked briefly round the restaurant, wondering now whether this was in fact the best place to meet and discuss business. However, using a private meeting room at Westminster would have precluded the opportunity to savour a fine Bordeaux, so he decided this was in fact preferable.

'Do tell,' said Brown. 'Nothing serious I trust? Where is that damn sherry?' He turned around and was pleased to see the sommelier approaching with a cold glass of the hotel's driest and finest.

'Ah, excellent. Thank you.' He turned back to Stone when the wine waiter was out of earshot. 'Now, you were saying?'

Stone cleared his throat. 'You're aware of course of the, er, retirement facility we've had running for about two years now?'

'Of course. I thought it a fine concept at the time. And it's working well I believe, especially now that it's become a joint services resource; greater and more secure level of funding.' He tapped the side of his nose.

'Indeed. And it's working better than we anticipated. The residents have settled in nicely, they are content, and see no need to be anywhere else. There was, as you know, some reluctance on the part of some of them to begin with, but – well, the right medication and... therapies... have proved very effective.'

'Excellent,' Brown said, savouring the chilled nutty bite of his sherry. 'But?'

'Well, as you also know the proposal for the community was that it would secretly double as an internment facility in the event any of our operatives, or indeed any of our employees, went "rogue" as it were. And of course if we ever needed to incarcerate foreign operatives there.'

Brown raised a bushy eyebrow as he stared at Stone over the rim of his nearly empty glass. 'Rendition. Naturally.' He nodded for Stone to continue.

'To that end we were fortunate to secure a secondment from the army of one of their most senior psychological bods, a Major Olivia Wilson. The name doesn't matter; what does matter is that she's a smart one, double-first from Oxford, PhD, the works. She's been largely responsible for how effective the facility has been over the past year. As well, she developed for us a robust and detailed strategy for managing any operatives who might prove... difficult.'

Stone could see that Brown was listening, even though he had already turned his head in the hope of catching the sommelier's eye again.

'But we have had to test Major Wilson's tactics sooner than expected. One of our field operatives – our best actually – resigned suddenly, on – we understand – a matter of principle.'

Brown gave up on the sommelier and put his empty glass down. He looked seriously through his tortoise shell-framed glasses at Stone.

'You have the situation in hand?'

'We do. We had it under control from the moment he handed his resignation to his superior. The problem – well, not so much a problem as a conundrum – is that his resignation said nothing more than "I resign, effective immediately." Although he did say – well, shouted actually – that we had gone too far – his words – and that he felt he could not work for us a minute longer.'

Stone now had the full attention of the foreign secretary.

'What matter of principle would galvanise one of your operatives, no, your *best* operative you say, to resign?'

Stone once more looked around the room to ensure no-one was within hearing. They weren't, but he nevertheless dropped his voice.

'We think he's somehow found out about Unity.'

Brown was silent. He stared at Stone for a moment, then folded his hands in front of him on the table and looked at them. He pursed his lips, then looked directly at his lunch companion.

'How much does he know?'

It was now Stone's turn to be silent, but only for a moment. 'That's the issue: we don't know. Possibly – and most likely – very little. Unity has been kept under the tightest security from the beginning. Even the boffins at the labs in Wiltshire have no idea of the end game of their current work, and those who are engaged on the delivery side, as well as those in manufacturing, are compartmentalised and have no knowledge of who their fellow team members are or what they're doing. Likewise, the various technicians in the facility are equally in the dark. It's like a jigsaw – the pieces themselves are unique but put together they form a complete and clear picture. Very, very few people know that full picture, and certainly none of the individuals working on the project do.'

There was a pause as George Brown twirled his empty sherry glass by the stem and thought. The waiter suddenly interrupted them, spotting the lull in the conversation as his chance to take their lunch orders.

But neither Stone nor Brown had chosen anything, their menus lying unopened on the table.

The foreign secretary said to the waiter, distractedly, 'Tell Silvino I'll have whatever he feels would go best with the '55 Cheval Blanc.'

'Same for me, thank you,' said Stone, mainly so that they could continue their conversation. The waiter departed after assuring Brown that the wine was being decanted and would be brought soon.

George Brown picked up the linen napkin and mopped his face with it.

'And you've got him secure you say?'

Stone smiled reassuringly. 'We have. He's safe, and Major Wilson's strategy is being applied as we speak. He won't escape, I can assure you.'

'But if he does? Have you any idea the damage he could do? Not only to you and me, but this whole country, the whole of Britain! My God.' Brown slumped in his seat and poured another glass of water, his hand shaking slightly.

Stone smiled again. 'Don't fret George. We need to find out what he knows first, that's our priority. From there we can decide how best to manage him.'

The wine arrived, the sommelier pouring a taste of the dark ruby liquid from a decanter for the foreign secretary. Normally he would have taken a sniff, held it to the light, taken a sip, swirled it in his mouth, sucked in some air, and then swallowed. This time he simply gulped it.

The wine waiter waited for his approval, but Brown was slow to give it.

'This doesn't taste anywhere near as good as I thought it would,' he grumbled. The sommelier looked crestfallen but Brown indicated to fill their glasses anyway.

He needed something to take away the bad taste in his mouth.

17

Tommy's flat, Stockwell, South London

Tommy stumbled from his bedroom into the kitchen, blinking against the strong morning light coming through the window. He robotically began making coffee, and listened for his flatmate. Not that they were in any kind of relationship; this arrangement was purely based on expediency, although as far as the landlord knew they were 'a couple.'

'Chris?' he called out tentatively.

No response. She was still asleep, or maybe already gone to work. He couldn't remember what shift she was on. He took his coffee, sat at the kitchen table and opened the map that Symes had returned to him.

Clever. That's what Symes had called him. So, did that mean that Charles's destination *was* actually within the arcs he'd drawn? He looked closely, but the map, he knew, wouldn't show specific government facilities, only towns, railway stations and roads. And churches, he thought, which could be useful; he could do with some divine intervention.

Seventeen miles or thereabouts. That's how far he'd gone. Tommy looked at the names within his arcs – South Ockendon, Brentwood, Epping, Watford, Rickmansworth... none of them meant anything to him.

He stared at the map, out of focus, his mind wandering. He closed his eyes. Now he was in the hearse with Charles, picturing him threading his way through the streets, across the river, turning this way and that. Suddenly he stood up knocking the chair over and rushed to the kitchen cupboard. 'No, no, no!' he said aloud. 'Wrong, man, all wrong!'

He took a saucer from the cupboard, went back to the table and drew another arc closer in. 'It would have been less than seventeen miles on the map because he didn't – couldn't – have driven in a straight line,' he muttered. 'Clever? Stupid more like.' He picked the chair up and sat again, and went through the names above the new arc: Waltham Cross, Potters Bar, Ruislip, Northolt... Northolt! There's an RAF base there, he realised. It was even named right there on the map!

Tommy took a long gulp of his coffee and sat back, thinking. Northolt. Planes, helicopters, hangars. A military facility, a Ministry of Defence facility. A *government* facility. He was sure he was right even though he had no more evidence than the odometer reading and some crudely-drawn lines on a map.

But why? he wondered. Why take the man there? To fly him somewhere else obviously. But that didn't help. If the man had been put on board an aeroplane or a helicopter he could be anywhere by now, maybe even another country. Unless they were holding him at the air base itself.

A key turned in the front door and Christine Watkins, Tommy's flatmate, swept in in a whirl of coat and scarf, a leather satchel in one hand and a portable typewriter in the other. She dropped her bag on the hall floor, though was more gentle placing the typewriter.

'God I need a drink!' she declared as she came into the kitchen. She saw Tommy's coffee on the table, grabbed it and took a couple of long gulps.

'Help yourself. Slake that thirst, baby!'

'Don't call me baby. Or I'll finish this whole mug.' She took another drink then gave it back to him. She looked at the map on the table. 'Are you moving out? Please tell me you're not?'

Tommy folded the map up and put it aside. He smiled his most charming smile. 'No man, chill out. I ain't going nowhere.'

'Anywhere,' she chided. 'And it's "I'm not going anywhere", but then I keep forgetting you didn't have a private education.' She liked teasing him.

'Which is why,' he chuckled, spreading his arms in submission, 'you are a newspaper reporter and I am but a humble garage mechanic. I do have class though – it's called working class.'

They went into the small lounge where Chris – rarely Christine – flopped on the couch while Tommy sat in one of the two old armchairs.

'It's been a hellishly long night shift. But I've got news,' Chris said, kicking her shoes off and curling her legs up under her. 'I've been promoted!'

'Yeah? That's gas!'

'Yes, isn't it? You are now looking at the paper's new assistant political editor!'

'Really?' Tommy was genuinely pleased for his flatmate. He knew she worked hard, and obviously her dedication had paid off. 'Wow. You've hit the big-time girl.' He raised his mug in a toast to her success. 'You had a better time than me then,' he smiled.

'Why, what did you get up to?' she yawned.

Tommy draped one leg over an arm of his chair and nonchalantly said, 'Oh, y'know, kidnapped a guy, nicked his car, got arrested and thrown in jail… that sort of thing.'

But Chris was miles away, possibly dreaming of her increase in salary and how she'd spend it. Or more likely looking forward to bed. 'Yeah? Sounds like fun,' she yawned, not believing a word he said, if indeed she'd heard him at all.

'Hey, Chris, what do you know about the RAF base at Northolt?'

Chris came out of her reverie and looked at him. 'Why? Are you going to join the air force?'

'Nah, but an old school mate of mine is in the RAF and I haven't seen him for a couple of years. Last I heard he'd been posted there,' he lied.

'I don't know anything about it much,' Chris said. 'One of our guys did a piece on it a while back. I do know it's used by all of the armed forces, not just the RAF, but that's all really. Why don't you just phone them and ask if he's there?'

Now it was Tommy's turn to be miles away as he pictured the base in his mind. He saw low buildings, hangars, runways, and a control tower. High fences and military patrols, a red and white barrier across the entrance, and a guard house.

'Yeah, maybe I will,' he said thoughtfully. 'Anyway, I've got to get to work. Well done on the promotion. Can I have one of your business cards?'

Chris was bemused. 'Why? I'll be getting new ones soon, with "Assistant Political Editor" on them, not just "Lowly Reporter."'

Tommy smiled broadly. 'Yeah, but we can stick the old one on the fridge and the new one next to it. And of course leave a space for the next one after that which'll have "*Chief* Political Editor" on it!'

She laughed and fished one out from her satchel.

'I'm happy enough with assistant for now,' she beamed. 'Here.' She handed him the card.

He looked at it. It bore the crest and name of the newspaper, along with her name: Chris Watkins. He went back into the kitchen to make some breakfast. Chris went upstairs to bed.

18

Century House, Stone's office

Stone swivelled his chair and faced Olivia Wilson across his mahogany desk.

'So, everything is "as expected" you say?'

Wilson sat ramrod straight on the edge of her seat, eschewing the inviting comfort of its soft leather. 'Yes sir, he's responding exactly as we thought he would, although…'

'Yes?'

'Well, he's an interesting mix; he's both captive yet in control at the same time. It doesn't surprise me given his psychological profile, but our first Number Two has handled it admirably.'

'What of Cobb?' asked Stone.

Wilson's shoulders slumped almost imperceptibly, but Stone noticed. He didn't say anything, merely raised an eyebrow.

'Cobb, yes. The ruse of getting Number Six to unquestioningly trust him as a friend and reveal why he resigned didn't work, so we've fallen back on the contingency and removed Cobb from the scenario. Six was suspicious of him I think right from the moment he saw him. Our aims of unsettling him might have backfired a little in that the environment and the people within it are so convincing that he doesn't trust anyone or anything, Cobb included. We staged Cobb's suicide per the contingency and brought his "grieving girlfriend" into play in an effort to win the subject's confidence.'

'And?'

'Again no luck I'm afraid. Once more he smelled a rat. Although she did try and help him "escape" as planned and he took the bait. The village's supervisor held the Rover security element back and allowed Six to steal the helicopter.'

Stone steepled his fingers, his elbows on the desk. His gaze at Wilson was unwavering. He was remembering George Brown's unease about the captive.

'I'm assuming he didn't get anywhere…'

'No sir. He got a brief aerial view of the village before being brought safely back down by remote control.'

'Excellent,' said Stone, leaning back in his chair. 'And you say the new Number Two has already taken over? I rather like your concept of constantly changing the authority figure, keeping our new resident guessing.'

Wilson permitted herself the briefest of smiles, but only for a millisecond. 'Thank you sir. It will be a vital role in wearing him down. As you know, we have quite a few top-quality candidates lined up for the Number Two role, so none of them will be exposed to the captive's defences for too long. While they retain their freshness, he on the other hand will, I believe, be worn down.'

Stone then did something out of character, Wilson noted. He shuffled the blotter on his desk, pretended to tidy the pens in their holder, and moved the telephone console so that it lined up with the corner of the desk. This, she knew, indicated that he was getting his thoughts in order. He spoke to the files and stationery in front of him rather than to Wilson herself.

'I'm curious, as are some above me, to know whether he has mentioned anything specific as regards his resignation.' Stone shrugged dismissively. 'You know, any reasons given, any phrases he's used, words he might have mentioned, operations he's worked on…'

His voice trailed off, although now he looked directly at Wilson again, his eyes piercing and unblinking through his rimless glasses.

Wilson considered this for a brief moment before answering. She didn't need a degree in psych training to recognise that Stone had something particular in mind and was reluctant to spell it out.

'No sir, nothing specific. He's railed against being given a number, emphasised quite vigorously that he is a "free man," and has naturally asked whose side we are on. Is there something we should be listening for in particular other than why he resigned?'

No, no, I don't think so,' said Stone, waving his hand dismissively. 'In the end, we want information. We are going to enormous lengths – and not insubstantial cost to get it – and you have all the resources you need at your disposal, so I expect you to succeed.

'If however he should mention anything to do with his work, or our work here, or any specific… projects, then you will notify me immediately. We know he resigned on a matter of principle; it would be helpful to also know exactly what drove that decision.'

Wilson felt she was sufficiently in the 'inner circle' of those in the know to ask, 'If I may speak candidly sir, it would help if I knew exactly what we might be looking for or listening for. If we did, then maybe we could drip-feed him some clues to gauge his reaction, see if we could maybe spur him into action.'

Stone's eyes once more searched his desktop before settling back on Wilson. He shook his head slowly.

'No. I don't want to be giving *him* information that might be… dangerous. Let's just say I have a feeling he knows something specific about a project that one of our departments is working on. It is not only classified, but above Top Secret. Therefore I'm afraid I can't discuss it with you even with the high-level clearance you have.' He drew a folder towards him and picked up a pen.

Wilson understood that the debrief was over. She stood, and for a moment she almost saluted, but squared her shoulders and said, 'Thank you sir. I'll keep you informed.'

19

The Lonely Pheasant Pub

Bill Riley was exhausted. He sat in one of the pub's booths staring at the glass of beer in front of him, his breathing deep and measured, his fingers twirling the glass round and round. He was reflecting on the shift in Sub-2 that he'd completed, and his handover to Anastasia Walker.

'And that's about it really,' he'd summed up to Walker. 'The new Number Two has taken over, our inmate has failed to escape from paradise, and so far we have failed to learn anything other than he is proving to be what the Americans call a "tough cookie."'

Walker seemed to take it in her stride. She'd asked him how he thought it had gone, and if he felt confident, whether he still supported the strategy. It was a strange question.

'I have every confidence both in Major Wilson's strategies and in our operational capacity to implement and manage them. How do *you* feel it's going now that we're underway?'

She had been non-committal. He therefore had nothing to report on Anastasia to Stone. He wondered idly whether she had been asked to report on him. He wouldn't be surprised.

But it had, he had to admit, been an action-packed start to the incarceration of the recently-resigned operative. Riley felt as though he'd just walked out of a highly emotional film rather than a work shift, and he was mesmerised still by the to-ing and fro-ing of events as they'd played out before him. Even Quentin McCauley the Sub-2 supervisor had been transfixed, and he was far more used to covertly watching on-screen antics than either Riley or Walker.

'I must say,' McCauley had remarked once the day's drama in the village had concluded and the prisoner was secure in his apartment, 'he's resilient and resourceful, I'll give him that.'

Absolutely, thought Riley as he now took a sip of his beer. Resilient and resourceful, as we always knew he would be. So much so that Number Six, as he'd been labelled, hadn't given a single clue as to his resignation, or what his intentions had been after he had stormed out of his superior's office.

Yes they'd found passports and travel brochures in his flat, indicating he'd been planning to go on a holiday, but knowing how clever he is, thought Riley, he could have planted those just so we would find them – to throw us off the scent.

Then an awful thought dawned on him: what if their top operative had planned all along to be taken? What if he already knew of the village and its dual purposes, and had deliberately planted himself inside to find out all he could? But to what end? And for whom? Earlier he had seen him ask the new Number Two, whose side are you on? Now he wondered the same thing about him.

Riley realised he should bring this up officially, and resolved to mention it the next day. Maybe to Stone himself, but certainly to Olivia Wilson, although he felt sure she must have considered such a possibility already. Mustn't she?

He placed a coaster over what was left of his beer, felt in his pocket for some coins, went to the pub's telephone at the back of the lounge bar and dialled Judith Tench's number. She picked up on the second ring.

'Ah, you're there,' Riley said, identifying himself.

'I know who it is,' Tench replied. 'I can tell your voice from a mile away. Where are you?'

'Not quite a mile away,' he said. 'In fact, just round the corner. Would this be a good time to pop over and see your new flat?'

'I'll put the kettle on,' she said. 'Unless something stronger is in order?'

'Something stronger,' said Riley. 'Definitely something stronger.'

*

It wasn't quite dark as Bill Riley made his way through the streets to the address she'd given him. He stopped a couple of times, pretending once to tie his shoelace, another time to look at reflections in a shop window. He didn't see anyone following, yet he had an uneasy feeling of being watched.

He deliberately took a circuitous route to Tench's flat, choosing some quiet streets so he could listen for any following footsteps, but he knew that anyone with tradecraft skills wouldn't be making any noise. He crossed the road to a phone box and went in, shutting the door behind him and coughing at the stench of stale and pungent cigarette smoke in the confined space.

He dialled Tench again.

'Not to be paranoid or anything, but is your place under observation for any reason?'

'Not that I've noticed,' she said. 'And I would notice. Why?'

'Oh nothing. Just my imagination playing tricks. It's been a long day. See you shortly.'

A tired face stared back at him from the small mirror in the phone box but showed nothing more. Still, he took a moment to glance around as he exited the kiosk. All quiet, no movement other than a cat slowly crossing the road. He set off again, walked five paces then stopped and quickly turned. Still nothing. Warily satisfied, he continued to his destination.

Tench opened the door and stood back as Riley entered. 'Here, let me take your things. Go through to the back,' she said as she hung his hat and overcoat on a hook in the hall.

Riley went through and into the back room, which he found both charming and warm. He missed a feminine touch in his own digs – the attention to colour coordination, table lamps rather than just a ceiling light, oil paintings of landscapes with brass picture lights over them, and an ornate drinks cabinet with the hinged door folded down on which was a tantalus with three decanters. Cut crystal glasses sparkled alongside.

'Are you still a whiskey-with-an-"e" drinker?' Tench asked as she went over to the cabinet. 'Sit down, sit down, don't clutter the place up!'

He sat. 'Yes, if you have it. Thanks. You've got a good memory.'

She poured out a generous measure of Powers and handed it to him.

'And one for yourself barman,' he smiled, but then his face hardened. 'You might need it.'

Tench poured a sherry, spooned some ice into it from a leather-bound ice bucket and sat opposite. 'Cheers.' She raised her glass.

'Sláinte,' he said and did the same. He took a gulp, feeling the warm liquid worm its way through him. He put the glass on a side table and intertwined his fingers, looking at her directly.

'Did you come alone tonight?' Tench asked.

'As far as I know. I checked, but if I was followed by someone I'd trained then I wouldn't know, would I?' he chuckled.

'No, you were a good instructor. Very good. But that was a long time ago, and now you're director, strategic. You've come a long way. I thought you were retiring soon?'

'I plan to. Just one or two things to take care of first.'

'And would either or both of those warrant your being followed, or my house being under observation?'

'Possibly. More likely me than you. I don't want to put you in an awkward position, maybe I should go…' He stood.

'Don't be ridiculous,' Tench said, 'sit down. We need to talk. A sweeper from Five came last week and the place is clean, so you don't need to worry about being overheard. And anyway,' she smiled, 'I don't mind the odd awkward position.'

Then her smile disappeared. 'Is this all about Unity?'

Riley let the word hang in the air for what seemed an eternity before deciding to continue.

'Maybe, maybe not,' he said. 'Hard to tell.' He sat down again.

Tench put her drink down; now it was her face that hardened. 'Bill Riley, what is the matter with you?'

'Me? Oh, there's nothing the matter with me. It's… how did you get on with Douglas-Home? Is... Unity a familiar word to the shadow secretary?'

Tench shook her head. 'Seemingly not. I dropped it into conversations a couple of times, but he didn't raise an eyebrow. It wasn't easy – you never told me anything about it – what it means, what it stands for. I didn't even know in what context I should bring it up. It's a common enough word, "one for all and all for one" sort of thing. The socialists must like it…' she stopped mid-sentence. 'Is this something to do with communism?'

Riley looked around the room, then deciding he could hold back no longer, stared straight at her.

'All right,' he said, 'I'll tell you what I know. How long have you got?'

'All night,' she said, returning his gaze.

20

Downing Street, London

Foreign Secretary George Brown needed a drink. It had been a trying day, meetings and more meetings, but worst of all was the one with the prime minister. He didn't particularly like the Yorkshireman, felt he was too… common? Was that the word? Certainly too manipulative. Yes, common and cunning he thought.

He descended the two steps of Number Ten and felt in his coat pocket for his hip flask. It wasn't there, and momentarily he panicked, then remembered he'd put it in his briefcase. He wouldn't take a nip now anyway, not here in broad daylight and in public, but once in the back of the car…

The chauffeur opened the rear door of the Jaguar and Brown entered, putting his briefcase on the seat beside him. He sank back in the leather upholstery, and not for the first time smiled at his good fortune and rise to power. And, he thought with some enthusiasm, the even greater power to come.

'Where to sir?' the chauffeur asked.

Brown thought for a moment. He really should go home, but he didn't want to, not yet.

'My house I think Daniel, but, er, take your time. Take a really long way home. I need to think.'

'Righty-ho sir,' the chauffeur said, adding mentally, *to think and drink*. He grinned as he started the engine and moved off.

Brown clicked open his briefcase, withdrew the hip flask and gulped down a mouthful. He looked in the driver's mirror to see if his chauffeur had seen him, but his eyes remained straight ahead.

As the limousine reached Whitehall a police car, followed quickly by a police van, both with sirens wailing and lights flashing, roared past. Daniel turned left and was instantly overtaken by two police motorcycles also at speed, and another van.

Brown didn't take much notice; this was central London after all and the police were always going somewhere at speed. He took another surreptitious swig from his flask.

As Daniel drove them closer to Trafalgar Square he could see that some police vehicles had stopped ahead at various angles across the road, the officers, truncheons at the ready, running towards a crowd of people. He slowed the car and said to his passenger, 'Seems to be something going on in Trafalgar Square sir. I'll see if I can get round it.'

'Right,' Brown said, not caring one way or the other. He took another swig and put the flask back in the briefcase.

The chauffeur drove forward slowly looking for a gap to the left further on. He saw one and aimed for it but a policeman stepped out and held his hand up for Daniel to stop. Daniel wound down his window as the officer came round to speak to him.

'I wouldn't come this way if I were you lad, bit of an unruly mob in the square.'

Daniel indicated his passenger in the back. 'Got Foreign Secretary Mr Brown to take home…'

The officer peered in the back, then saluted. 'Oh, good evening sir, sorry, didn't recognise you. Bit of a demonstration going on, protest against the Vietnam war apparently. Mainly young people. Let me see what I can do.'

Brown waved him away nonchalantly.

The officer went and spoke to the two police motorbike riders then came back. 'All right lad, the motorbikes will give you an escort past the mob. Shouldn't take long.' He once more saluted to Brown, but the foreign secretary didn't notice.

Daniel wound up his window, the police riders kicked their machines into life and the officer waved the limo to follow them.

It went wrong as soon as they moved off. Whether someone in the crowd recognised Brown, or simply (and rightly) assumed that a posh car with police outriders must mean somebody important inside was never ascertained, but a brick suddenly smashed through the driver's window, smacking Daniel in the head.

The mob surged forward. The two police riders stopped and looked back, but first one, then the other was pushed from their machines by the crowd. The riders picked themselves up and drew their truncheons.

Now Brown was fully alert. He hastily locked the rear doors with trembling hands. 'Damn it! Get me out of here!' he shouted to Daniel, but the driver was shaking his head, stunned by the blow. Blood seeped from a gash in his temple and he was covered in broken glass.

However, he was army-trained and had passed the diplomatic protection driving course with distinction. He knew the situation would only get worse if they didn't get away immediately.

Brown looked back and saw more police come running, yelling at the crowd to get back. The mob was having none of it. They waved placards declaring their dislike for the Vietnam war, demanding peace, demanding Britain withdraw its support for American armed forces taking part in the conflict. They chanted, they yelled, they gestured.

The police tried to form themselves into a barrier between the limousine and the crowd, but the blue line was far too thin. Brown looked out at the ugly rabble, his hands shaking.

Suddenly there were faces pressed up against his window – ugly snarling faces, mouthing obscenities, fists hammering on the glass, boots kicking the doors. One long-haired skinny youth spat at the window and the gob of saliva dribbled down the glass. Brown raised his arm, withdrew further into his seat and once again shouted at his driver.

'Come on man! Get me out of here! Get a bloody move on!'

Daniel shook his head and blinked, wiped the blood from his eye, wiped his hand on his jacket, then turned round. Brown thought it was to talk to him but he shouted, 'Get down!' Brown did as he was told. It was partly for added protection, but mainly so that Daniel could see through the rear window.

The engine was still running, the road behind was relatively clear. Daniel saw his opportunity. He slammed the car into reverse and hit the accelerator. The car shot backwards, and Brown's briefcase tumbled to the floor spilling its contents. A young woman threw herself onto the bonnet. She screamed as Daniel increased speed and spun the car round. The girl was thrown off onto the road, her placard cartwheeling across the pavement.

The mob was enraged. The yelling swelled in volume, the sticks and poles of placards and banners were turned round to become weapons as the crowd surged forward through the police line running for the limousine. Another brick hit the car and bounced off the rear as Daniel engaged first gear and gunned the engine. Smoke flew from the rear tyres and the car leapt forward.

In the rear mirror the chauffeur saw the mob get smaller as he flicked through the gears. He slowed as he approached Downing Street, thinking to take Brown back there, but he could see a line of police vehicles had blocked the road off. He was waved urgently on by a uniformed sergeant.

'Are you all right sir?' Daniel asked his passenger, glancing in the mirror.

Brown slowly got up from the floor and cautiously looked out of the back window at the mob, now in the distance. He was pale, shaking, sweating. His life was one of comfort, and privilege. He'd never been subjected to such rage or hatred before. He turned to Daniel and blinked.

'I said are you all right sir?'

'Yes, er yes, I'm fine. Fine'

'Oh don't worry about me sir, it's just a scratch,' Daniel said sarcastically when Brown failed to return the query. 'But the car's a bit of a mess.'

'Yes, yes, I suppose it is.' Brown robotically picked up his briefcase and the various files and pens on the floor of the car. He found the hip flask and this time didn't try to hide the generous swig he took.

Daniel eventually saw a quiet place to park the car and brought it to a stop. If Brown noticed he didn't say anything. The chauffeur switched off the engine and got out, glass falling from his jacket onto the road, the brick tumbling out also. He looked at his face in the wing mirror. A bloody mess looked back at him. He went to the back of the car and took a bottle of water and a cloth from the boot, wetted the cloth and began to wipe the blood from his face. He did what he could to stem the bleeding but knew he would have to go to the hospital.

Still holding the cloth to his head he walked round the car surveying the damage – panels dented, his window smashed, scratches, a dent in the boot where the second brick had hit, but basically all superficial.

However, not suitable as a limousine for the foreign secretary until it was fixed.

Daniel went to the rear door and opened it. Brown was still staring as though hypnotised. Shock, Daniel thought. He'd seen it before in battle, knew the signs. He offered the bottle of water to Brown.

'Water sir? It might help…'

'What?' Brown turned slowly as though seeing his driver for the first time. Then his eyes focused on the bottle. 'No, no thank you. I say, are you all right Daniel?'

'Yes sir, as I say, just a scratch. But I should get it looked at.'

'Bloody savages!' Brown growled. 'Get in,' he said, gesturing for Daniel to join him in the back. This was against protocol, but the circumstances were exceptional. Daniel moved the briefcase, got in and closed the door. Brown drew the hip flask from his pocket and offered it to his chauffeur.

'Here, you look like you need a drink…'

'Well, I… I'm not supposed to drink on duty sir.'

Brown however wasn't standing for it. 'Then you're fired, at least for the next few minutes. Here, while you're unemployed, have a bloody drink…'

Daniel took the flask and had a sip. It was whisky and it burned his throat. He was more of a lager man. But it helped. He handed it back. 'Thanks.'

Brown wiped the neck of the flask with his coat sleeve, took another large gulp himself and screwed the cap back on.

'Bloody damn savages, that's what they are. They have no idea about international politics, and even less about wars and why we fight them or support them. That's the problem with young people today, they think they know everything, think they can change the world,' he growled. 'Well they can't, and we won't let them. They'll see. They'll soon see who's in charge.'

Daniel didn't know what to say. He decided nothing would be the safest bet.

'You wouldn't join a rabble like that would you?' Brown turned to Daniel.

'No sir, I don't think so…'

'No, you wouldn't. You were in the army weren't you? Properly trained. Know how to take orders. Know not to question authority. Obedience, that's what's needed. We need this country to come together, to be all facing the same direction.'

Brown was rambling now and Daniel wondered if the incident at Trafalgar Square had maybe affected him more than he'd realised.

Brown pounded his knee with his fist. 'Order! Uniformity! Obedience! That's what the youth of today needs: Unity! And by God they'll get it. Whether they like it or not, they'll get it!'

21

RAF Northolt, West End Road

Tommy switched off the ignition of his Triumph, flipped the side stand down and leaned the bike over. He lifted his goggles and took off his helmet.

He was parked a hundred yards or so from the air base's main entrance, and he could see now that what he'd envisaged the day before had been about right; there were the red and white barriers at the main gate, a central guard house between them, and a high chain-link fence all along the boundary in both directions.

A muted roar caught his attention, and he shielded his eyes against the late morning sunlight. In the distance through the fence he could make out a twin-engined jet with high tail wings hurtling down the runway, rapidly picking up speed. Its torpedo-shaped engines roared loudly, its nose lifted and then it shot up into the sky, banked left and flew north. Tommy didn't know much about aircraft but this one looked old, certainly not one of the experimental fighter jets that were rumoured to be able to take off and land vertically. Still, the mechanic in him appreciated the chunky design, and the roar of the engines appealed as their thunder eventually dissipated in the blue sky.

He wondered what to do next. He was hardly going to be welcomed onto the base, and had no real reason for going there. He didn't, as he'd told his flatmate the evening before, actually have a friend in the RAF who had been posted there. He felt guilty about the fib.

Tommy shaded his eyes and looked again towards the hangars and other buildings. There was nothing to see.

He started to put his helmet back on, then he remembered he needed petrol. He unscrewed the petrol cap on the tank and wobbled the bike side to side. The meagre amount of fluid inside made a hollow splashing noise – confirming there wasn't much in there. Definitely time to fill up. He kicked the bike into life again and headed down the road towards a garage, pulled in, and an acne-faced forecourt attendant began filling the tank.

'Nice bike,' the young man said, his voice breaking in that adolescent way. 'Goes okay?'

'Yeah, not bad for a 500,' Tommy replied, looking towards the back of the forecourt area. He could see a couple of men sitting on folding camping stools, cameras with long lenses in hand. Just the fence between them and the air base perimeter.

'Plane spotters?' he asked the attendant. The youngster nodded.

'Yeah, that's one of their favourite spots, bein' at the end of the runway and everything.' He pronounced it *everyfink*. 'Those two are 'ere most days. Can't see the point meself. You seen one plane you seen 'em all, aintcha?'

Tommy paid for the petrol and wheeled his Triumph over to a corner of the forecourt, put it on its stand and sauntered over to the plane spotters.

'Hello gents,' he said amiably. 'Is this the best spot for it then?'

The pair looked at each other then back at Tommy. The larger of the two, bearded, unkempt hair, and with what Tommy thought was possibly a personal hygiene problem said, 'Plane spotting you mean? Yeah, this is all right, but you can see lots from all around 'ere. Specially Ickenham Marsh over at the other end, if the farmer will let you on 'is land.'

'Will he?' Tommy asked.

'Nah,' said the spotter. We tried, din' we Wayne?'

Wayne huffed, then reached for a thermos flask beside him and began pouring himself a coffee. 'Waste of time. Shame really 'cos it's a better spot than this. Good luck if you wanna try it.' He took a sip and sighed.

They turned their attention back to the runway ignoring Tommy.

'What was that jet that just took off before?' Tommy asked. They looked at each other again.

'So you're not a spotter then, obviously?'

Tommy shook his head. 'No, but thinking of taking it up. Only military aircraft though.'

This seemed to mollify the pair. They nodded slightly to each other. Tubby turned on his camping stool and faced Tommy. He spread his hands.

'That's the only sort there is, my son. Sod the civilian stuff. Anyway, that was a Gloster Meteor. F8 Wayne reckons.'

'F8, definitely,' Wayne nodded, sipping his coffee. 'Great aircraft. Old now, but great aircraft. Saw service at the end of the war. Made my day that has. Got a good shot too I reckon.' He held up his camera as if to prove he'd taken a good photograph.

Tommy's eyes scanned the air base. The hangars and control tower seemed far away. He understood their need for long lenses.

'D'you ever see anything else interesting?'

The spotters looked at each other again. Wayne turned back to the runway and muttered, 'He's all yours Derek.'

Derek the tubby one said, 'What are you? A reporter or sunnink?'

Tommy fished his flatmate's business card from his pocket and handed it to him. 'Yeah, actually, I am. Chris, Chris Watkins.'

Derek fingered the card, showed it to Wayne, then gave it back to Tommy. 'So, what, you working on a story of some sort?'

Tommy looked right and left, then crouched down so he was at Derek's level. He lowered his voice.

'As a matter of fact I am. But it's in its early stages right now. Don't want the other papers to get hold of it if you know what I mean.' He tapped the side of his nose conspiratorially. 'Could be a good breaking story – an exposé if you like – if it works out.'

Now it was Wayne's turn to turn around. Tommy had their attention. Wayne asked, 'So what sort of other things might we have seen? Watcha looking for?'

Derek added, 'Yeah, what? And what's in it for us, Mr… er, Watkins?' He looked at his friend and they nodded at each other again, then looked back expectantly at Tommy.

Tommy stood and scanned the air base again. 'Fame, maybe. Can't promise you fortune, but I could talk to the editor. Depends what you can give me.' He checked his watch. 'Anyway, I've got other stories to file so can't stay here all day…'

Sensing the prospect of losing some easy cash, and maybe getting their names in the paper, the pair now didn't want Tommy to leave.

'No wait!' Wayne said. 'If we can help in some way we'd be glad to. Wouldn't we Degs?' Derek agreed and nodded enthusiastically. A Vulcan bomber could have taken off behind them now and they wouldn't have noticed. Their attention was firmly on Tommy.

'Well,' said Tommy, again checking around him as though to assure himself nobody could overhear, 'unusual activity for example. I can't tell you too much about the story, but let's just say that RAF Northolt could be being used for… well, purposes other than aircraft landings and take-offs.'

The two looked at each other for a moment. They thought hard. A couple of times they looked like they were about to say something, then didn't. They could see the chance of a fee for services rendered disappearing in front of them, like a plane vanishing into cloud.

Derek sighed. 'Sorry mate, no. All we see is aircraft takin' off or landing. There's been nothing unusual. How far back are we going?'

Tommy started to put on his crash helmet. 'Over the last six months say, but the last few days in particular. Any comings and goings, interesting people, strange cargoes being loaded, that sort of thing. No?'

They shook their heads. Inwardly Tommy sighed; for a moment he thought he might have found some witnesses to what happened to the man from the flat he'd helped extract.

'Never mind. Thanks for your time gents. Good luck with the spotting.'

He turned and walked back to his motorbike, pulled it off its stand, turned on the ignition and kicked it into life. He snicked it into first gear and was about to pull away when some movement caught his eye. In his handlebar mirror he could see Derek running after him, puffing and waving as he did so.

Tommy put the gears in neutral and turned towards him as he reached the bike, already badly out of breath even though he'd run only a few yards. His face was flushed.

'There… there was one thing…' Derek puffed. 'Wednesday last week… Wayne and I was walking down the road, past the main gate, on our way 'ere for a twilight session, an' we saw an ambulance leaving the base. With a hearse behind it. Is that of any use?'

Tommy switched off the ignition and began unclipping his helmet.

22

Century House, Sub-basement 2

The large central screen showed the new Number Two having breakfast with the latest arrival in his apartment. As with the previous village authority figures, he was smooth talking, cultured, charming.

In the observation lounge, Olivia Wilson watched with interest, Bill Riley seated beside her.

'He seems to be handling it very well,' Riley remarked.

'Who? Two or Six?'

'Six,' said Riley. 'Very self-assured. But Two also. Evenly matched I'd say. You pick them well.'

Wilson failed to rise to the bait and said nothing, her eyes fixed on the screen. Riley also went quiet as they watched Number Two introduce the concept of a democratic election within the village, and then suggested that Six should run for office. Riley turned to Wilson with raised eyebrows.

'Seriously? You plan to give him a chance to take control?'

'Not at all,' Wilson countered, still watching the interplay between the two characters. 'It's another ruse. Give him a taste of power, a chance of freedom, then sweep it away again, just as we did after his arrival. He may seem self-assured now, but it won't last.'

Riley looked as if he was about to say something but thought better of it.

As the morning wore on, Number Six did indeed decide to run for office, for the position of the next Number Two, although Riley suspected he was merely playing them at their own game. They saw him address the villagers, talking of freedom and individuality. The villagers laughed at the very prospect.

Number Two advised his opposition that he would be required to meet the community's 'Council,' but it didn't go well. Riley became increasingly uncomfortable as he witnessed Six ranting at the so-called council members in one of the official buildings, calling them brainwashed imbeciles, becoming agitated and – Riley feared – on the edge of losing control.

Number Two appeared equally unsettled and in danger of losing direction. Wilson's forehead creased in an almost imperceptible frown. Riley squirmed with discomfort in his seat as he watched Number Two subject Six to some disorientating spinning, dropping him in a confused state through the floor to an area directly below the council chamber.

Here Six underwent psychological testing by a man wearing a badge proclaiming him to be Number 26. Riley noted he was superbly and formally dressed in a three-piece suit with tails, his tie immaculately knotted, his manner warm and friendly.

'Remind me never to get on your bad side,' Riley quipped to Wilson. He made it sound like a joke but inside he was more than half serious.

Wilson reached for a cordless red phone in front of her and pushed a button.

On a separate screen they saw Number Two, now back in the control dome, answer an identical phone as it beeped.

Riley realised Wilson was speaking directly to him. No going through an operator, no dialling required, it was a direct connection. She didn't introduce herself.

'I rather feel you were a bit heavy handed in the council chamber. He might come across as confident but he's also fragile.'

She paused as Two made his excuses.

'Just be more careful,' she admonished, and again listened to his reasoning. 'All right, but I'm relying on you to keep things on track. Warn 26 not to go too far either. I want him undamaged.'

She ended the call and turned to Riley. 'We mustn't over-stretch him. The core staff are aware of his value, but some of them are a little over-enthusiastic. I can't be here twenty-four hours every day so you and Walker keep an eye on Number Two, the psychological staff and anyone in direct contact with Six and let me know immediately should they appear to overstep their mark. Any time, day or night.'

'Sure,' said Riley. 'Do they know we're watching them?'

'Not always. They know we have cameras and microphones everywhere but they can't tell when they're on.'

'Don't you trust them?'

Olivia Wilson sighed. She didn't appreciate her expertise being questioned. 'Yes, I trust them. They've been highly trained and are completely up to speed on what's required. They're basically working to a script. But they also have to be flexible and adapt to circumstances. To ad lib if you like. It's those situations I am less confident of.'

She stood and said, 'I'm just going to have a chat with the supervisor,' and left the observation lounge. It was the moment Riley had been waiting for. He watched until he could see her talking to McCauley out in the main monitoring section, grabbed his coffee mug then quickly went over to where the major's satchel was, on the floor nearby. He placed the mug on the floor under the window.

He opened the satchel, rifled through the various files inside until he came to one in particular – as usual, marked Top Secret, but also in this case with the title 'Number Two' – and withdrew it. He placed it on the floor and opened it. There in front of him was a list of names and addresses with telephone numbers alongside. He briefly checked through the observation window and saw Wilson still talking to McCauley.

Quickly returning to the file, Riley took out a miniature Minox camera from inside his jacket, and photographed the page of names, three times in case any might be blurred or out of focus. He replaced the page in the file and glanced again out of the window.

To his horror he saw McCauley on his own. He dived for the floor, threw the file back in the satchel and replaced it where it had been beside her chair but was still on his knees when he heard the door open. He tipped over the coffee mug and got out his hankie, started mopping at the spillage.

'What *are* you doing?' Wilson demanded as she came in. He looked up.

'Sorry, knocked my mug off the ledge. Careless of me. No harm done, it didn't go on your coat.' He carried on mopping at the dark brown stain expanding across the carpet.

Wilson tutted at his clumsiness and gathered her satchel, and her coat from the back of her chair. 'I'll leave you to it. The election in the village will be in a few days. Six will win, but don't worry. He'll be compliant, malleable. The taxi driver you saw engage with him earlier, Number 58, she's a key player.'

'What language…' Riley began but Wilson cut him off.

'Again, fabricated. She's rather good, I think. Right, I'm off. I hope I don't hear from you.' And with that she walked – almost marched, Riley thought – out of the observation lounge.

'Be seeing you,' Riley whispered under his breath, echoing the mantra that the village residents frequently used as a parting aphorism. He went back to his cleaning chore, smiling for once.

23

Virgil Street Garage

The Jaguar limousine glided almost noiselessly up to the open garage door and the driver switched off the engine, engaged the handbrake.

Charles turned from the workbench, wiped his hands on a cloth and walked over to the car as the driver got out. He could see both the man and the vehicle looked a bit worse for wear.

'Daniel!' Charles said in surprise, 'What have you been up to? Boxing? And what *have* you done to the motor car?'

George Brown's chauffeur walked round the bonnet and shook Charles by the hand. 'Hello Charles. Yes…' he patted the bonnet, 'bit of a kerfuffle. Got caught up in an anti-war protest in Trafalgar Square, taking the foreign secretary home. Crowd turned ugly, especially when they recognised Brown.'

'You all right?' Charles asked, examining the stitches above Daniel's right eye.

'Fine. Nothing that can't be fixed. Brown's unscathed, though understandably shocked. Anyway, speaking of fixing, take a walk round the car with me.'

He led Charles on a tour of the damage, pointing out the dents, scratches, the broken window and so forth. Charles opened a door and peered inside.

'Looks all right in here apart from the broken glass everywhere. But quite a bit of work on the outside. I hope you've got a replacement vehicle – this could take some time.'

Daniel nodded. 'Yes, all sorted. I'll leave it with you.' He handed Charles the keys. 'Good to see you again. Wish it were in happier circumstances!'

Charles chuckled. 'True. Next time don't leave it till the braying mob sends you here! I'll get my lad onto it.'

They shook hands again and Daniel left. Charles called to Tommy who was once again down in the inspection pit under a vehicle.

'Tommy! For your sins you can clean this Jag up and itemise the damage for me.'

Tommy grunted acknowledgement but was pleased that at least Charles was talking to him. Ever since he'd been released from the police station following his episode in the Lotus his boss had been very quiet.

'I hear you've been a naughty boy,' Charles had said softly when Tommy returned to work. 'Broke the rules, drew attention to yourself, and…' – here he paused and talk a deep breath – 'had to be rescued. I'll say no more about it for now, I'm sure Mr. Symes has said everything that needs to be said. But just know that I am not well pleased.'

Other than that Charles had let the matter drop, but he had hardly said a word to Tommy since, apart from telling him what work to carry out in the garage, and to send him back to retrieve the Lotus from the police station. He'd wagged a warning finger at him and told him not to break any traffic rules on the way back.

Tommy saw the arrival of the damaged government limousine as possibly a way to break the ice. He climbed out from the inspection pit wiping his hands and strolled out to the car, peering in where the driver's window used to be.

'Start with the inside, get all that broken glass out,' instructed Charles.

'Sure, will do. No problem man,' said Tommy, trying to sound enthusiastic and compliant. He really didn't want to be on the wrong side of his boss.

Charles grunted and went back to the workbench. Tommy got a brush and pan from the back of the garage and slid the front seats of the Jag back as far as they would go. For the next few minutes he carefully brushed up – sometimes picked up with his fingers – as much broken glass as he could find.

He called out to Charles as he worked. 'Did I hear that bloke say the car had been in a riot?'

Charles didn't turn from the workbench but did at least reply. 'Yes. Something about a protest in Trafalgar Square. Daniel had George Brown the foreign secretary in the back and the crowd didn't like him apparently. I dunno, the young people today – present company included,' he added, and actually chuckled.

Tommy finished clearing up the glass from the front, took out the floor mats and shook them as well, then decided to move the seats forward as far as they would slide on their rails in case some glass had fallen behind them, which was how he found the book.

There, under the driver's seat at the back was a black official-looking notebook, with the government crest embossed in gold on the front. He was about to pick it up and shout to Charles, but suddenly thought better of it. Instead, he whistled a tune as he worked hoping now that Charles would continue to leave him alone.

He opened the book on the floor of the car and took a quick look inside. It was full of scrawled notes – likely Brown's and presumably from meetings he'd attended – but now wasn't the time to do any in-depth reading. However, he flipped through to the last few entries, where one word caught his eye because it was underlined three times: Unity.

Easing the notebook under the dustpan and holding both in one hand, the brush in the other, Tommy backed out of the rear of the vehicle and walked over to the rubbish bin and slid the broken glass into it, but kept hold of the book underneath.

Charles stayed at the workbench. Tommy slid the book under his motorcycle jacket which was lying on the seat of his bike, popped into the office for a clipboard and a pencil and went back to the car to begin the damage report. Chris his flatmate would be very interested in what he'd found – she was after all a newly-appointed assistant political editor – but first he needed to find time to read it himself.

He resumed his whistling as he walked slowly round the car, drawing a diagram of the vehicle and noting the dents and scratches.

24

Century House, Sub-basement 2

'Running for the position of Number Two?' Anastasia Walker was incredulous.

'That's right,' Riley acknowledged. 'Wilson says it won't matter, he won't take control, but…'

Walker turned and looked out into the monitoring room. Riley stole a glance at his watch and hoped the handover wouldn't take much longer; he had a date, sort of.

Walker turned back and sat in one of the monitoring office's chairs. 'What do you think of Wilson?'

Riley was caught unawares. 'Well, I…' he glanced around the room, through the window to the surveillance monitors and large screens, then back to Walker.

'What I think is that she has the whole thing planned out in minute detail, and not much fazes her. She actually admitted that the key players in the village are basically working to a script. Her only concern is where they are forced to "ad lib," as she called it, which is why she asked us to keep a watchful eye on Number Two and the other senior personnel in that respect.'

'Did she indeed? So we're answering to her now are we?'

'Well, no, not really. I rather think we are the key link with Stone on this, but Wilson is obviously high up in his estimation.' He paused as Walker absorbed this.

Riley decided to finally broach the subject that had been in the back of his mind for some time. 'Do you think she knows about Unity?'

Walker looked directly at him. 'Unity? Why do you ask?'

She always was one for answering a question with another question Riley thought. It annoyed him.

'Because Stone has engaged her – along with all the skills and experience she brings to this role – to prise information out of our top man. Ostensibly to find out why he resigned, but you and I already know it was on a "matter of principle," – as does Stone – and that that principle quite likely is that he found out about Unity.

'I mean it would make sense that Olivia Wilson knows just what sort of information we're looking for. And she was present at the joint directorate meeting the other week as you know.'

'Yes, and when we were all summoned to attend we were asked not to mention or discuss in any way the subject of Unity,' responded Walker tersely. 'So on that basis I'd think she *doesn't* know about it. I doubt many of the directors themselves do. It's way above top secret as you know – you and I are among the very few who are party to it. Apart from the technical boffins of course, but even they are privileged to only isolated pieces of information, so I doubt many of them can piece together the whole project picture, or its aims and outcomes.'

Riley nodded thoughtfully. He was about to say something, but Walker spoke first.

'Are *you* comfortable with Unity? With the concept?' she asked.

Riley now realised he was being interrogated. Maybe he was right, maybe Stone had also asked Walker to report on him, just as he was supposed to do about her.

He cleared his throat and walked the three paces over to the main window, looked out at the operators in front of their monitors. On the big screen he could see a wide view of the village, the pathway lights coming on as evening approached. All was quiet.

'I'm increasingly concerned about it, if I'm honest Anastasia.' He turned to her, leaned back against the window and folded his arms. 'I mean, look at this surveillance here,' he waved a thumb behind him, 'it's all-seeing, all-hearing. The residents have no freedom of thought; in fact they have little or no freedom at all. And Unity is taking advantage of that; they've become guinea pigs, lab rats…' his voice trailed off as he turned and looked back at the big screen. 'Have you thought about that?' he said to the observation window.

He wondered if he'd gone too far, whether he should have expressed supreme confidence in the project, pretended it was the greatest concept in the world, but it was too late. If she was reporting privately to Stone, she was sure to tell him.

Maybe his retirement would be brought forward; maybe he would be forcibly retired to the village, like so many of the others. A bead of sweat ran down his temple and he wiped it away, pretending to be brushing his hair back. Walker hadn't noticed.

She stood and joined him, her face stern. 'Of course I've thought about it. But the positives outweigh the negatives. You know Bill Riley, you're beginning to sound like you're also disagreeing with the project. This is a matter of defence, remember. It's a prudent and extremely clever strategic… advantage. Don't you agree?' She looked at him.

Riley realised he needed to divert her.

'And have you thought that maybe our Number Six is a plant? That he knew when he resigned he'd be taken to the village? That he's not there to give us information but to find out as much about the place as he can, before somehow escaping and blowing the lid off the whole thing? He's the one you should be worried about, not me.'

He let the concept hang in the air. Neither spoke. Walker turned and once again looked out into the monitoring room at the big screen which showed a still frame of Number Six addressing the villagers through a megaphone.

'If that's the case,' she said quietly, 'who's side is *he* on?'

25

The Foreign Office, Whitehall, London

Judith Tench sat upright in one of the chairs in the small reception room next to the larger office of the Shadow Secretary of State for Foreign and Commonwealth Affairs. A secretary sat at a desk nearby, typing rapidly. A light on a console next to her suddenly glowed green and she paused in her work.

'You can go in now Miss Tench,' she said, pointing to the connecting door.

Tench picked up her leather briefcase. 'Thank you,' she said, but the woman had already resumed typing.

Alec Douglas-Home stood as Tench entered, indicating a chair in front of his desk.

'Ah, Judith. Good to see you again. Please, sit…'

Tench sat and Douglas-Home did likewise, but picked up a file and quickly glanced at it before closing it and putting it back on his desk. Tench, who was very good at reading upside down, could clearly see it was stamped 'Secret', but couldn't see what else was written on the cover. She hoped it wasn't her personnel record.

Douglas-Home turned his skull-like head in her direction and smiled.

'And what brings my most senior principal advisor here this morning?' he asked, trying to sound pleasant, but failing.

Tench wasn't one for pleasantries, and she didn't have a great deal of respect for Douglas-Home, but he was instrumental in maintaining some important checks and balances against the ruling Labour government, and in that role he was not only valuable, he could be just the leverage she needed if what Bill Riley had revealed to her the previous evening was true.

'I'd like to speak candidly if I may sir,' she said.

If the smile on Douglas-Home's face had been forced, it now disappeared altogether. 'Of course. Go on…' he said, steepling his fingers in front of him, his elbows on the arms of his chair. A clock ticked loudly on the wall to one side, the only other sound was the muted traffic outside the windows, and the muffled clack-clack of the secretary's typing beyond the door.

'I'm hearing rumours of something going on that has relevance to your shadow responsibilities in the security intelligence area,' said Tench. Douglas-Home's eyebrows rose marginally, which she took as a signal to continue.

'It seems a department within MI6 has lost its top operative. He resigned recently, on what I understand was a matter of principle. He was apparently planning a holiday abroad somewhere, but his employers intervened and are holding him against his will in a classified facility.'

Douglas-Home's face was now a mask of stone. He stared at Tench for a moment, then said, 'Why?'

'I'm given to understand they want to find out what information he's got in his head, and maybe what he was planning to do with it.'

'But he signed the Official Secrets Act surely, just as all employees of the security services must do when they are first employed?'

Tench sighed inwardly at the shadow secretary's naivety. 'Yes of course, but that could be meaningless if a foreign power were able to get to him and extract the information… very sensitive information I might add.'

'Of course, but that's hardly likely is it, especially after the lessons we learned after Philby,

Maclean and so on were uncovered. It sounds to me like the security service has him under their control for protective purposes, to ensure he comes to no harm. Why should I be worried about that, or need to raise it as a concern officially? Or, for that matter, interfere in the routine work of the SIS?

'And what do you mean by you're "given to understand" that they want to discover what information he has? Who told you?'

Tench looked at him directly. 'I'm sorry, I'm not at liberty to say. But I can assure you that my source is impeccable and at a very high level.'

'I'm sure,' Douglas-Home said, 'but what do you expect me to *do*, Judith?'

'Nothing immediately sir, I hope to have more information very soon. For the moment I'm giving you a heads-up. But it seems that MI6 - and MI5 might be in with them in this for all I know – have a classified facility designed to hold ex-operatives and others who have either retired or resigned, a place where they are on the one hand cared for but on the other are held captive.'

'Where is this place?'

'I can't say sir,' she said, and saw exasperation begin to cross his face. 'No, I mean I really can't say because I haven't been told. What I do know is that it's a sort of retirement village with very high security. In fact it's even referred to as exactly that: the village.'

Douglas-Home sat back in his seat and sighed. 'Well Judith, it sounds perfectly sensible to me really, a comfortable and secure facility where ex-operatives can live out the rest of their lives in perfect safety, among their own kind, wanting for nothing…'

Tench knew it was time to play her ace card. 'They're drugged sir. They're being used as human guinea pigs. For physical and psychological experiments. The residents in the village are like sheep, fully compliant, shepherded by those who guard and oversee them, their… warders. They do as they're told and don't ask questions, don't query their incarceration. They have no freedom. I believe they are part of a much bigger strategy to…'

'To what?'

Tench realised she would need something more concrete for the shadow foreign secretary, but listening to herself she also realised she sounded unconvincing.

'A bigger plan that could have implications far beyond the retirement facility,' she blurted, and immediately felt guilty because she might have told Douglas-Home too much.

Douglas-Home absorbed this for a few moments. Tench thought it best to stop talking. The clock ticked slowly on. The shadow foreign secretary finally stirred.

'But you can't tell me what the plan is. Nor who gave you your information. Nor anything, in fact, of substance,' he growled.

'I'm not one for game-playing Judith, as well you know. I like facts, truth and clarity. What I'm hearing from you is rumour and conjecture from the sounds of it. And,' he raised a hand when he saw she was about to interject, 'I'm not sure there's anything to be concerned about from what little you've told me. It even sounds to me like a sensible and well-executed facility if it guarantees the safety of ex-security intelligence personnel and protects them from foreign agents or interference.

'I suggest you come back when you've got sufficient reason to do so, with some evidence of wrongdoing, evidence of… malpractice, or of a breach of security protocol at a high level. I have heard nothing of the sort today. You're my senior principal advisor, come back when you're ready to advise me.'

With that Douglas-Home picked up the file in front of him and opened it once more. The meeting was over.

Tench stood, clutching her briefcase. 'Thank you sir,' she whispered, and left.

26

Tommy's flat, Stockwell, South London

The government notebook – George Brown's notebook – lay open on the kitchen table. Tommy stirred his third coffee of the day at the kitchen counter, before returning to it. He resumed reading.

It wasn't the most riveting of books he'd read; scrawled notes, some dated others not, but obviously based on meetings that Brown the foreign secretary had attended. Harold Wilson's name showed up frequently – usually Brown referred to him as 'HW', or 'the PM' – and there were lots of acronyms and other initials which he expected his flatmate Chris would be able to interpret. She will definitely be interested in this, he thought.

He reached the end of the notes for a second time and once again looked at the last few pages, seeking to make sense of them.

Stone for lunch, SG. Problem - top man resignation.

May know about Unity. The Village. Interrogation. Priority!

The word Unity – with a capital 'U' Tommy noted – was underlined three times. 'The Village' was underlined once. Obviously important, he thought, but at this stage meaningless. However, the note about a 'top man' resigning made him wonder if in fact that was who he and Charles had extracted. Tommy sighed, sat back and sipped his coffee, grimacing. He didn't usually have more than one a day, and the taste of this third mug was bitter.

He returned to the book and looked at the very last entry, which seemed to be about a meeting he'd had with the prime minister, Harold Wilson.

Argued yet again. Too cautious. Commie?? Bring Unity forward?

He leaned back in the kitchen chair and rubbed the bridge of his nose between thumb and forefinger. It had been a busy day at the garage – along with his usual work he'd had to take Brown's limousine to a specialist panel repairer that Charles used occasionally.

He'd half expected the chauffeur to return looking for the lost notebook, but he hadn't shown. Which was a relief to Tommy as he was feeling somewhat guilty about having kept it. Well, stolen it, he admitted to himself. But he had every intention of returning it once Chris had seen it.

A key turned in the front door and Chris entered.

Tommy picked up the notebook and waved it at her. 'What would this be worth if you won a prize for your political journalism?' he cheekily asked. 'A tenner? Twenty? A kiss?'

Chris kicked off her shoes, dropped her bag, and began taking off her coat.

'What are you talking about?'

Tommy smirked and riffled through the book's pages. 'Well, I have here the private notebook of the foreign secretary.'

'Sure, of course you do. All mechanics have one,' Chris chided. 'Stop being an idiot. I've had a rubbish day, I'm tired, and I have a headache. The tube was packed and I had to stand under a man's smelly armpit the entire journey from Tottenham Court Road, so please don't play games.' She flopped onto the couch in the lounge and ran a hand through her hair.

Tommy came in from the kitchen and put the book on the couch beside her.

'Well, take a look and then tell me I'm an idiot.' She picked it up and flipped through the pages, then turned back to the cover and ran a fingernail over the embossed government crest. She then looked more closely at some of the notes, turning the pages slowly as she read. Tommy relaxed into an armchair and waited.

'Gordon Bennett!' Chris said.

'No, George Brown. Apparently.'

'No, I mean, well, Jesus! Is this for real?' She looked more closely at the handwriting, the notes, and particularly the entries that referred to 'HW.'

'How the hell did you get this?'

Tommy smirked. 'The quickness of the hand deceives the eye!'

Chris glared at him. 'Seriously, if this really is George Brown's it's, well, it's worth gold. But I have to know how you got it. Are you in trouble?'

'Not now that *you've* got it,' he smiled. 'You're the one holding it, and – I'm assuming – the one who can do something with it. I merely delivered it,' he shrugged.

He could see she wasn't amused by his performance so he told her about Brown's limousine being brought in for repairs, how it had got damaged and how he'd found the book on the floor under the seat. She listened without interruption, but kept looking at the notes in the book as he talked.

'Has anyone been in touch with your garage about the book? I mean, he must have realised by now that he doesn't have it.'

'Nothing so far, but his chauffeur might ask. The car's away having the dents taken out of it so we don't have it in the workshop.'

'That's probably a good thing,' Chris said, chewing her lip.

'Why?'

'Because it means more than one person could have found the book, not just you, or your boss. But it's only a matter of time. I need to show this to my editor, and we might have to photograph all the pages, then give it back to you so you can put it back where you found it. Can you do that?'

Tommy assured her he would be able to.

'Have you read it?' Chris asked.

Tommy shrugged. 'I flipped through it. Meaningless to me,' he said. 'But I'm sure you and your boss'll be able to get something from it. What do you make of the notes towards the end, about this Unity thing, some bloke resigning, and that village reference? Anything in that?'

Chris turned to the page in question and looked at the scrawl again.

'Well, he's had lunch with someone called Stone obviously, and we can assume this man told him about the resignation of a top official – that much seems clear, although I have no idea who Stone is. I'll ask around at work. But the resignation is a problem obviously. SG? Don't know. And the resigned man might know about something called Unity, but again…' her voice trailed off. 'Six could be MI6. Brown has ministerial oversight of the Security Intelligence Service, I know that much.'

Tommy tried to act nonchalant. 'The village?

She looked at Tommy, then back to the book. 'Could be any village anywhere. Maybe my boss will know more.'

'Yeah, maybe. Strange that Brown spelt it with a capital V though.'

Chris shrugged and closed the notebook. 'I'll show it to the editor. In fact, I'll take it to him now, get it copied and get it back to you as soon as possible.'

She got up and slipped her shoes back on. 'Hopefully the tube won't be as packed, or as smelly.

Damn it, the last thing I feel like doing is going back into work. But thank you for this Tommy.' She walked over to him and gave him a peck on the cheek. 'This could be big.'

Tommy wasn't one to blush easily, but he did so this time. Maybe finding the foreign secretary's notebook would be rewarding for him too in some way. He smiled as Chris shut the door behind her.

Then the smile dropped from his face. Suddenly some of the jigsaw pieces were beginning to fall into place.

27

The Lonely Pheasant Pub

Tench took a diplomatic sip of her sherry, then put her glass back on the table.

'Anything?'

Riley finished his casual survey of the room, taking in those at nearby tables, others sitting further away, ignoring big groups and looking for the more out-of-place people, individuals, anyone taking an interest in him or Tench.

'Not that I can see,' he said, his eyes swivelling back to his date. 'I think we're all right.' He smiled.

She took a quick glance around just to reassure herself.

'No, it didn't go well, to answer your question,' she said. 'He's a cold fish at the best of times, but I certainly couldn't get him on the hook. He even thought the services were doing a good job of protecting your man, for God's sake.'

She took another sip of her drink, then realised she was looking way too serious to be on a date. Her face softened and she took his hand. She had suggested that to all intents and purposes it should seem as though they were romantically involved. Riley was happy with that.

'So, what next?' Riley asked. As far as dates went, this wasn't the most exciting. But it was important.

'You'll need to get me some evidence,' Tench said very quietly, as though whispering an intimacy to him. She stroked his hand, and he wondered for a moment how much of it was acting. 'AD-H won't bite until there's something to bite on.'

Riley surveyed the room again as he replied. 'Thing is, there's nothing to show. Very few people are party to the project,' – they'd agreed the word Unity was out of bounds in public – 'and security is extremely tight. Anastasia Walker's not likely to blow the whistle, she's playing it dead straight, for now anyway. However, I do have something that might be of help to us…'

Riley paused. Tench felt it was for dramatic effect. She tightened her grip on his hand. 'Don't play the enigmatic spy with me Bill Riley or I'll have you kidnapped, hooded, and taken to a mouldy basement with a single bare light bulb and interrogated to within an inch of your life.'

'I have no doubt you would. But you don't need to. I managed to sneak a photograph of Major Wilson's "cast list" of those who play Number Two, including those who are currently waiting in the wings.' He paused again.

'Impressive. You've not lost your touch then. Are you going to tell me who's on it or shall I get the pliers out?'

'Do you carry them in your handbag?' He leaned forward slightly. 'Most of the names are meaningless to me, although I will run a security check on them. But one does stand out – the name rings a bell.' He leaned forward further, kissed her affectionately on the cheek and whispered it in her ear.

He sat back and Tench stared at him. 'I know that name,' she said. 'I believe we've…'

Riley waited, but Tench was biting her lip. 'We've what? Shall I get *my* pliers out now?'

Tench reached a decision. 'Damn it. We've used him before, a couple of times. Nothing dramatic, just keeping his ears open and reporting to us. But he was good, reliable.'

Riley smiled. 'I don't think I need to ask who "we" are. I know you're MI5.'

'Is it that obvious?' she smiled. 'I really must go on a refresher course. Anyway, how do you think he can be of use?'

'Well since he's scheduled to do a stint in the village he could maybe get us all the evidence we need. And I'll give you a copy of the list too – you can do your own checks. But I'll have to be very careful not to alert Wilson, or raise her suspicions in any way.'

Tench nodded agreement. 'From what you told me that night at my flat she's the director of this whole piece of… grand theatre, isn't she?'

She recalled how Riley had talked until the early hours, Tench interrupting only occasionally for more information or to ask him to clarify something. The bottle of Powers was half empty by the time he'd finished.

Riley nodded. 'Director – that's a good way of putting it, yes. And sticking with the theatre analogy we don't want this turning into a horror show. I wouldn't want to get on her wrong side. At the moment she's got the whole village round her little finger, and as I told you, the permanent residents are medicated and therefore not likely to question anything or pose a risk. The others – those you might call actors and extras – are only brought in for brief appearances; enter stage right, exit stage left, that sort of thing. Wilson says they're told an absolute minimum, although obviously some of them must be more clued-up than others. She even got rid of one, chap called Cobb, after he'd completed his "walk-on" part.'

'Got rid of him?' Tench asked, startled. 'Whatever do you mean?'

Riley patted her hand and smiled. 'Don't fret my dear. He's been transferred to our High Commission in

New Zealand, put in charge of the cipher clerks for a few months. Keeps him out of the way. But I get the impression that Wilson is ruthless. She giveth and she taketh away, if I may be so biblical.'

'Well I think we have our answer,' she said, then dropped her voice. 'We need to get that man on our side and into the village, as a sort of *deus ex machina* who drops from the skies and solves everything.'

Riley shook his head. 'This isn't a stage drama, despite the analogies. It presupposes that he'll agree to work with us, and anyway, on his own he'll be most unlikely to solve everything, as you put it. But he might get us the evidence we need to expose the whole… conspiracy. And I do believe we need to do that. If Unity is allowed to continue, who knows where it will end?'

They both fell silent for a while, sipping their drinks, busy with their own thoughts, analysing how 'their' Number Two might help them.

Riley was the first to break the silence. 'There is someone else who might prove to be of use.'

Tench raised an eyebrow. 'On the list?'

'No.

'Who then?'

'The captive. Our top man. Well, former top man, let's say.'

Tench withdrew her hand and sat back, thinking about what Riley had suggested. She leaned forward again.

'How? How do we know he'd also agree to be on our side?'

'Well, he's certainly not on the side of his captors. So in that respect he's against them, as are we Judith, even though I am – technically – one of them,' Riley whispered. 'He might even – and it's just my theory – have had himself taken to the village deliberately in order to expose it, but if that's the case he doesn't seem to be getting very far. Either way we might still need AD-H's help from a political standpoint sooner or later, so let's do some deep thinking about how we can achieve that.

'We need evidence. And as I said, we need to be very, very sure of what we're doing. I'm close to retirement, so I don't mind going out with a bang, but you've still got a few years ahead of you.'

'Oh bugger that,' Tench snarled. 'From what you've told me about Uni… the project, it's far more important that we stop it in its tracks.'

28

Daniel Forbes's house, Wandsworth, London

For a man employed to drive elegant motor cars, chauffeur Daniel Forbes's own vehicle, a Mini, was a stark contrast. He smiled to himself as he washed it now, parked outside his terraced house, and patted the car's roof.

'When you grow up, you're going to be a Bentley,' he whispered. Nothing wrong with ambition, he thought; all he had to do was become wealthy, but he knew that was unlikely on a government driver's salary.

He caught his reflection in the side window as he ran his cloth over the surface and saw that the cut to his temple was healing nicely. His headache had gone too and although he'd been given a few days off following the Trafalgar Square incident he was looking forward to getting back to work.

'Mr Forbes? Daniel Forbes?' a woman's voice asked behind him.

He turned, wringing his cloth out as he did so. A dark-haired woman of average height looked at him. Her clothing was nondescript. Her voice was neutral. She was as run of the mill as they came, he thought, and knew immediately she was security intelligence.

'Who's asking?'

'Mr Forbes? Yes?'

He nodded slightly, and the woman brought out a small identification card in a plastic wallet and flashed it at him.

'Lillian Grimes,' she announced. He looked at the card which announced her role as an 'intelligence officer' with the security service. Which most likely meant MI5. Which confirmed… what? He raised his eyebrows and went back to wiping down the car.

'How's your head?' Grimes asked.

'I'll have to declare a distinguishing feature when I renew my passport,' Forbes said, continuing his wiping. 'Other than that I'm fighting fit.'

'Good. No memory problems then.'

He stopped and turned again.

'No, why? I've already put in my report about what happened with Mr Brown and the Trafalgar Square mob.'

Lillian Grimes put the identification card back in her pocket. 'Is there somewhere we can talk?'

'Here's fine,' Forbes said, looking up and down the street. 'Nobody to overhear us if that's what you're worried about.'

She sighed, realising that Daniel Forbes was one of those people with an innate distrust of the security services, possibly because of his experience in the military, possibly because he'd watched too many spy dramas on television.

'The foreign secretary has misplaced a notebook. We wondered whether you might have found it. In the limousine after the riot, after you'd arranged a taxi to take him home.'

'Notebook? Nope. Is it important?'

She ignored his question. 'Did you check the vehicle?'

Forbes nodded. 'Yeah, checked the damage. Lots of broken glass from the smashed window inside, but I didn't see any notebook. Why d'you think it would be in the car?'

'Mr Brown's briefcase fell to the floor when you escaped from the crowd. He says items were scattered around. The notebook might have fallen out too.'

'As I said, I didn't see it, haven't found it, don't know anything about it, can't help.' He furiously wiped the roof of the Mini.

She stared at him, her eyes boring into the back of his head as she tried to gauge whether he was telling the truth. She dropped her gaze and pulled out a small notebook of her own, referred to a page, then looked back to him.

'And you took the car for repair to one of the government garages, the one in Virgil Street yes?'

Now it was Forbes's turn to sigh. 'Yes. You know all that, it was in my report. Why am I being interrogated?'

'If this was an interrogation you'd certainly know about it,' Grimes spat. 'I'm just making friendly enquiries. Following up. That notebook contains important information of the foreign secretary's and it would be… worrying if it fell into the wrong hands.'

Forbes wrung his cloth out again, with slightly more force than was necessary.

'It went to the garage – an approved garage as you know – for repair. The chief mechanic said he'd get his lad onto it. That's all I know. Now unless you want to help me polish my own motor…' He flicked the cloth like a whip, turned back and began a final wipe-down of the Mini, indicating the meeting was over.

He gave the car another few seconds' attention before looking round. Grimes had walked down the road and he saw her turn the corner. Leaving the cloth on the car he trotted down the street in her wake, then pulled up and quickly glanced round the corner.

He saw her get into a waiting car, then watched as it indicated and pulled into the traffic. He whispered the number plate to himself as he returned to his house, ignored the cloth on the car roof and went inside.

Daniel picked up the phone from the hall table, flicked out the index below it and ran his finger down the list till he found what he wanted. He dialled and waited.

The phone was picked up after just a few rings.

'Yes?'

'Charles? It's Daniel Forbes.'

'Daniel! I'm afraid your car isn't back from surgery yet, probably not till next week…'

'That's all right, no hurry. I have a favour. Nothing to do with the motor, just wondered if you could help…'

'Hang on.' He heard Charles put the phone down, then close the door of the office in the garage. He picked up again.

'What can I do for you? Nothing's too much trouble for the son of my best friend, you know that.'

'Yeah, thanks. Dad sends his best by the way. He's doing okay, but, well, you know…'

'I do, son, I do. Tell him I'll come and see him soon. Now…'

Daniel got to the point. 'Charles, do you still have access to vehicle registrations? Are you able to check a number plate for me? Owner? That sort of thing?'

Charles was quiet for a moment.

'Are you in trouble son?'

'No, not at all,' Daniel said confidently, twisting the handset's cord in his other hand. 'Just had a minor scrape with some bloke who didn't stop. Nothing serious, but he owes me for a new wing on the Mini.' He looked at his reflection in the hall mirror, the reflection of a liar. He turned away.

'Blimey. You do know how to wreck motor cars don't you? That's two in two weeks! Go on then, give it to me,' Charles said, and took down the number that Daniel had memorised.

'I'll get back to you.'

'Thanks Charles, appreciate it.' He returned the handset to the cradle.

Daniel chewed his lip and thought. Then he picked the phone up again and dialled the number he'd remembered from Lillian Grimes's identification card. A woman's voice answered, giving only the phone number. So at least the number was real. Maybe.

Daniel said, 'I'd like to speak to one of your officers who visited me a short while ago. She said to call if I had any more information for her.'

'The name?' the woman asked.

'Grimes. Lillian Grimes.'

There was a pause on the end of the line. Daniel assumed the woman was checking her internal directory. When she put him through he would hang up. But he wasn't put through.

'I'm sorry,' the woman said. 'There's nobody here by that name. Are you sure it's Grimes?'

'Er, no, that's fine, thank you. I must have got it wrong.' He hung up. But he knew it was no mistake. Lillian Grimes wasn't MI5, and she probably wasn't called Lillian Grimes. So who was she?

29

Century House, Sub-basement 2

Anastasia Walker was annoyed. Olivia Wilson annoyed her. The supervisors in the monitoring facility annoyed her. And she was still angry that she'd foolishly volunteered the first shift after the subject had been taken to the village because it had meant she'd worked nights for far too long now and she was tired.

But this would be her last graveyard shift for a while, and it was almost over. She had spoken to Stone and he'd authorised her to bring Rupert Symes on board so that the three of them – she, Riley and now Symes – could do eight-hour shifts each.

Stone had been sympathetic, possibly because Symes was also party to the village project and was therefore no threat to the security of the operation.

She'd also taken the opportunity to report to Stone on her interpretation of how things were going, both in the village and in Monitoring.

'And what of Riley?' Stone had asked.

'I worry still about his commitment, as you'd mentioned,' she'd said. 'The way he talks, it sounds to me like he has a problem with the Unity project.'

'A problem?'

'He doesn't seem to be… at ease with it; the medications applied to the residents, the goal of compliance and acquiescence, and the ultimate application of Unity in a defence context. All the same things that we suspect drove our top man to resign, if he in fact knows that much.'

'Do you trust Riley?' Stone had asked directly.

Walker had pondered this for a moment before answering. 'I do… for now. As he pointed out – and I thought this quite astute – the one we should be suspicious of is Number Six.'

'Why? He's in one of the most secure locations in the country, monitored twenty-four hours a day with little or no chance of escape. Trust doesn't come into it, since there's nobody he can talk to in confidence, nobody he can tell anything to.'

Walker had thought of proposing the theory that Six might actually be a plant – that he had offered his resignation knowing that he would be taken to the village – but she decided there was little evidence of it, at least not at this stage. Olivia Wilson was convinced he was simply a rat in a trap, as she'd called him once. Walker had therefore decided to say nothing.

'No, you're right sir. He's in a safe place. The safest,' she'd smiled.

Stone had nodded, and purred, 'Well, if you're concerned, bring it up with Wilson. She's in charge of his interrogation, and I'm sure she'll manage him… accordingly.'

Accordingly. Walker recalled how the pause before the word had added enormous, crushing weight to it. *Accordingly.*

Now she shivered as she checked the clock on the wall to see how long she had before Riley took over.

She glanced out into the room where the large screen showed the village grounds, early morning sunlight shafting through the trees, two gardeners already at work trimming hedges, another worker sweeping a path. Such a beautiful place, she thought, hiding such an ugly truth.

The 'election' of the new Number Two was about to take place, and Olivia Wilson was due in also to monitor proceedings, but all Walker really wanted to do now was go home and sleep. Riley could keep an eye on things, and Symes could have the dreaded night shift.

But she found the activities of the village mesmerising, and even during the night shifts she'd been impressed with the level of security and vigilance of the on-site control room. Stone had been right: there was little chance of the captive escaping. So if he really was there on purpose, what was he planning to do? And how would he blow the lid off, or even destroy the village, if indeed that was his goal? Especially as he seemed to be acting alone.

The door behind her opened and she turned, relieved that Riley had arrived at last. But it wasn't him, it was Wilson. The air in the room crackled with unseen electricity as she walked in and stood facing Walker.

'Good morning,' Wilson said, without any hint that she meant it. 'A big day in the village. Anything of interest overnight?'

Walker wondered why Wilson seemed on edge and searched her face for a clue, but there was nothing.

'All quiet,' she reported. 'The evening medication obviously works well – he slept soundly for eight hours so I've had little to do or worry about.'

Walker brought Wilson up to date with Symes's appointment to the monitoring team but she appeared neither concerned nor interested.

Wilson turned her attention to the screen in the monitoring room. 'Election Day,' she said, mainly to herself.

Walker took up a position beside her. 'Yes. And you're not worried about the outcome?'

'Not remotely. The villagers will vote for Number Six and give him a landslide victory. Number Two will concede.'

Walker was confused. 'So what stops Six from taking over?'

Wilson sighed inwardly yet again at having to explain details. She turned and faced Walker.

'Number 58, the taxi driver, is our ace card in the pack. All through the electioneering and the voting she'll be supporting Number Six, encouraging him, befriending him, even though they don't share a common language. Once he wins he will be more relaxed in her company, and will let his guard down. Yes we'll give him a small taste of authority, of control, but he will not be in charge. I am in charge.' Wilson turned back to the screen, and Walker was left in no doubt the conversation was over.

Riley finally arrived, bundling himself into the room and apologising for his late arrival.

Walker quickly grabbed her coat and satchel and as she passed him whispered, 'Good luck. You'll need it,' then more loudly called to Wilson, 'Be seeing you.'

30

Virgil Street Garage

Chris Watkins had been to Tommy's workplace only once before. Now that she was close she put her Bacon's Atlas of London and Street Index back in her bag and headed off down the road towards where she remembered it was and turned the corner.

It was a short road that quickly disappeared under the railway bridge carrying trains to and from Waterloo Station. The garage was about halfway down on the right, two cars parked on the pavement outside, along with Tommy's red motorcycle. Another car was parked in the gloom under the railway arch. Apart from that the street was deserted.

The garage roller door was up and Chris peered inside.

Charles saw her out of the corner of his eye as he worked under the bonnet of a Wolseley. He backed out from under it and straightened up, a spanner in his hand.

'Yes Miss? Can I help you?' He thought he recognised her, but wasn't sure.

'I was looking for Tommy. Just wanted to give him something he forgot. It won't take long.'

'Tom!' Charles called into the gloom of the interior. 'Young lady here to see you.'

Tommy emerged from the back and nodded his thanks. Charles said out of the corner of his mouth, 'Don't be too long son, there's still half an hour till your lunch break,' and went back to his engine tinkering.

'Chris! What brings you here?'

Chris grabbed a sleeve of his overalls and drew him out into the sunlight and away from the opening. She took George Brown's notebook out of her bag and furtively handed it to him, blocking the line of sight from the garage so that Charles wouldn't see, although he wasn't watching anyway.

'Here. For you to put back where you found it. Is the car here?' she asked, looking round.

'No, still at the panel place, but I can take it there during my lunch break. Did your photographer work his magic?'

'Yes, every page. My editor's ecstatic, thinks I'm the bee's knees. He also thinks he can decipher a lot of what's in the book, and yes, there is some good juicy stuff about Harold Wilson and the Cabinet.'

'You make them sound like a pop group,' Tommy smiled. 'But good, thanks.' He slid the book inside his overalls. 'I'll have it back in the car within an hour or so.'

'Okay, good luck. See you later,' Chris said, and walked back the way she'd come.

After Tommy managed to sneak the notebook inside his motorbike jacket he returned to his work. Charles didn't see him, but did ask, 'That your girlfriend then?'

Tommy laughed. 'Nah, we share a flat. Purely platonic, unfortunately.'

He went back to replacing a set of spark plugs and cleaning a dirty distributor until his lunchtime came around, then cleaned up and grabbed his keys and jacket. He called out to Charles, 'Just going out for a while. Won't be long.'

Charles nodded, as Tommy donned his jacket and helmet, climbed onto his bike and kicked it into life. Charles preferred motor cars to motor bikes, but he admired how Tommy kept his in good condition, regularly servicing it, tuning it, and polishing the chrome and paintwork.

He ambled out to the road and watched as Tommy revved confidently down towards the intersection, and then he jumped as a car loudly beeped its horn behind him. He leapt back onto the pavement as a green-grey Ford Cortina roared past and squealed round the corner in the same direction that Tommy had gone, not even pausing to give way to other traffic.

'Maniac!' Charles shouted after it. He turned angrily and went back into the garage, then paused and looked back at the now quiet street. Something about that car, he thought. What was it? Something familiar, even though he was sure he'd never seen it before.

Didn't see the driver, he thought, or the passenger – just shapes really, but almost certainly a man and a woman. Colour of the car was non-descript. He leaned on the workbench and closed his eyes replaying the scene from just a moment ago in his mind.

Then his eyes shot open. 'Bloody hell!' he said aloud. 'No. No! Too much of a coincidence. It can't be…'

He quickly wiped his hands on a rag, almost trotted into the office and picked up the phone.

*

Tommy flicked through the gears and concentrated on the road ahead. Traffic was reasonably light, and he was able to give the bike a decent workout, at least in between traffic lights. He knew the way to the panel shop where Brown's limousine was, and also that it wouldn't take him more than about fifteen minutes.

Once there his plan was to ask the boss if he'd mind if he checked inside the car for something he'd lost. He was sure he'd agree, and then Tommy would be able to slide the notebook back where he found it. He'd even thought of using a train ticket as his pretend 'find', just to add a sense of reality to the charade. The boss wouldn't question his wanting to access the vehicle.

With Tommy mentally rehearsing his upcoming performance he didn't notice the Cortina racing to catch up with him. Even though the car had gunned down Virgil Street quickly, Tommy had already weaved his bike three or four vehicles ahead on the main road, so the Cortina was having to play catch-up.

The driver revved the engine, chopped through the gears, and drove with expertise, as he'd been trained to do. His passenger, a woman, had a London city map open on her lap and called out how the road would turn ahead, or what intersections were coming up. They hoped Tommy was carrying what they wanted – they'd seen the girl pass him something; the problem they faced was not knowing where he was going, but they desperately needed to get him in a quiet street with few pedestrians. Or witnesses.

'*Cyka blyat!*' the driver muttered under his breath.

'Language please, Dmitri,' the woman who called herself Lillian Grimes admonished in perfect English. 'We'll get him.'

Dmitri dropped a gear and floored the accelerator. The car lurched forward. He pressed the horn as a van blocked his view of Tommy. The van pulled over slightly and the Cortina swerved round and overtook, narrowly missing a central road bollard. The van driver yelled an obscenity as the Cortina sped past.

The horn made Tommy glance in his handlebar mirror, and he could see a car in a hurry behind. His instinct was to move to the left and allow it to overtake, knowing from experience that motorcycle riders were more vulnerable than car drivers. But it wasn't a police car – which had been a brief but genuine worry – so instead he wound open the throttle and sped up to put some distance between him and the Cortina.

Dmitri slammed the steering wheel in frustration and once again put his foot to the floor. Grimes put a steadying hand on the dashboard in front of her. The car's engine roared, but they got no closer to the motorbike ahead.

Tommy glanced in his mirror again and saw that the car was still not far behind him. He decided to get out of the way after all to let it pass, so he sped up more, pulled in front of a lorry, then indicated he was turning left onto a side street. The lorry braked slightly to let him manoeuvre and as Tommy turned the corner he heard another loud blaring of horns behind him as the Cortina swerved in behind the lorry and made its own rapid turn.

The car's front wheel bounced off the kerb and the driver straightened up. Now they were off the main road and on a much quieter street. Dmitri gripped the wheel in determination. Grimes stole a glance at her map.

'This is it,' she shouted over the engine noise. 'After the next intersection it becomes one-way. If he goes straight through we'll take him there!'

Tommy quickly glanced round and saw that the Cortina had followed him. His first thought was that he'd somehow annoyed the driver, who now wanted to have words with him, but he had a gut feeling that this driver wanted something else, and it probably wasn't to give him friendly advice on his road craft.

The Triumph bucked as Tommy opened the throttle and roared down a street of warehouses. Dmitri dropped a gear and sped after him. Pedestrians crossing the road ahead turned in alarm towards the noise of the bike and car and leapt back out of the way as first Tommy then the Cortina roared past.

Seeing an intersection ahead Tommy quickly wondered what to do. It was unfamiliar territory and he didn't know these side roads well. He needed to find somewhere that offered him an escape – an alleyway or some other narrow passage wide enough for a motorcycle but not a car. He looked left and right, then the intersection was upon him. Decision time.

Looking ahead he saw the street directly across was one-way, so less chance of oncoming traffic. He chose it and, slowing only slightly to check no cross traffic was coming, accelerated ahead. But he hadn't looked properly; a van coming through the intersection only just missed hitting his back wheel, the driver braking sharply, but it gave Tommy a chance.

Dmitri cursed as the van blocked the intersection momentarily, then he wove round the vehicle and once again floored the accelerator.

Tommy was dismayed to see the Cortina still behind him and gaining now. The road ahead turned slightly and he skidded round the bend, his rear wheel sliding out until he corrected the handlebars to compensate. His mind rapidly computed all the obstacles, the road surface, the risks, the hazards: loose dog, two pedestrians, man with a handcart, pile of bricks and sand beside the kerb. And then ahead, at last, sanctuary.

A bin lorry was stopped in the middle of the road, the two binmen emptying bins into the open sides. Tommy bounced the bike up onto the pavement, beeping his horn repeatedly as he closed on the lorry.

The binmen dived out of the way, yelling both in fright and anger, but Tommy scraped past, roared along the pavement and down onto the road again.

He risked a glance back and was about to smile in satisfaction that the Cortina would never be able to follow him, but when he turned back again he saw an elderly woman carrying a shopping bag crossing in front of him.

He slammed on both brakes, then aimed the bike behind the woman to go round her, but he put too much pressure on the back brake and the rear of the Triumph slid. He felt the bike begin to tip, tried straightening the handlebars, put his left foot down to try for balance but it was too late. His footrest hit the cobbles, the bike fell over and slid along the road, throwing Tommy onto the road and into the gutter.

Tommy bounced once, then rolled and slammed into the kerbstone, his helmet hitting the road, and the bike skidding away from him showering sparks as the metalwork ground against the surface.

With the breath knocked out of him Tommy tried to get up but couldn't. The elderly shopper looked at him, unsure what to do, frightened by the noise of the crash and the near miss. He could see her standing there, helpless, and then behind her, running from round the bin lorry, two people, a man and a woman. They rushed up to him and the man knelt down.

The man said nothing, but unzipped Tommy's leather jacket and reached inside checking – Tommy thought hazily – for injuries, but that wasn't his aim. Tommy tried to speak but words wouldn't come.

The woman remained standing, looking around her, biting her lip. '*Davay, Dmitri, nam nuzhno ubirat'sya otsyuda!*'

The man's hand found Tommy's inside pocket, reached in and felt the notebook. He drew it out, saw the government crest on the cover and showed it to the woman.

'*Ponyatno. Poydem!*'

Tommy made another feeble effort to get up, wanted to shout after the couple, but he saw them run back round the bin lorry and disappear. He heard a car engine revving, a crash of gears as it went into reverse, and then it was gone. Along with George Brown's notebook.

The old lady dropped her shopping bag on the road and stared open mouthed at him. Tommy's head fell back into the gutter, and his world faded to black.

31

St. Thomas's Hospital, London

Charles counted off the cubicle numbers as he peered through the doors to the accident and emergency ward till he saw number five. The curtains were drawn back, and he saw a face he knew – Chris, he remembered now, Tommy's flatmate. She was sitting beside a bed talking to the young man in it. He recognised the tousled red hair of the patient and pushed through the door.

Chris and Tommy both turned towards him as he entered, Chris standing and Tommy waving lazily.

'Can you never keep out of trouble?' asked Charles when he reached the bed, but with a kindly look on his face. 'Hello Miss,' he said to Chris.

Chris shook his hand. 'Hello Charles. We've never been formally introduced. I'm Chris Watkins, Tommy's flatmate. And now nurse,' she said, looking at Tommy who was sitting up and not looking too bad considering he'd been bouncing on cobbles a couple of hours earlier.

'Thanks for calling,' Charles said to Chris. 'I had wondered where he'd got to.' He turned to Tommy. 'You all right son?'

'Yeah,' Tommy nodded slightly, careful not to strain his neck further. 'Not bad thanks, just a bit bruised. And my pride's hurt too. I thought I was a good rider…'

Charles picked up a scratched crash helmet from the bedside cabinet. 'Good job you wore this. They ought to make them compulsory.'

'That's what the doctor said,' Tommy nodded carefully. 'Said it might have saved me from concussion, or bleeding on the brain, or something like that. Anyway, I'm all right I think. I have to wait for the results of the X-rays.'

'So what happened?' Charles asked, folding himself gently onto the edge of the bed.

Tommy told him about being pursued by the car, trying to evade it, and failing. He stopped short of telling how the driver had stolen the notebook, or that he and the passenger had failed to come to his aid.

Charles listened intently, nodding now and then, his eyes searching Tommy's face as though looking for something more.

Chris said, 'It must have been scary. Have you any idea why they were chasing you? Did you annoy the driver somehow?' She said it somewhat robotically, almost like she was reading a script.

Tommy looked down at the bed sheets. 'Nope, no idea.'

Charles was still looking at him. He broke his gaze, quickly glanced around the room, then lowered his voice. 'Did they get the book son?'

Tommy felt himself go red. He looked from Charles to Chris with a raised eyebrow. 'Chris, did you…?'

'No! I didn't tell him!' she said. 'You said to keep quiet, so I did…'

'How d'you…' he began asking Charles, but he put up a hand.

'It's all right Tommy. I know about Brown's notebook, and I also know who the car belongs to. Do you want to tell me the bits you missed out?'

Tommy did, this time omitting nothing. He also included how he'd found the notebook in the back of the car.

Charles listened, maybe raised his eyebrows once or twice, but he didn't interrupt or say anything until Tommy had finished.

'Foreign you say? Russian?'

'Maybe. I don't know any Russian, never been there obviously. But the bloke's name was Dmitri, I'm pretty sure of that. The woman said it when she was yelling at him. Who were they?'

Charles again looked quickly round the ward and said quietly, 'Not here. I need to talk to Mr. Symes about this first, and I need to find out how much you can be told.'

Chris looked confused. 'What? What do you mean "how much he can be told?" He's just been thrown off his bike after being chased by some, some... thieves...' She realised her voice was getting louder. She dropped it to an angry whisper. 'And you're acting like it all has to be hushed up or something. What's going on? The police should be told...'

Tommy and Charles exchanged brief glances and looked uncomfortable.

'I can't say, Miss. Not at the moment. Our garage is a government garage, as I think you know. All the vehicles we service are government cars – some used by those in the public eye – ministers of the Crown, that sort of thing – and others are used by, well, people whose job it is to stay under the radar so to speak.'

Chris still looked confused. 'But what's that got to do with the foreign secretary's notebook? And Tommy being chased and almost killed?'

Charles sighed and looked down. Tommy took Chris's hand and squeezed it. 'It's okay girl, relax. Let Charles talk to his boss and then maybe things will become clearer. I don't know any more than I've told you,' he lied. 'Do I Charles?'

His boss nodded. 'That's right, Miss. Like Tommy says, give me some time to find out more and then maybe things'll become clearer. Thanks again for calling me. Tommy, let me know how it goes with the X-rays. Take a few days off if you want, I suspect you'll have bruises tomorrow in places you didn't know existed.'

Charles left and Chris withdrew her hand from Tommy's.

'You're not telling me everything Thomas Deighton, are you? We'll be going public with some of what was in Brown's notebook in a few days, and I won't be able to stop my editor, so if there's anything else I should know you need to tell me. And soon.'

32

Stone's office, Century House

'A D-notice?' repeated George Brown. He finished pacing up and down and slumped dejectedly into one of the two couches in the plush office. 'Will they comply?'

Stone stood and came round from behind his desk. This was the top floor room he used for special meetings – his more usual work office was one floor below and away from distractions. The Foreign Secretary however deserved – nay craved – special treatment, and Stone knew how to calm troubled waters.

'Yes, the media generally respond well to a formal request.'

Brown grunted. He swivelled round, his eyes taking in the cocktail cabinet, but then settling back on the director general. 'But what about that kerfuffle earlier this year?'

Stone smiled and walked over to the drinks cabinet. He could tell Brown needed reassurance both mental and liquid. He prepared a large whisky.

'Yes, that was rather unfortunate, the whole thing about the Daily Express and the cables. What was the journalist's name? Pincher, wasn't it?'

Brown gratefully accepted the cut crystal glass and drank. Stone sat on the opposite couch, his own drink untouched.

The foreign secretary ran a finger under his collar, then took another gulp.

'Well, if you think it will work. I suppose it's all we can do – gag the media and hope they keep the whole thing quiet. And you've not managed to retrieve it?'

'Not the actual notebook, no. Nor has MI5 I believe. Ever since you alerted me to losing it I've had people chasing it but to no avail. All we know is that it appears to have fallen out of your briefcase during your escape from the protest.'

'Riot you mean!' grumped Brown.

'Riot then,' Stone acknowledged. 'When you escaped from the riot. But in the aftermath you didn't notice it was missing. You can't blame yourself George, you'd just been through a terrifying experience.'

'You can say that again! Bloody young people!' Brown's face turned red as he recalled the Trafalgar Square incident.

Stone smiled and pretended to take a sip of his own drink. It was however just to put Brown at ease. He put the glass down and interlaced his fingers.

'I shouldn't worry. The newspaper concerned photographed the whole notebook and by this evening we'll have a copy of those images even if we don't have the notebook itself. It helps to have operatives in various strategic places.'

Brown nodded, but still wasn't mollified. 'That's all very well, but what about the original for God's sake? It's full of all my notes!'

'I realise that. But at least having the photographs will mean we can actually know what was in it, what you'd written, and then we'll know whether to worry or not. The original is more of a problem I admit. But we're working on it – along with MI5 – rest assured.'

'The thing is,' Brown looked around the office once again taking in the decanters behind him – Stone stood and refilled Brown's glass on cue – 'The thing is… I, er, I'd written about Unity after our meeting at the Savoy.'

Stone turned from the decanter and scowled at the back of Brown's head before striding back to the couches and handing the foreign secretary his refreshed glass, by which time he was smiling again.

'Oh don't fret dear chap! It's a common enough word. Anyone reading it will just assume you're talking about the cabinet needing to be working together. Unless…'

'Unless what?' Brown asked nervously.

Stone shrugged. 'Well, unless you were very specific in your notes about what Unity is.' He raised an enquiring eyebrow.

'No, no, I wasn't,' Brown assured him. 'Not that I can recall. But anyway, why wasn't it handed back to me or my office when it was found? You said something about a mechanic?'

'Yes. As I explained, your chauffeur took the car to one of our approved garages for repair – not far from here actually – and we've confirmed that the chauffeur didn't find it. But now we know that the mechanic who was given the job of cleaning the car up *did* find it, and gave it to his girlfriend or whatever who works for the newspaper. Perhaps he thought he was doing her a favour. I don't think it was malicious.'

Brown squirmed. 'Bloody scoundrel! Thief, that's what he is. Should be prosecuted, taken to task!'

'Oh don't worry, we're keeping an eye on him, and her. And with the paper having been served a D-notice there's nothing they can do with any of the information they got from the book anyway.'

Brown was unmoved. 'But if they don't have it, where is it?'

'The mechanic actually attempted to return it to your car but… never made it.' Stone kept the details deliberately vague; the less Brown knew the better. In reality, and despite Stone's composed face and assured manner, inside he was worried.

'Let's just say it's been… mislaid. Look, George, don't fret. We'll know exactly what was in the book very soon – you can see the photographs too – and then, as I say, we'll know whether we need worry or not.'

After Brown had left, Stone checked his diary, and his watch. He had half an hour before his next appointment. During this time he put a call through on the scrambler to his opposite number in MI5. The conversation was slightly tense, though Stone never once lost his temper or even showed strain. However, since his domain was 'foreign affairs' rather than domestic he was having some difficulty maintaining control of the situation.

MI5, with oversight of domestic intelligence, felt it was their role to manage the foreign secretary and his 'lost' notebook. They wanted full control over the operation to retrieve it, and to keep tabs on those involved.

Stone on the other hand was very aware that the notebook had been taken by what appeared to be Soviet agents, which meant a conflict of interest between the two agencies. In principle, Russian spies on British soil fell under the bailiwick of MI5, while MI6's role was to monitor enemy activity and gather intelligence on foreign soil. But Stone's close association with George Brown changed the dynamics somewhat, especially in relation to Unity, so he was determined to retain as much control as possible.

The call ended in a stalemate. Stone returned the handset to the cradle, sat back and stared at nothing in particular while he thought.

This whole village thing was in danger of getting out of hand, he feared. The original concept was sound:

a secure and isolated facility in which retired or recalcitrant operatives from any of the security services could be held and monitored. But it had also been used as a site for rendition, where enemy operatives caught on foreign soil were brought. And it had, as a matter of financial expediency, become a joint services facility, which complicated things further.

And then there was Unity. The project that could see defence transformed, battlefield collateral dramatically reduced, invasions stopped in their tracks, wars maybe even a thing of the past. It was, he believed, masterful, but it was also a plan that required all those involved in the village to work together, in harmony. Ironically, in unity.

The intercom on his desk buzzed.

'Yes?'

A woman's voice announced, 'Anastasia Walker is here to see you sir.'

'Send her in.'

33

Century House, Sub-basement 2

Symes yawned and stretched. It had been a more eventful night than any so far. Riley had told him that with the village's residents drugged, little happened after lights-out, so he wasn't expecting any action. But last night the captive had resisted sleep, escaped from his apartment and headed for the beach.

The latest Number Two, a small but forceful female, had been unconcerned about the attempt, though she had activated the Rover security element to intervene, the 'blob' as many called it – the large white pliable orb whose role was to prevent escape, and certainly to deter any thought of it.

Two's concern, rather than Number Six escaping, was that one of the village's doctors – an overly-keen clinician – would damage the captive with his invasive mind-probing experiments. She had, as instructed by Major Wilson, cautioned him that Six was not to be harmed. Duped maybe, but not drugged into a husk of a man, nor subject to still-experimental mine-bending techniques. The doctor had reluctantly acquiesced, at least for the moment.

'I gather it's a new tactic,' Supervisor McCauley had told Symes as they'd observed the action. 'Major Wilson is trying this novel approach apparently, adding value to the prisoner. Taking a less commanding, more coercing approach. It's all rather fun,' he chuckled.

Symes frowned. 'Hardly what I'd call entertainment, old boy.'

'Well, quite,' admitted McCauley, backtracking slightly. He felt somewhat threatened by Symes's public school persona, his posh way of speaking, his tailored suit and his smooth demeanour. 'What I mean is, well, it's very much a game of cat and mouse.'

Symes wondered if McCauley was referring to the fact that the new Number Two was accompanied by a black cat, a traditional omen of evil, and yet also elegance. If the cat was Wilson's idea it was clever one.

He reflected on the progress with the captive to date, if progress was indeed the right word. The prisoner had been non-compliant from the start, had outwitted or outworn three number Twos so far, but had also been thwarted in his attempts to escape, discover where he was, or indeed learn anything about his captors. Six had won the village so-called democratic election, yet had gained nothing at all. Nor, it had to be said, had those in charge. It was, if anything, a stalemate.

Riley's arrival broke his concentration. Symes and McCauley both turned as he entered the monitoring room. Riley smiled briefly at Symes and nodded to McCauley.

'Give us a moment would you?'

It took a second for it to dawn on McCauley that he was being dismissed. 'Oh right. Message received and all that. I'll be on the floor.'

After he'd left and gone back to the tiered monitors in the main room Riley slumped down into one of the chairs. He looked at Symes. 'We don't seem to be getting very far with him do we? Our Number Six.' Riley nodded towards the main monitor showing the village. 'I suppose you'd better fill me in on the night's activities. Oh, and maybe let's catch up for a drink later – it's been a while. All work and no play and all that. Usual place, say seven o'clock?'

34

Villiers Cocktail Bar, London

Symes arrived on the dot of seven, impeccably dressed as always, his pinstriped suit looking as new as the day he'd had it made, his manner that of a man of supreme self-confidence. He shot his cuffs, glanced around the room, saw Riley and headed towards him, ducking his head under the low brick arches as he went.

Riley looked up and gave a brief smile as Symes sat down.

'Got you a cheap yet cheerful Portuguese rosé,' Riley said, pushing the glass towards him. Symes grimaced.

'If I'd needed mouthwash I'd have stopped at the chemist. But thanks.' He took a sip, grimaced again, and looked around, either for a spittoon or to check who was there. His head swivelled back and he stared at Riley.

'So, all work and no play? I suspect this meeting isn't exactly going to be a jolly little sing-along, so I'm guessing it's work.'

Riley chuckled. 'I taught you well. Yes, it's work, and it's serious. We're on the edge of something bigger than we realised and I need you in on it.'

'Hard to imagine anything much bigger than the village project at the moment, and what's-his-name, Number Six. But he's safe enough where he is, so…?'

Riley looked at Symes, as though weighing up what to tell him. In fact that was exactly what he was doing – wondering whether he could be trusted. He decided he'd have to take the chance.

'You were at Eton weren't you?'

Symes smiled, his dimples two deep craters. He patted his striped tie and said in a voice as rich and smooth as a fine vintage port, 'Obviously.'

'Turn over your coaster.'

Symes moved his glass and palmed the coaster before taking a quick look at the underside. There was a name: Barnaby Carrington-Hall. His only reaction was to raise an immaculate eyebrow.

Riley watched him. 'Was he there with you?'

Symes nodded and surreptitiously moving the card under the table tore it in half, then into quarters. 'Indeed he was, and I'm sure you know that. Why do you ask?'

'Just wanted to be sure, that's all,' shrugged Riley. 'Tell me about him.'

Symes rubbed his chin and sat back in his seat. He slyly put the torn-up coaster in his inside pocket. The pieces would be distributed in various rubbish bins on his way home later.

'Top scholar. Very clever. Good sports all-rounder – beat me at fencing, the bastard. Education interrupted by the war – like mine – but then while I went on to Cambridge he went to Oxford, read PPE – philosophy, politics, and economics – graduated with first class honours, and straight into the civil service. Worked his way up quickly and held a number of attaché posts. Very much a man of principle. High values. Totally straight. Extremely well-connected in high places. Yes, Westminster, since you're about to ask. Last I heard he was a defence attaché, and highly regarded too.'

Riley smiled. '*Defence attaché*. Well, we all know what that means. So he's an intelligence officer?'

Symes took another sip of the Portuguese rosé, drew in some air to aerate it in his mouth, then swallowed. 'God, I might take some of this home.'

'Really? So you like it after all?'

'No,' said Symes, 'but I do need some paint stripper.' He thought for a moment. 'Is he one of us? Maybe. I wouldn't know – I haven't seen him for a few years – and why is it important?'

'I'll get to that in a moment.' Riley leaned forward and dropped his voice. 'You're one of the few people in our organisation who knows about Unity.' Symes nodded slightly and held his gaze. 'But I'm not sure you – or any of us apart from those at the top – fully appreciate the extent of the project, or the implications if it's allowed to go ahead.'

'But it is going ahead,' shrugged Symes. 'That's what the village is all about, as you know: an experimental retirement home for ex-operatives and other staff with invaluable knowledge in their heads.'

'And...?' Riley asked.

'And... well, it's a testing ground – field laboratory if you like – to try out new interrogation techniques, some of which are, shall we say, unusual?'

Riley looked down at his glass then back up. 'Mind-altering drugs, sleep deprivation, the use of twins for experiments, gas, electro-shock so-called "therapy", psychological manipulation, hypnosis, and that, that *thing*, that Rover... a bit more than unusual I'd say. And I haven't even mentioned rendition. There's more than a handful of residents there who've been forcibly brought in from overseas you know. The whole thing is illegal.'

Symes tutted. 'Oh come on Riley, a lot of what we do is illegal. That's why it's secret. That's why most of us signed up. What's your point? And what's...' he patted his pocket, 'our alumnus got to do with it all?'

Riley sighed and knocked back the remainder of his drink. 'The outcome of what's happening in the village has ramifications far beyond its pretty cobbled streets and gaily-painted walls. The plan isn't to stop at the village. The people there are a litmus paper of society; they're lab rats, guinea pigs…'

Symes nodded. 'Yes, yes, I've heard that before. But compliant lab rats. The way they're controlled makes them docile, unquestioning, malleable. They're no threat to anyone and, importantly, they're most unlikely to break the Official Secrets Act or put any of us in danger. They're as one, all facing the same direction, all thinking the same thing. They're unified. That's what Unity is…'

He realised he might have been talking too loudly. Riley held up a hand in protest. 'All right, all right, no need to tell the world Symes. But you're wrong; that's not only what Unity is.'

'Then what…?'

'I'll tell you what I know, and even that might not be the full story. But first, let's talk some more about your Etonian chum.' Riley nodded towards the coaster pieces in Symes's pocket. 'Olivia Wilson has him lined up to be a new Number Two apparently. He'll be going to the village.'

This time Symes raised both eyebrows. Then he nodded, smiled, and said, 'I see. And you want me to have a word with him first, is that it?'

Riley nodded. 'More than that, Symes. You need to engage all that persuasive charm of yours. We need him on our side, because if what our newest resident knows about Unity gets out and reached, say, a less than democratic power, we could find ourselves in deep trouble…'

35

Tommy's flat, Stockwell, South London

'A D-notice! A bloody D-notice!' Chris slumped onto the settee and folded her arms, stared at the television screen even though it was off. Her eyes smouldered.

Tommy rubbed the back of his neck – it was still sore from falling off his motorbike – and regarded her from the kitchen where he'd just put the kettle on. He walked quietly through to the lounge and picked Chris's coat and bag off the floor where she'd thrown them as soon as she'd got in. He hung them up in the hall and came back in. She hadn't moved.

'Er… what's a D-notice when it's at home?'

Chris picked up the cushion next to her and strangled it. 'Aaaargh!' she shouted, and threw it across the room.

A moment later she seemed to realise where she was, looked up and saw Tommy, sighed, then rubbed her face and tucked her hair behind her ears.

'A D-notice is issued by the government to stop publication of sensitive information or material. We have to abide by it – it's law – and they've slapped one on the publication of Brown's notebook.'

The kettle whistled and Tommy went back into the kitchen. As he made a pot of tea he called out, 'So there *was* something in it then. Did they tell you what?'

'No. Just said that as foreign secretary his official government notes were off-limits and not in the public interest. A "matter of national security."'

Tommy came in and handed her a steaming mug. She nodded acknowledgement. He sat down next to her. 'Safe to sit here or do you still feel like punching something?'

She laughed and gave him a pretend thump. 'You'd better watch it.' Then she paused and thumped him again, harder. 'Which reminds me – sensitive information – what have you been getting up to? What was all that stuff in the hospital when your boss came to visit?'

Tommy looked sheepish and dropped his eyes to the floor. 'It's… difficult,' he stammered. Chris raised a fist again and held it mid-air.

'I can't tell you!' he blurted. 'I… signed the Official Secrets Act. I'm not allowed!'

'You *what*?!'

Tommy took a sip of his tea. It was tasteless. Chris turned fully to face him.

'Tommy Deighton! What the hell? First the government comes down on us at work like a ton of bricks, now I come home and you've gone all *Danger Man* on me. I am not going to let this go Tommy. This could be the biggest story of my career…'

Tommy interrupted, 'Or it could be nothing at all!'

Chris wasn't in a listening mood. 'The *biggest* of my career, and I need to do it. Don't you understand? I need to put some pieces together, I need to find out what some of those things in Brown's notebook mean, and I need… I need… oh God I need something stronger than bloody tea.'

She went into the kitchen and poured the remains of her mug away, got a glass from the cupboard, and a bottle of sherry from another cupboard – the Bristol Cream she kept for when her mum came to visit – and poured herself a generous amount. Tommy hadn't moved when she returned to the couch and sat down.

'Look, we've got the photos of what's in the book, we know some Russians stole it from you and – need I remind you, could have killed you in the process – and you know a lot more than that. Bugger the Official Secrets, Tommy. Help me with this!'

'But Charles said he was going to check how much you could be told, about… well, me, what's going on and everything, so shouldn't we wait until…'

'No! No, I can't wait! Something's going on at a very high level in government, and I think you know what it is, somehow. God only knows how…'

'To be honest Chris, I don't know a great deal myself, I…'

'*Seriously?* You expect me to believe that? You're not a mechanic, that's for sure!'

'Yes Chris, I am a mechanic, really I am. It's just that the garage that Charles runs is a government garage and… we have to do some extra work sometimes…'

'Extra work.' Chris said it flatly. 'What sort of extra work, and how does it relate to this… this bloody notebook of George Brown's? Come on, *tell me!*'

'Off the record?' pleaded Tommy. Chris rolled her eyes. 'All right,' she said. 'Off the record. For now.'

Tommy took a deep breath and told her: how he got the job, what his conditions of employment were (which, he reminded her, he was breaching just by telling her), that most of the work involved being what he called a 'grease monkey' but that every now and then Charles and he would set off in the hearse and render an anonymous person unconscious. They would load them into a casket and into the hearse, and Charles would drop Tommy off back at work.

Chris's mouth dropped open as he spoke. He continued, telling her about the most recent assignment, and how he'd got curious and tried to find out where

Charles had taken the 'body'. He even showed her the map with the arcs he'd drawn, and she stared at it, fascinated.

'See? I wasn't looking for a new flat,' he smiled. She didn't smile back.

He told her about getting arrested, being sprung by Symes, and what Symes had said. He left nothing out, and finally reached the point where he'd found the notebook. He shrugged his hands.

'That's it,' he said. 'Really, that's everything. You know the rest.'

She looked at him and smiled. 'You know, you're really quite smart for a boy who went to a secondary modern.' Then her face turned serious. 'But what about the man you... gassed? And this Unity thing? And the so-called village. What do you know about them?'

Tommy shrugged again. 'Nothing. No really, nothing – don't hit me! Charles hasn't said where he took the hearse, even though I know it was the RAF base at Northolt, but I have no idea where the ambulance went after that, or even if the man was actually in it. I suspect even Charles might not know. As for Unity... I have no idea.'

Chris bit her lip and thought.

'Well,' she announced finally. 'You've obviously got more than one brain cell, and I'm an assistant political editor, and we know what's in the notebook, so...'

She got up, grabbed pens and notepaper from a drawer, cleared the kitchen table and set everything down. She looked at Tommy.

'Well come on then!'

36

The Savoy Grill

George Brown drained his glass and placed it definitively on the linen tablecloth so that the waiter would see it and refill it. He wiped his lips on his napkin and shook his head.

'It's taking too long. Much too long,' he seethed.

Stone gave a slow nod and put down his knife and fork. 'Some things can't be rushed.'

Brown growled, 'But you've not broken him? He's told you nothing? I thought we were at the forefront of interrogation techniques. I mean, you've got everything at your disposal – the latest technology, scientific equipment, the finest brains, computers – what more do you need?' He quickly scanned the room, then lowered his voice. 'Can't you just… you know, stick needles under his fingernails or something?'

Stone sighed inwardly, but picked up his cutlery again and went back to his mixed grill.

'You must remember we're dealing with someone who's been trained to withstand the very interrogation techniques you mention. He has an inordinate ability to manage pain, and to endure… whatever we throw at him. We always knew he'd be a difficult nut to crack.'

'Well then stop!' Brown hissed. 'Maybe it doesn't matter what information he's got about Unity. Maybe he never got the chance to pass it on. He's a captive for God's sake. In which case Unity is still viable, and the sooner we get it operational the better. Defence is straining at the leash, and I'm just as keen to see it tested.'

The wine waiter appeared by his side and poured more burgundy. He moved round to Stone's side of the table but Stone put his hand over his glass and the waiter nodded and moved away.

'And really George, how practical would it be for us to bring the project forward?' Stone asked. 'In real terms. Weeks? Months? A year or more?'

The foreign secretary twirled his glass on the table and stared at it. 'You know I've been quietly diverting funds to Unity for some time now. The PM looks the other way of course, but he's under increasing pressure. There are rumours of a coup to oust him – you must know about that – and if that happens I could lose all control of the purse strings, unless of course...'

He thought for a moment, then leaned forward and continued. 'So I'm thinking weeks, two months at the very most.'

Stone almost choked on a piece of lamb. '*Two months?* Are you serious?'

Brown once again quickly scanned the nearby tables for eavesdroppers – just as Stone had been doing since they arrived – but didn't see any. He lowered his voice further nonetheless.

'Secretary for Defence Denis Healey tells me that both the Royal Aircraft Establishment and the Ministry of Aviation Supply, along with the boffins at Porton Down confirm that the delivery system and payload are nearly ready. The dispersal system is undergoing testing as we speak. The… arrow can be fitted to the bow in a couple of weeks, and once the final tests are complete the payload can be added. I'm told that the guidance systems are solid – all we have to do is confirm a target. And make sure that your captive stays where he is.'

Stone sat back in his chair and looked at Brown. This was the first time he had been given it straight;

usually Brown beat about the bush, talked in metaphors – *bows and arrows* – and was reluctant to supply any detail. But now, here it all was, laid out on the table, so to speak. He noticed a beading of sweat on Brown's forehead, and watched as his dining companion took yet another gulp of the burgundy. The air of increasing desperation was palpable.

'Oh come on man,' sneered Brown, 'it's not like we haven't done this sort of thing before. We've been trialling germ warfare on the British public in various places since 1940 – they just don't know it.'

'What's your ultimate end game George?' Stone asked directly.

Brown stared back, spreading his arms wide. 'I should have thought that was obvious; a happy, stable, productive and unquestioning society. A commendable goal I should have thought.'

Then he shook his head, threw his napkin on the table, rose from his seat and turned to leave. But he suddenly stopped and turned back. He swayed slightly as he focused on Stone.

'Oh, and I want to lead that society,' he growled, leaning on the table with both hands, his florid face just a few inches from Stone's. 'I want to be prime minister.'

37

Battersea Park, London

Symes sat on a park bench, *The Guardian* newspaper in front of him. It was open at the finance section, but he wasn't reading it, merely waiting.

Hopeful pigeons hopped near the bench on the off chance of a morsel, except Symes didn't have any sandwiches with him even though it was nearly lunchtime. The birds quickly lost interest and flew off.

A slightly portly man in his 40s came into view along the path. Well-dressed in a three-piece pin-stripe suit, bowler hat and jauntily swinging a tightly-furled umbrella as he walked, Barnaby Carrington-Hall seemed to make a last-minute decision to stop and rest for a while. He pulled out a pocket watch from his waistcoat, glanced at it, and then aimed for the vacant space on the bench beside Symes.

Carrington-Hall unfolded the newspaper he'd also brought, *The Times*, and held it out in front of him, just as Symes was doing.

'You know how obvious we look, don't you?' grumped Carrington-Hall. 'This is what they do in those dreadful spy programmes on the television.'

Symes chuckled. 'Terribly nice to see you too Barney.'

Carrington-Hall swiftly turned a page. 'This had better be worthwhile Symes. I have things to do, meetings to convene, reports to write, people to influence, agendas to keep.'

'Sounds like you need a holiday old bean. Maybe somewhere by the sea, some charming coastal village perhaps, with little cobbled streets and pastel-coloured buildings. A beach, fresh sea air. Do you the world of good.'

There was silence for a moment from behind *The Times*, although Symes noted his fists tightened slightly on the pages he held. Carrington-Hall flicked his paper out to straighten a crease and turned another page.

'So you know I'm rostered to go to the retirement village. No surprises there. What do you want?'

'I – we – need your help. What do you know about the facility?'

Carrington-Hall sighed audibly. 'Symes, it's all hush-hush as you know. I'm not sure I'm at liberty to discuss it with you, despite your position in the organisation.'

Symes chuckled. 'All right, I'll do the talking. And then you can decide whether you think it's safe to discuss it with me. Are you sitting comfortably?'

And so Symes précised the recent developments from the moment their top operative had resigned, through his being taken to the village, the various attempts at interrogation to find out why he'd quit, and the oversight of the whole operation by Olivia Wilson. He explained about his, Walker's and Riley's observation roles, and how they were increasingly concerned about how the village residents – and the recent arrival – were being manipulated and used for experimental purposes. He revealed what they knew so far about Unity. He left nothing out, and even included Judith Tench's involvement.

At last Carrington-Hall's interest was piqued. 'Tench? MI5? I know her. Top drawer. All right, let's talk. But I have to say a lot of what you've told me so far I already know, and the rest sounds like conjecture.'

'Which is why we need you to get us what we want: hard evidence.'

There was a momentary silence from behind Carrington-Hall's newspaper. Then he said, 'I've been there before you know, seconded – actually more like kidnapped – and taken there as an observer, just over a year ago. I wasn't happy with what I saw then and made it clear in my report. You should be able to find it if you search hard enough, although it didn't seem to make any difference. I was thanked for my input and that's the last I heard, until your Major Wilson contacted me a while back, asking if I'd be interested in "an assignment." She told me about your man resigning and that my job would be to break him.'

'That doesn't sound like you Barney. Not your style. Why'd you agree?'

'Because it gets me back in there. Thought I might be able to do something this time, from the inside. Exactly what you want, coincidentally.'

'So you'll help?'

There was another pause, but then he said, 'From what you've told me, you need all the help you can get. So yes, count me in. But remember, I'm only at this stage waiting in the wings; I can't just go there tomorrow, guns blazing as it were – I'm on stand-by, waiting to be summoned. I'm one of many, as you pointed out earlier. But I don't like Wilson. I did some digging – she's not… ethical. She wasn't in charge when I was there last time, but my network contacts tell me she's dangerous, and everything you've just told me confirms it.'

'The only risk,' said Symes, 'is that our man is broken before you get assigned as Number Two. If that happens it'll be too late.'

Carrington-Hall folded his newspaper, picked up his bowler hat from beside him and put it on. He stood, looked at the Thames on the other side of the path that ran in front of them, and turned to go.

'Then we'd better hope he holds out.'

38

Century House, Sub-basement 2

The chess board in the village grounds was literally life-size. As Wilson and Walker looked on from the observation lounge, the two men playing the game called for their human pieces to move to particular positions on the board, the players doing as they were bid.

'Never liked chess,' noted Walker, her arms folded across her chest as she stood next to Olivia Wilson looking out through the observation lounge window.

'Oh it's wonderful!' Wilson turned briefly to her then back to the main monitor which showed a wide shot of the figures on the board. Their main subject was one of them.

Wilson continued. 'It's so… alive and exciting. The twists and turns of the play. Teasing your opponent with a sacrificial move, having to think five, ten moves ahead, then coming out of nowhere to claim checkmate! Wonderful!'

Walker had never heard Wilson so animated. 'Is that what you're doing here, in the village – planning five or ten moves ahead? Is this whole thing a game to you?'

But she realised she'd gone too far. Wilson broke away and went to pour a coffee. When she came back she took a seat as far away from Walker as she could, and resumed watching the action. Walker's question went unanswered.

Walker saw that another new Number Two had been appointed. There must be an endless supply, she thought, and wondered where Wilson got them from.

'He's rather dashing,' Walker commented, moving back closer to Wilson and nodding towards the clean-shaven man with black glossy hair who was also watching the chess game. Wilson remained silent and sipped her coffee.

Suddenly they noticed one of the chess 'pieces' – a short thickset man in a striped top – run from the board in fear or panic. Wilson's mug paused halfway to her mouth as she watched a couple of the village's security people intercept him. Then she continued sipping her drink.

'Another renegade,' observed Walker.

'Not for long. He'll be dealt with accordingly.'

'How?' asked Walker.

Wilson's eyes remained on the screen. Once again she inwardly seethed at having her tactics questioned, particularly by Anastasia Walker. She really must have a word with Stone about whether he could help reinforce her – Wilson's – authority.

'Re-education,' Wilson spat. 'He'll learn.'

Orwell, thought Walker with a shiver. *Nineteen Eighty-four*. Winston Smith. Re-education.

'How?' she asked.

Wilson sighed, clenched her coffee mug and stood to face Walker. 'I have multiple means at my disposal. Which I use is up to me. Or rather, in this case, the expert clinicians at the village hospital. They're aware of the outcomes I require, they are on the spot, and they know their subjects, *intimately*. They take appropriate action according to the individual concerned. Some require little intervention – perhaps gentle persuasion – while others need urgent and direct invasive medical procedures. Whichever end of the spectrum of treatment, the patients *will* conform. They *will* obey. Now, Miss Walker, if you have no further questions, I have work to do.'

With that, Wilson turned, slammed her mug on the monitoring desk, gathered her satchel and coat and stormed out of the observation lounge.

Walker sighed and rubbed the back of her neck. She went out into the main room where she found Holland on duty, and stood beside him. She needed a distraction.

'Another lead player,' she muttered, as they both looked at the new Number Two on the large screen.

'Yes. Handsome chap, quite the dish.'

'Where *does* she find them all?' Walker wondered aloud.

Holland glanced up at her, then back to the screen. 'Civil service, many of them, apparently,' he said. 'They're all hand-picked, all… what you might call the cream of the crop.'

'Does *she* pick them?'

'Major Wilson? I believe so, likely with the boss's approval. But ask her, she's the one you should be talking to.'

Walker looked down at him. 'I might.' And she walked back towards the lounge. Inside she glanced again at the main screen to see that the errant resident had been taken to the village hospital where, for some unfathomable reason, Number Two had invited Number Six to watch his treatment.

'This is bizarre…' Walker muttered to herself. Over the course of the next few hours she observed the man in the striped top undergo a type of Pavlovian shock treatment, overseen by a male and a female psychiatrist, until a point where the female informed Number Two that the subject would now be cooperative.

Walker tutted to herself, then sat at the mini-monitoring desk. She went to pick up the phone, then paused and looked once again at the screen. The man in the striped top looked broken, defeated.

She picked up the handset and dialled. She heard the phone picked up at the other end.

'I think we need to talk.'

39

Stone's office, Century House

'Yes, that's right,' Stone said into the mouthpiece. He leaned forward to double check that the scrambler light was on and that the conversation he was having was definitely secure. It was. He stiffened as he listened to the protesting voice on the other end of the line.

'I can take care of that from this end. Look, you're Defence, and in the end that's what this is all about: defence of the realm. It's your job as much as it is mine, and the project needs to be brought forward. Those above us in Westminster and Whitehall are insistent.'

Stone listened some more, then picked up a fountain pen and threw it across the room where it hit the wall and fell to the floor.

'I don't bloody care what testing phases still have to be done! Get on to Porton Down and get them to pull out all the stops. Now!' He cut the connection.

His intercom immediately beeped and he flicked a switch. 'What?'

There was a split-second pause as his secretary assimilated the unusually aggressive response from her boss. 'Er, Major Wilson asks to see you sir…'

Stone closed his eyes briefly and tried to clear his mind, then blinked and sat upright. He took a deep breath. 'Very well, send her in.'

Wilson swept into the room with less than her usual military precision. Her hair, despite its shortness, was tousled, there were dark shadows under her eyes, and her satchel slipped from her shoulder as she shut the door behind her, hanging awkwardly in the crook of her elbow.

Stone smoothed down his tie and regained composure. 'Olivia, lovely to see you again,' he purred. 'Please, sit down…'

She did, and made an attempt to tidy herself. She lowered her satchel to the floor beside her and clasped her hands in her lap.

'I… I'm sorry to bother you at short notice Sir, but I just wanted to…' Her eyes searched the carpet in front of her for a prompt.

Stone nodded for her to continue. 'Yes?'

'I just wanted to say… wanted to say that I'm finding the presence of Miss Walker, Mr Riley and Mr Symes in Monitoring a distraction. You told me you'd appointed them as observers, but they ask too many questions. If they were just to observe maybe that would be fine; however I find that they frequently question my authority and methods. It's not helping. I need to concentrate if we're to get anywhere, especially with our latest resident.'

Stone pondered her deluge of disenchantment for a moment; this was not the usual, unflappable Wilson he'd come to know, and admire. His appointment of Walker and Riley in particular was to determine whether they were trustworthy when it came to maintaining secrecy about and, importantly, support for, the Unity project. Symes he had no qualms about. But interruptions or dissonance so close to the ultimate Unity mission was the last thing he needed at this particular time.

'Do you think they're doing this to deliberately distract you, or out of a genuine interest in your methods?'

The question took her by surprise. She bit her lip and thought. 'Well, Sir… I don't know. I… they seem unconvinced that the work I've been tasked to do for you is, well, worthy. Or worthwhile. Or even warranted. I'm not questioning their seniority or experience, or their own authority… I'm sure they're among the finest people you've got. But…' And once again she scanned the carpet looking for help.

'But?'

She could contain herself no longer and stood up to pace back and forth in front of his desk. But he allowed her the freedom to talk.

'The subject – Number Six – is proving far more resistant and resilient than I'd anticipated. He is at once a captive and a warden himself. He is manipulating those around him as much as they – we – have a hold over him. He crumples, then revives, he is thwarted at every turn yet remains buoyant, full of confidence and determination. It's hard to tell sometimes who's the cat and who's the mouse. I have never, in all my experience, come across a subject so tough.

'And, you'll recall you asked me to let you know if he used any repetitive phrases or words? Nothing. I mean, I don't even know what I'm supposed to listen for! Multiple times we've asked him why he resigned and he's never given us that information.'

Stone watched her. She paused in her pacing and looked at him.

'Have you tried all the methods at your disposal?' he asked. She sat down again, leaned back in the chair and rubbed a hand across her eyes, and sighed.

'Not quite. I still have a few tricks up my sleeve.'

'Good,' said Stone. 'And the role of Number Two… I do like the way you refresh them regularly. But I wonder whether we've been pitting the right people against him. You have the list. Go through it again and see if there's someone on it who might be more his equal. Move them up, bring them in sooner rather than later. We need to act.'

Wilson saw that Stone's face had hardened, and the purr had gone from his voice. The psychologist in her took in his body language in a flash and she realised that he was uneasy, under pressure, and not in a mood for failure.

'Is there something I need to know Sir?'

Stone sat bolt upright in his chair and clasped his hands on the desk in front of him. He looked at her unblinkingly.

'Yes. But I can't tell you right now what it is. Need-to-know and all that. What I can say is that we're going to have to bring our man back to London, as we discussed some time ago when you formulated your strategy. Just temporarily while some things need to be done in the… facility.

'Meanwhile, I'll take care of Walker and Riley, and Symes too. You'll be able to continue your work uninterrupted. But continue you will. In fact you must. And send reports to me daily, and copy Walker in. That'll be all.'

Without a further word Stone opened a file on his desk and reached for his fountain pen, then realised it lay in two pieces on the floor, the ink slowly seeping into the carpet like blood from a wound. Wilson slipped out of his office.

40

Judith Tench's flat

'And that's the gist of it,' said Riley, taking a sip of Earl Grey at Tench's kitchen table. Outside a blackbird sang its goodnight song as darkness descended on the neat lawn stretching back to the hydrangeas at the end.

Tench leaned back against the kitchen countertop and regarded Riley. 'So she's becoming unhinged? Wilson I mean.'

'I'd wondered that for a while. Maybe. Or perhaps she's just passionate about her job. Some people are, to a concerning degree. I've seen it. We've had to let a couple go during their training for just being too… eager.'

'Because it makes them unfit for the job.'

'Yes, as you say, unfit. Enthusiasm is one thing, but an obsessive drive for results or perfection is something else.' He finished his tea and gently placed the cup back in its saucer on the table. 'So the call from Anastasia Walker wasn't too much of a surprise, although I am still a bit wary of her.'

Tench took his cup and saucer and put them on the draining board, then turned back. 'Can we trust her?'

Riley looked off into the distance for a second, then back to her. 'Honestly? I don't know. Stone asked me to keep an eye on her during this operation, and I'm almost a hundred percent certain he asked her to do the same about me. Playing one off against the other.'

'What have you told him so far?' asked Tench.

'There's been very little I could tell him. I've reported that she seems fully engaged with her observation role. That's it. Not sure she'll have said the same about me though. And yet…'

'Well?'

'We've all – me, Walker and Symes – just been taken out of the loop. No longer needed in Monitoring. A memo came round from Stone. Seemed to take Walker as much by surprise as the rest of us, so at least there's no more spying on each other. Unless of course the director's playing a game – you know, that he needs *me* removed from Monitoring, maybe because of something Walker's told him – but can't just take me out as that would be too obvious. So he removes all of us.'

Tench considered this for a second. 'A bit counter-productive though, if he wanted you all to observe the goings-on in the village community and report to him. Who's going to report to him now? Wilson?'

Riley only got as far as opening his mouth to answer when the doorbell rang.

Tench looked at her watch and pushed herself off the countertop. 'That'll be your Symes. You're absolutely sure it's okay to let him in, in both senses of the word?'

Riley crossed his fingers and held them up.

When she opened the door Tench found a dashing man in his mid-40s, smiling with perfect teeth, standing on the doorstep. He proffered a small but pretty bunch of flowers and said, 'Symes. Rupert Symes.'

Tench, mildly flustered for a moment, let him in and took the flowers. 'That's very kind, and somewhat unnecessary given we've never met.' She shut the door, hung up his coat and directed him towards the kitchen. Despite herself she smiled behind his back.

Riley and Symes greeted each other while Tench took a vase down from a cupboard and a knife from the drawer to cut the stems down. She arranged them loosely, added water, then placed the vase on the table.

'Are you flirting with my friend?' Riley stared at Symes.

He chuckled. 'Dear boy. If I were, she wouldn't be *your* friend for long.'

Riley shook his head. 'Right, to business.'

But Symes interrupted. 'Before we start, aren't you supposed to ask me if I was followed here?'

Riley and Tench glanced at each other, then back to Symes, who didn't wait for the question. 'Because I've taken almost an hour to get here, checking reflections, tying shoelaces, crossing roads and crossing back again, doubling back, catching a bus one stop – all the usual things – and if there was anyone following me then they are very, very good.'

Riley raised an eyebrow. 'I'd have expected you to do nothing less, Symes. And?'

'Not a chance old boy.' Symes's dimples worked overtime.

'Good,' said Riley.

At which point the doorbell rang again.

Riley and Symes looked at each other, then Riley said, 'That's not Walker – she's not due here for another hour.'

Tench hissed, 'Out the back. Stay behind the shed. It's probably nothing. I'll call you when it's clear…'

They quietly eased themselves out through the back door. Tench watched as they made their way in the gloom across the patio and behind the shed, then the doorbell rang again. When she was satisfied they were out of sight she dropped the blind and went to the front door.

She opened it tentatively, ready to peer round it but the door burst open and a man pushed her forcibly back into the hall, keeping one hand on her and closing the door behind him with the other. She staggered back and tried to take in the details: black oilskin-type jacket, black woollen hat, dark green scarf over the mouth and nose, brown slightly-scared eyes that never left her face.

She tried to yell, but her shout was cut off before it started. His left hand was at her throat now, still pushing, and to relieve the pressure Tench continued backwards into the kitchen until she was backed up against the kitchen table which scraped against the tiled floor. The vase of flowers toppled, rolled, spilt its water but remained on the table.

Using both hands now, the stranger spun her to the left and pushed her back against the countertop where he increased his grip on her throat. Tench tried to force his arms away but he was much stronger and pinned her left hand down. His grip on her throat was fierce and dark spots began to dance at the edges of her vision.

He pushed his face up against hers. 'Give it up,' he whispered. Even through the increasing fog she recognised it as an English voice, London accent, not cultured. She tried to speak, couldn't. But he wasn't there for a conversation.

'Drop it. Walk away, and nothing will happen. You and your mates, give it up. Understand?' He tightened his grip further and Tench knew she would soon pass out, or worse.

With her right hand she reached behind her, felt the cup on the countertop, gripped it and in one move smashed it against the front of the counter then swung up the piece in her hand and slashed at the man's eyes with the shard. He flinched back, but held his grip. The broken cup's edge grazed across his forehead, a trickle of blood forming above his left eye.

You bitch!' he hissed, and released her left hand as he wiped the blood from his forehead and eyes with his hand. It was all she needed.

Tench knew the knife she'd used for the flowers was also behind her. She dropped the shard, again reached behind, felt the knife, found the handle. She curled her fingers round it and just as the man drew his fist back to strike her in the face she stabbed him in the ribs, rapidly, once, twice, three times.

His eyes widened, his fist poised mid-air, the pressure on Tench's throat eased, and he looked down at his side. Tench quickly brought the knife up to his throat, the tip just penetrating through the scarf. She didn't care whether it punctured his skin, but it must have because he instantly drew back, looked at her with a mixture of surprise, then rage, then… fear?

The man said nothing more. Clasping his left hand to his side both he and Tench looked down to see blood seeping through his jacket. He looked back up once more, eyes wide in panic, then quickly turned. Clutching his side he ran down the hall and out of the front door and disappeared into the night.

*

Outside Riley and Symes had hidden behind the shed as Tench had ordered.

'Who…?' Riley whispered, looking at Symes.

Symes shook his head. 'No idea old boy.'

'You're sure you weren't followed? Absolutely sure?'

Symes shook his head. 'Not a chance. Probably just coincidence, a neighbour or someone.'

He slowly eased his head round the edge of the shed, but could see nothing. The kitchen blinds were down, the sitting room curtains drawn. From inside he heard a scraping noise, like a chair on a floor.

'Anything?' asked Riley. Symes shook his head. 'Can't see. Might be sitting down for a cup…' but he was interrupted by a noise that sounded like something dropping or smashing. They looked at each other in alarm. Riley was first to move. He grabbed Symes by the arm and hissed, 'Let's go!'

The two men crept rapidly across the grass and onto the patio. They stopped either side of the back door and listened. Nothing. Then… a sob? It was all they needed. Symes grabbed the handle and the two of them flew through the door and into the kitchen.

Tench was still leaning against the countertop, holding her throat with one hand, rubbing it, her face flushed and blotchy, her hair in disarray. In her other hand was the small knife she'd used on the flower stems, its blade covered in blood, some of which dripped from the tip onto the floor.

Riley went to her. Symes looked down the hall and could see the front door slowly swinging shut. He leapt down the hall and threw it open, flew down the steps and looked up and down the street. Nothing, and nobody. He checked again, then slowly turned to go back inside, which is when he saw drops of blood on the steps. Another check of the street, still nothing. He stepped around the blood, went back inside, and closed and locked the door behind him.

In the kitchen Riley was helping Tench into one of the chairs. The knife was now on the countertop.

'Get some water!'

Symes did as he was told. 'What the *hell* just happened?'

Tench coughed, rubbed her throat some more, then took the glass of water and drank. Her eyes were glassy, but smouldering. She grimaced – it was painful to swallow.

'Some… someone…' she wheezed, 'Someone wants us to stop.'

41

Century House, Sub-basement 2

Olivia Wilson was much happier. She sat alone in the observation lounge and flicked through the various feeds on the small monitors before her. She looked at the different external views of the village, then found some live coverage from interior cameras, including a couple in the hospital and the village control room.

She was further pleased to witness the debonair Number Two countermanding a female psych specialist who suggested performing a leucotomy on Number Six. Wilson had instructed Two directly to focus on co-operation with the prisoner rather than conflict – or worse: intervention. The specialist defended her recommendation, declaring that Six showed 'aggressive tendencies' – which made Wilson chuckle.

'Of course he does you idiot,' she muttered aloud. 'He's a caged animal, trapped, behind bars; of course he's aggressive!'

She sat back and picked up a manila folder stamped Top Secret. The circulation list on the front showed the date and time it had left Personnel, and the same information alongside her own name about when she'd received it. It would go no further.

Wilson opened it. Inside was a file, the many pages held together with a large paper clip. On the front was simply a name: Carrington-Hall, Barnaby, and a file number.

Attached to the inside cover was a black and white photograph, a head-and-shoulders shot of a man in his mid-to-late 40s, although he looked older. She noted his medical record showed that his left eye was, in fact, false, the result of a school fencing accident at the age of fifteen.

Although it wasn't the first time she'd viewed the file, she hadn't previously considered Carrington-Hall as a rebel. In the photograph he wore a short beard and moustache but his hair was surprisingly long for a man of his age, and status.

A bit of a renegade, wondered Wilson, like our Number Six? Maybe that's exactly what we need, she pondered. Pit like against like, fight fire with fire. She nodded to herself. Stone's intuition was right, and this might be just the man to match the prisoner, and either break him, or… or what?

Her jubilation was short-lived, however. That night she watched as the captive made another bid for freedom, having recruited a cohort of what he believed were like-minded inmates from the village residents and staff. One of them was the man who had fled the chess board and been subsequently 're-educated' at the hospital. So, she wondered, had his treatment failed?

During the night she learned that Six had managed to locate a fishing boat not far offshore, had headed out to it on a makeshift raft, and had boarded the vessel.

But, as she knew, it was to no avail. The man who had undergone re-education had revealed Six's escape plan to Number Two. And anyway, she thought with satisfaction, the boat he'd boarded was under their control. He was never going to get away.

Remote-controlled by Number Two the vessel was brought back inshore, the prisoner recaptured. It was, she thought, drama on the high seas, and yet another masterful illustration of just how total and uncompromising the captive's incarceration was. And, she smiled, how many resources and how much funding were being invested in the village project. It was, for her, the case study of a lifetime, and she was determined to make the most of it.

Now all she had to do was keep Stone happy by turning the thumbscrews a bit tighter on Six. She then did something totally out of character and put her feet up on the monitoring desk, leaned back further in her chair, and lit a cigarette. She inhaled, stretched for a moment, then returned to the manila file.

Thumbing through the pages she came across a timeline of the glass-eyed man's involvement in operations and had to shake her head to believe what she was seeing: he had previously been assigned to the village just over a year ago – just before she was given the oversight role for the experiments on the residents.

So, she thought, our man is a veteran. Even better – no need to bring him up to speed or to induct him in the ways of the village.

She read further and discovered that he'd been seconded there as an observer, but only for a limited time. He had filed a report, and had then returned to his role as a defence attaché.

She made a mental note to follow up on his report and closed the folder. She closed her eyes, took another drag on her cigarette and visualised the various steps she would now have to go through to bring the prisoner back to London, as Stone had requested. Then her eyes flicked open, she swung her legs off the desk, reached for a notepad and scribbled on it hastily.

She looked at what she'd written: *Six must escape*. Then, after a short pause, she began writing a list of names underneath, along with other words, boxes, arrows and lines which would make little sense to anyone reading them, but which – to her at least – added up to her biggest and most complex piece of theatre yet.

42

Century House, Sub-basement 3

Those present around the oval conference table could tell that Stone was not his usual calm and commanding self. While they waited for the final attendees to take their seats, they watched as he talked animatedly in hushed tones to Olivia Wilson seated to his right. Between them was a large ring-binder to which they referred often.

Stone nodded at something Wilson had just pointed to in the file then glanced around the room. If he was satisfied that everyone was there his face didn't show it. He cleared his throat.

'Right, let's get started. The first thing you'll be aware of is that we have some extra attendees today, and some from the last directorate meeting who are… missing. This is deliberate on my part. You will understand why in due course. But first I've asked Major Wilson here, our director of psych ops, to give you a rundown on where we are up to with developments in the facility, and our newest resident. Please keep any questions until the end.'

He turned to Wilson and nodded. She stood, just as she had done at the first meeting weeks – or was it months ago? – and began.

There was silence in the room as she spoke, and she used the large screen to display images from the hillside village to illustrate various points. Had they been allowed, some of those attending would have been scribbling notes furiously, but since pens, paper and any recording devices were prohibited from the room they could do nothing but sit and listen. Stone had given Wilson dispensation to bring in her folders for reference.

It took Wilson forty minutes to cover everything that had happened since the operative had been taken to the village, and her update was comprehensive – apart from one or two aspects that Stone had said he would 'prefer' she didn't cover. She knew 'prefer' wasn't a request; it was an order.

There was silence when she finished.

'Thank you. So,' said Stone, 'any questions?' A number of hands went up. The questions weren't difficult and generally sought more details, but the final one threw Wilson.

'What,' asked a stern-looking man with a jutting chin and piercing blue eyes, 'will you do with your Number Six if you don't break him? What if after you carry out this – and I have to say it – this rather unbelievable – plan to bring him "back to London" he still doesn't give us what we want?'

Wilson looked to Stone for guidance. He smiled at everyone around the table. 'I shouldn't worry about that. Major Wilson has various means at her disposal to ensure that he will be dealt with.'

'Dealt with?' the man queried.

Stone's mouth tightened into a sharp line. 'Let's put it this way: the facility's hospital has methods and equipment that can ensure that a… patient… remembers nothing. In the end, if necessary, his memory of his incarceration, even his work for us in the past, can be erased.'

'But that's barbaric!'

'Given the information in his head I believe it's… appropriate, although admittedly very much a last resort,' countered Stone.

'But you're talking about turning him into a vegetable!'

Stone turned to Wilson. 'Then we'd better hope it doesn't come to that. Thank you Major. That will be all.'

Wilson realised she'd been dismissed. She gathered her files, mumbled her thanks in return, and left the room, disappointed that she wasn't to be party to the rest of the meeting.

After the door had hummed shut Stone looked at the faces around the table.

'I hope that gives you a clear idea of the state of play. Now, you're all here today because I – which means all of us – face increasing pressure from our government sponsors to bring Unity forward.'

He scanned the faces, each representing the highest levels of authority within defence, intelligence, home and foreign affairs, and Cold War strategic planning. The others represented the village community operations itself.

'Why?' demanded one of the strategists. 'We have no indication of any changes to the status quo in the Soviet Union. Kosygin is pliable, Andropov slightly more concerning, but overall there's no indication of any particular arms build-up or increase in tensions beyond the normal.'

'I agree,' chipped in the Ministry of Defence representative. 'Also, the project at Porton Down is incomplete. Bringing it forward just isn't practical – they're working as hard as they can.'

'It's nothing to do with what's happening in the Soviet Union,' Stone hissed.

'Then why the urgency?' asked the strategist.

Stone slammed the table with his fist, his eyes glaring at each person before him. 'I will NOT have my orders questioned!' he shouted. 'When I say bring the programme forward, I mean BRING IT BLOODY FORWARD!'

The silence was complete, the room seeming to drop in temperature a few degrees.

Stone glared at them some more, then waved a dismissive hand. 'Get out.'

43

Chemical Defence Experimental Establishment
(CDEE)
Porton Down

Dr. Sarika Khatri turned off the valve and the spray ceased. She stepped out from the decontamination shower, unclipped her air hose, then her transparent helmet and lifted it off her head. She placed them, followed by her white airtight suit in a special cupboard where they would be dried with a blast of warm air, which would be filtered multiple times before being tested and discharged into the atmosphere some floors above.

At her locker she slipped back into her regular day shoes, shrugged into a jersey, took her purse from the shelf, then closed and locked the door. Her last act before leaving the decontamination room was to go back to near the shower chamber where there was a transparent panel in the wall. It gave access to a type of dumb waiter. She pressed the 'up' button beside it, and machinery whirred into life. Within a few seconds a compartment arrived from the laboratory one level below; it contained her notes, clipped to a board, all of which had also been decontaminated.

Sliding the panel up she retrieved her paperwork, closed the door and left the room.

She took the lift three floors up and stepped out. As she walked down the corridor towards her office a man's head popped out of the director's door ahead. He saw her, and pointed into his office, then withdrew. She sighed and wondered what it would be this time. Just recently she had had a fraught conversation with the boss about her work, and having just finished her shift in the lab the last thing she wanted was more of the same.

'Ah, Sarika. Come in, come in,' the director fussed, trying too hard to be affable, she thought. 'Would you like tea?' he asked, pointing to a pot on the table next to his desk. 'Freshly made…'

'No thank you sir,' she said.

'Oh, right. Right. Well, do sit down.'

She did as requested and waited. The director fussed with the things on his desk, straightened his blotter, adjusted the perpetual calendar so that it lined up with the blotter's edge. He avoided looking at her, and she realised he was holding something back.

'Was there something sir? Only I…' She waved vaguely in the direction of her office where she had a report to type up, bar charts and graphs to update, and test results to duplicate and file.

'Oh right, right. Of course. Busy, you must be busy. Well,' he said, finally looking at her, his beady eyes blinking rapidly, his hands fidgeting, 'I just… wondered whether you'd given any more thought to our little chat the other day…'

Sarika's heart sank. So it *was* about the meeting she'd had with him after all. She'd hoped the issue had gone away. Obviously it hadn't.

'I have sir.'

'Good, good. Splendid. And…?' He raised his eyebrows, his mouth forming an anticipatory smile.

'And I haven't changed my position,' she declared. 'I will not fast-track the work on Eirene-3, nor will I cut it short. I thought I'd made that clear when we talked last time… sir,' she added acerbically.

The director stopped fidgeting. His smile, what there was of it, disappeared and his eyes dropped to the desk. He placed both arms on the desk and clasped his hands, then looked at her directly. He had stopped blinking. But, she noticed, his brow was shining under the fluorescent strip light – sweat?

'The thing is Sarika,' he said in a low almost whispered voice, 'the thing is, I'm getting a lot of pressure from London to deliver the "finished product" sooner rather than later. No, wait, hear me out! I know Eirene's not *completely* finished final testing yet, but there's not far to go, and all the results to date have been very positive. Haven't they?'

Sarika shifted in her seat. 'Yes but…'

The director held up a hand. 'Yes, satisfying results. And we've gone from a solid to a liquid to a gas with no discernible drop-off in efficacy. We know that the product can be scaled up without issue, and that it can be compressed. You've done excellent work Sarika. Exemplary.'

She stared back at him. 'Sir, I will not breach the professional standards to which I have adhered all my working life by taking… taking shortcuts. I will not sacrifice my integrity just for some head honcho in London who wants this project completed before his performance review. There are required formal stages, steps… you of all people know this. I told you two days ago that I could not in all conscience speed up the research, take short-cuts or declare it finished. I have not changed my mind. The answer is no.'

She stood up. The air between them was charged, the hum of the fluorescent tube above their heads the only sound. For what seemed an eternity neither of them spoke nor moved.

Then the director slowly nodded. Sarika picked up her purse, turned and put her hand on the door handle. As she turned it, she heard the director say, 'Oh, Sarika: one more thing.'

She looked back. He picked up a manila envelope from his in-tray and held it out. 'This came for you.' She took it. It bore her name, along with 'Personal and Confidential' in large letters, underlined.

She turned and left.

Back at her desk she let out a long breath. This was worse than the last meeting with him, and she wondered just what sort of pressure London was applying, and why the project's completion was so urgent. But of course the staff at the establishment were rarely given the full picture of the work they were doing. Project Eirene was no exception.

She massaged her temples; a headache was coming. Then she saw the envelope on her desk and picked it up.

It was foolscap-sized, fully sealed, and other than her name and 'Personal and Confidential' bore no markings. She took a paper knife from her drawer and slit it open.

She put her hand inside and withdrew a white blank piece of heavy paper, then realised it was the back of a photograph. She turned it over and let out a cry, then dropped it on the desk in front of her. Her hand went to her mouth, and tears began forming. 'No!'

The picture was a candid shot in black and white, taken with a long lens. It was of her parents who lived in London. They were side by side and walking along a street. It had been taken probably from the other side of the road, but was clear and sharp. She was in no doubt: these were definitely her parents.

Also sharp were the two gun sight targets that had been drawn across their heads, the cross hairs lining up with their temples.

44

Virgil Street Garage

Tommy saw the highly polished shoes from where he was working in the inspection pit beneath a dark green and silver Bentley. He knew immediately who they belonged to: Symes.

'I'm down here,' he called. 'Give me a moment.'

The feet walked in and stopped near the workbench. Tommy wiped his hands on his overalls and crept up the steps at the back of the car. Symes was running his finger along the bench, then held it out in front of him, examining it.

'I must say you do keep a very clean workshop,' he smiled. 'You obviously pay attention to detail.'

Tommy ignored him and went to a clipboard hanging on the wall and wrote something on it. 'What d'you want?' he asked without turning.

'Oh, just a little chat with you, and Charles.'

Tommy turned round, but Symes continued. 'And Chris.'

'What d'you mean man? Charles is out – he'll be back soon – but *Chris*?'

Symes flicked an imaginary speck off his sleeve. 'Well Tommy, it seems you and she know far more about… things… than might be good for you. You've already been knocked off your motorbike and managed to give the foreign secretary's notebook to the Russians…'

Tommy flushed, his hands clenched into fists. 'I never gave it to them! They stole it from me, and you know it! I was trying to return it!'

'What's going on?' It was Charles, coming in through the open garage door.

'Ah, Charles, just the man.' Symes smiled. Charles grunted.

Then Symes leaned over slightly and added, 'And just the woman too. Hello Chris, come in, come in.'

Chris tentatively entered the workshop looking bewildered. 'Was it you who phoned me?' she asked.

Symes chuckled. 'Yes my dear. Sorry I couldn't be more informative on the telephone, but anyway, here you are. I'm Symes.' He held out his hand but she ignored it.

'What's this all about?' Charles asked.

Symes looked at him and chuckled. 'Oh come on Charles old thing, you know very well. Now, close the door and we'll talk.'

Reluctantly Charles closed the big roller door and switched on the workshop lights.

'We might want to sit down,' said Symes looking around and taking in the office at the back.

'Not enough room in there for all of us,' grumped Charles.

'Well, we need to be comfortable.' Symes continued to look around, his eyes stopping on the Bentley. He pointed at it. 'This will do. Hop in.'

Chris stared at Tommy with raised eyebrows but he just shook his head and mouthed, 'I don't know,' and opened the rear door for her. He slid in after her, Charles took the front passenger seat and Symes the driver's seat. Symes turned and faced them all.

'That's better.' He looked around the inside of the car. 'Rather like a gentleman's club, this. All leather and polished wood. Very plush.'

'Get on with it,' snapped Charles.

Symes didn't react. He looked at Chris and Tommy for a moment, then tutted.

'Tsk, tsk. What are we going to do with you two?'

Tommy looked at Chris, but she just silently stared at Symes. He continued.

'I must admit you've both been very clever. You've pieced together quite a bit of what's been – or in fact is – going on. Very impressive.'

Chris broke her silence. 'What do you mean? We've done nothing!'

Symes didn't respond. Instead he reached inside his coat pocket and brought something out, held it up for them all to see. It was the smallest tape recorder any of them had ever seen, and beautiful. The engineer in Tommy admired the sleek design, the shiny – what appeared to be – stainless steel or alloy, the perfect tiny spools that held the brown tape. Symes switched it on to play. The sound was surprisingly good quality.

'So, we know the man you… kidnapped… was taken to Northolt Air Base.' Chris's voice.

'Yeah, and that he was probably then taken in the ambulance somewhere else.' Tommy.

Chris couldn't contain her anger. 'What the hell? That's us! Where did you get that? How?'

Symes stopped the tape. 'Well, as I think you're aware, the flat next door has had workers in recently…'

Tommy and Chris nodded.

'Except they weren't builders. They work for us. Not so much builders as monitors. Surveillance.'

'You've been *spying* on us?' Chris was incredulous. 'Recording us?'

'I'm afraid so. Tommy, you did sign the Official Secrets Act remember, and this shows you are now in breach of it. That's a crime. And you,' he said, looking directly at Chris, 'have been helping him. You've been interfering in matters of national security, also an offence.'

Charles cleared his throat. 'Er, I'm sure they didn't mean any harm Mr. Symes. They're just young 'uns…'

'They may not have meant any harm Charles, but my problem now is what to do with them.'

Tommy's fists were clenched again. 'What do you mean "do with us"? We haven't discovered anything. Much.' He looked at Chris again but her smouldering gaze remained on Symes.

He put the recorder back in his pocket. 'No need to play you the rest. You know what we've heard. It's all recorded and transcribed. You've managed between you to work out that the man you and Charles rendered unconscious was taken to the airbase, and yes he was transferred into an ambulance. Don't worry, he wasn't harmed, although he was kept unconscious for his journey.

'You also, thanks to your having stolen the foreign secretary's notebook Tommy – another offence – worked out that there's something called The Village, and that our man was likely taken there. Guesswork on your part maybe, but an excellent guess. And then you wondered what Unity was, and here…' he looked at Chris again 'you've excelled in your reporting and deduction skills… you reached a conclusion that there's a government project by that name and that it's somehow linked with the man you took, Tommy. And that Unity also somehow ties in with the village.'

'Is this right?' Charles asked them.

They both looked down and then Tommy stared back up at Symes. 'You can blame me. It wasn't Chris's fault. I was the one who wanted to know what was going on. I mean, I know I'm employed as a mechanic, and that there's more to the job than that. I'd already worked out you lot are spies or whatever, but that didn't worry me particularly. What I was worried about was what happens to the poor blokes Charles and I take care of. Like, what happens? Do you shoot them, torture them, what? I just wanted to know. Chris had nothing to do with it.'

Symes's smile didn't touch his eyes. 'Oh, but you got her involved, by showing her George Brown's notebook. I know, I know, you thought you were doing her a favour. But look where it's got us: a major national newspaper now has copies of it, we've had to come down hard on them to stop publication, the Soviets have stolen the actual book from you and they might well reach some of the same conclusions that you have. It's all got very messy.'

'I was doing my job,' Chris spat. 'I'm a journalist. A political journalist, so Brown's notebook and its contents were well within my remit. You can hardly call that a breach of the Official Secrets Act.'

'I can call it what I like young lady,' responded Symes coldly. 'But it remains a national security issue. So, we have two choices. We can prosecute you both, which would also be very messy – you could both lose your jobs at the very least – or… we can bring you on board.'

'Meaning?'

'Meaning, young Tommy, that we use your cleverness to our advantage. You get to work for Queen and country, and when it's all over your slate is wiped clean. And yours Chris,' he added.

Charles cleared his throat again. 'You might want to consider what he's offering,' he said to the two of them in the back seat. 'It's not a bad place to work – I know, I've been involved with the organisation for quite some time now.' He turned to Symes. 'Would they be getting a job for life, or just till this "mess" as you call it is cleared up?'

Symes looked from Charles to Chris and Tommy. 'Depends. Normally they'd have to go through the whole recruitment process, and then – if they passed – spend months in training. And even then they could fall at the last hurdle. But in this case expedience is necessary, so we'll dispense with any formalities. As for the future, that will depend on how well you both perform.'

'But you're basically blackmailing us,' Chris sneered. 'We don't have a choice at all; it's either play ball with you or we end up in court.'

'That's still a choice,' said Symes.

45

Century House

Bill Riley listened to the caller on his desk phone, then said, 'Right. Understood. Thanks.' He replaced the receiver in its cradle, sat back and steepled his fingers, then swivelled his chair to gaze out of the window across London.

Good, he thought, one more piece in the game. Or two in this case. He knew Symes would do well taking over his position when he retired. And then he shuddered – what most of us call feeling like someone has just walked over our grave – as he again considered what 'retirement' could mean in the intelligence community. He certainly didn't want to end up in the village.

He picked up the handset again and pressed a button on his phone, got put through to Walker. 'Anastasia? Care for a stroll? Why? Because I think it will be good for you. Excellent. Front door five minutes? Fine, see you there.'

Finally, he thought, a plan was coming together, and he was relieved to have Walker on board. Along with, as he'd just heard from Symes, the assistant funeral director Tommy and his flatmate Chris. Better them in the fold than snapping at their heels.

*

They walked to a nearby small park and sat on a bench. A few pigeons flew in hoping for some crumbs. They were to be disappointed.

'Sorry about the other night,' Riley said. 'Glad I was able to phone you in time, save you the trip.'

Walker nodded. 'So what happened? You were vague on the phone. Rightly so of course.'

Riley told her the events of the evening at Tench's flat, leaving nothing out. He passed on Tench's description of the fight in the kitchen almost word for word, blow for blow, stab for stab.

'She's quite some girl your friend!'

'Turns out she was in Section VII during the war,' Riley said. 'As an instructor.'

'Section VII? What's that?'

'Ah well, if I told you I'd have to kill you and all that. Top secret, even to this day.'

'Seriously Riley. Have you forgotten where we work? Secret is our middle name. You've just told me the name of the outfit. Come on, spill the beans!'

'Sorry, I really thought you knew. Seven was a military unit – one of ours actually – that trained young people in the event that the Nazis successfully occupied Britain. They were a sort of resistance, trained to disrupt, disturb, disarm and even dismember if necessary. Also, trained to kill with whatever came to hand.'

'Which includes tea cups and fruit knives,' said Walker matter-of-factly.

'Exactly. He's lucky he didn't get a vase smashed over his head as well, or a tea towel down the throat.'

'And when you say young people…'

Riley looked over her shoulder for a moment and paused.

Walker pressed him. 'How young?'

He looked back. 'Well, children, basically.'

Walker couldn't hide her shock. '*Children*?' she hissed. 'We recruited *children* to kill the enemy?'

'Yes, apparently. So Tench knew her stuff; she taught it for two years, and obviously hasn't forgotten any of it. He picked the wrong woman to… harangue.'

'She's Five isn't she?' said Walker. It wasn't so much a question as a statement.

Riley as usual looked off to one side and back again. 'Possibly. Hard to say. Well-connected though.'

'Five then.'

'Yes, I suppose.'

'Oh Riley, for God's sake, of course she is. Don't play games with me, I – we – haven't got time. Has she told you how they're involved in this?'

'I don't think they are, officially. They're busy enough with counterinsurgency, counterespionage and so forth, although they have been following up Brown's stolen notebook. He might be foreign secretary but he's a top politician and the theft involved Soviets on British soil, but…'

'But what?'

'There're rumours of a plot against the prime minister. No, nothing like that, apparently just to get rid of him politically. And of course there's increasing unrest domestically what with the anti-war protests. Harold Wilson's not having an easy ride at the moment.'

Walker shook her head. 'No, Five must be involved in the village in some way. I mean it's a joint intelligence "retirement" facility remember, so they've got some of their own in there. And who attacked Tench? You say she didn't recognise him, yet he told her to give up, which presumably means stop what you and she have been doing: plotting to stop Unity. Why her? Why not grab *you* round the throat and warn you off? Or Symes?'

Riley shrugged. 'I really don't know.'

'What's she done about it? Reported it to the police?'

'No. She said she'd… take care of it. And I'm sure she will.'

'Well there you are then,' smirked Walker. 'She's definitely MI5, and her job as Douglas-Home's senior advisor is just a cover.' Riley didn't respond, other than to give a slight shrug again. A pigeon pecked at his shoelace. He shooed it away.

She looked at him again. 'Well come on Bill Riley, what next? Our last scheduled meeting was rudely interrupted, so when – to quote Macbeth – shall we three meet again? Or four in this case.'

'Six actually,' said a voice behind them. Riley and Walker turned, startled, to see Symes standing there, his hands in his pockets.

'How long have you been there?' Walker demanded, embarrassed that they'd failed to hear him arrive.

'Long enough to learn an awful lot of interesting stuff. Good job I'm not a Soviet spy.' He walked slowly round the bench, looked up and down the path, then faced them.

'Yes, we've got two new recruits. I'll tell you about them, but first – hot off the press – we finally have our own knight in the game: Barnaby Carrington-Hall is now in the village.'

46

Aerospace Facility, Stevenage, Hertfordshire

Bob Harvey peered out of the gatehouse into the night. He checked his watch against the clock on the wall – almost one o'clock – and stepped outside, breathing in the fresh night air.

He checked his full field of view, slowly turning and taking in the fence line that surrounded the huge factory, the main administration and auxiliary buildings, the car park, and the approach road. Arc lights bathed the whole scene as bright as day, so the fox trotting across the approach road stood out like a silhouette in a Chinese shadow play. Other than that all was quiet, yet Harvey knew there would be activity soon enough.

He went back inside the wooden gatehouse and picked up a clipboard. On it was his shift schedule – a timetable of anticipated arrivals and departures over the next eight hours, names of expected visitors (sometimes not named, merely labelled 'VIP' or 'Support'), the number of vehicles, what type and so forth. He noted again the major activity scheduled for one a.m., the arrivals due imminently, and checked his watch once more.

The sound began quietly at first, in the distance, then slowly increased to a muted roar, and he again stepped out of the gatehouse. On the road beyond the security barrier he could see the glow of headlamps, first two, then four, then more as a convoy of vehicles approached.

The first to arrive at the barrier were two large military BSA motorcycles, their riders kitted out in identical helmets, goggles, gauntlets, khaki uniforms and motorcycle boots. The one nearest him reached inside his jacket, pulled out a sheaf of papers and jerked a thumb behind him.

'These are for us and the rest of the convoy,' he barked. 'Four motorcycles, four Land Rovers, twelve personnel in total.' He patted his side where Harvey saw a pistol in a leather holster. 'We're all carrying sidearms, and the Land Rovers have one general purpose machine gun in each, just so you know. I'm sure you don't want any surprises.'

Bob Harvey looked down the row of idling vehicles, past the Land Rovers to the two other motorcycles at the rear. He walked down the length of the convoy and stopped at each vehicle, checking the paperwork on his clipboard against the papers he'd been handed by the motorbike rider. 'Morning,' he nodded to all the occupants as he looked into the vehicles, but none returned the greeting and remained staring straight ahead.

He returned to the gatehouse, picked up the phone and dialled a number. 'Security here. Convoy's arrived as scheduled,' he announced. 'Yes sir, right away.'

Stepping out once more he handed the papers back to the motorcycle outrider and began to point to one of the large factory buildings. 'Right, go along the access road, then…'

But the rider waved him away and revved his throttle. 'We know where to go.'

Harvey nodded and went to the barrier weight, pushed on it with both hands, then as it raised he waved the riders and the rest of the convoy through. The bikes and matt green Land Rovers roared past – their GPMGs invisible behind their canvas covers – and headed directly for a set of large sliding doors in the centre of the main factory building. The doors began to slide open, but only wide enough to let the convoy through, then closed again once the rear riders had entered, swallowing the whole snake of vehicles. The exhaust smoke from the vehicles slowly dissipated in the calm night air.

Harvey shook his head. 'Arrogant sods,' he muttered under his breath. Back in the gatehouse he noted the arrival time of the convoy against the schedule, hung up his clipboard, and turned on the gas ring in the corner to make a cup of tea.

Fifty minutes later Harvey yawned, stretched, and swung his legs off the gatehouse desk. He rubbed his face and wondered if he had time to make another brew but decided it could wait.

The phone trilled. He picked it up and listened, then said, 'Right you are sir. I'll get the barrier up now.' He stood, and picked up his torch.

As he stepped outside he saw the large doors of the main building begin to slide open, the inside largely in darkness apart from the glow from various headlamps. He raised the red and white striped barrier to its full height and secured it in place. Suddenly – and it took him by surprise even though he was expecting it – all the compound lamps went out, plunging the whole area into darkness.

A roar made him turn once again to where the doors had opened, and he saw two of the military motorcycles move out and stop just before the approach road. Behind them two of the Land Rovers took up position, their engines also idling. And then, something large, something enormous began to slowly creep out from the cavernous interior. 'Here she comes,' thought Harvey, his heart rate increasing.

A large metal beast gradually emerged, a heavy-duty Thornycroft Antar transporter, and as it did so Harvey could see its massive load was supported by a specially constructed framework of steel girders, the whole covered by equally massive tarpaulins the size of circus tents. On and on it came as the Thornycroft cab slowly turned and headed to where the Land Rovers and motorbikes waited.

Bob Harvey removed his cap and smoothed back what was left of his hair as he watched in awe as the procession lined up. The transporter's tarpaulins covered something long and cylindrical, lying on its side – it must be three or four times taller than me he thought, and the trailer unit must be a hundred feet long if it's an inch. He let out a low whistle, knowing he was witnessing a piece of history, but not entirely sure if it was actually something worth celebrating.

He shook his head and replaced his cap. 'Pity the poor sods on the receiving end of that,' he muttered.

The huge transporter was now clear of the doors. It came to a stop behind the front vehicles as the two remaining Land Rovers took up position behind it, with the remaining motorcycles at the back. The building's doors slowly rolled shut. The driver of the front Land Rover spoke into his radio, there was a revving of engines, and the convoy began to move.

The front motorcyclists roared past Harvey and out onto the main road where they stopped, their role at this point being to halt any traffic. There was none. The riders waved the Land Rovers and the transporter on.

The security guard was deafened as the Thornycroft inched past in a fog of exhaust fumes, but he didn't really notice, so in awe of the payload was he. He almost saluted, but realised it wasn't necessary. The tarpaulins didn't quite come down far enough to fully hide the ribbed surface of the stainless steel cylinder, nor, as Harvey saw, the two huge nozzles at the back of the object. He again shook his head in disbelief.

The transporter turned left and followed the lead vehicles. The final two Land Rovers and motorbikes slid by, and once the whole convoy was on the road the first motorbike riders gunned their throttles and roared off to take up their positions at the front again. As the convoy disappeared down the road, silence once again descended and Harvey let the barrier back down.

He returned to the gatehouse, grabbed his pen and clipboard and noted on the schedule: *0155 - Blue Streak Missile convoy departed on time*. Then, checking that nobody was in view or watching him, he picked up the phone.

47

Century House, Sub-basement 2

Wilson heard the door behind her quietly open. She turned from where she was sitting at the monitoring desk making notes and was surprised to see Stone walk in. He softly closed the door behind him, making sure it was properly shut before speaking. Wilson stood, almost to attention.

'Sir. I wasn't expecting you.'

Stone gestured for her to sit. 'It's all right Olivia. I'm not here to intrude on your work. I just wanted to have a chat. My turn to apologise for the surprise visit.'

Wilson resumed her seat and saw by Stone's body language that he was tense. He briefly glanced out at the main screen in the monitoring room then took another chair, sat and faced her.

'Thank you for your latest report. In it you elaborated on the situation where you've arranged for our man to escape from the facility, and that he will soon be "in transit" shall we say?'

Wilson nodded. 'Yes, the ruse is working, as far as we know. He has no concept of what's really happening, thanks to the girl he believes is helping him – Nadia. He's convinced she'll be able to get him back to London, and safety, by the two of them travelling hidden in a large cargo crate. He believes she's part of a sort of resistance movement and that it's helping him.'

Stone nodded enthusiastically. 'And I believe you've installed the latest Number Two…'

'Yes sir, and to give him credit, he's proving to be a real diplomat' – she proffered Carrington-Hall's file and Stone casually flipped though it – 'and an ideal match for our captive. He's not one to be unnerved or unsettled in any way. I believe this time we will crack the nut, as it were.'

'Yes, that's excellent. Your plan of simply pretending our man's being returned to London, while never actually escaping the village, is commendable, especially as it might well result in his telling us what we want to know, as you say.' Wilson allowed herself the briefest flicker of a smile.

Stone laid the file on the desk. 'It also, importantly, buys us the breathing space we need to… take care of some things in the facility.'

Wilson raised an eyebrow by way of query.

'I'm afraid I can't tell you what; it's classified. And with that in mind, you will not have access to this area tonight or tomorrow. In fact, all the staff in monitoring have been given the night and most of tomorrow off; a surprise holiday, a reward for their diligence and sterling work. So please don't feel aggrieved. It's nothing personal. Once the girl and our man are on their way you must leave sub-basement two.'

Wilson nodded. 'I understand sir,' even though she didn't. Soldiers don't question orders. But she did feel irritated, she did take it personally, and she desperately wanted to know why Stone needed the prisoner 'out' of the village for, so she realised, a minimum of twelve hours. But it wasn't her place to ask, and anyway she knew she wouldn't be told. She could only guess that something important was going to happen that required no external witnesses. She was, however, concerned about her charge, and was about to raise the issue when Stone continued, as though he had read her mind.

'And don't worry about your Number Six,' he said. 'The facility's controller will be watching his every move, as will your new and very capable Number Two.' He placed an emphasis on the word 'capable.'

'Speaking of whom, I'd like to know more about him and what you've told him.'

'Well sir, I…' Wilson was lost for words. She thought she'd covered everything in her reports, and the file he had just reviewed had all the background information on him.

Stone gave her a prompt. 'I hear that Number Two and Number Six had a – how shall I put it? – a private chat down near the beach recently, out of range of cameras or microphones. I'm also told that Nadia overheard what they were talking about. It seems,' he said, pushing his rimless glasses up the bridge of his nose and staring at her in that disconcerting unwavering way, 'that your Number Two told him the whole purpose of…' and here he paused, having almost used the word Unity – '… told him far more than he needs to know.'

There was silence. Wilson dropped her eyes as her mind raced: why hadn't village control told her about this? Why was she finding out about it from Stone? What had Number Two said that was so critical? All these thoughts tumbled through her mind in a millisecond.

'I'm sorry sir, I haven't been told about this and wasn't here to witness it. Is it a problem?'

Stone lived up to his name: he was motionless, and again didn't blink. The only part of him that moved was the thin slit of his mouth.

'Let's hope not. For your sake.'

Wilson dropped her eyes to the floor so that Stone wouldn't see the blaze in them, wouldn't see the anger that was causing her temples to pound, or the rage that was now welling up inside her.

48

Amesbury, Wiltshire

Sarika Khatri wiped her hands on a tea towel as the knocking on her front door was repeated with some authority. She opened it to find a dark-haired woman in her mid-thirties on her doorstep.

'Dr. Khatri?' the woman asked, and Sarika nodded. The woman smiled and held out an identification card, which declared her to be one Lillian Grimes of the security services. She said as much, and asked if she could come in.

'What's this about?' asked Sarika. 'Is it to do with my parents?'

'Yes, partly. Can we go inside?'

Sarika held the door open, then ushered the visitor into the lounge. Grimes looked around the pretty cottage, having already admired the thatched roof and half-timber framing outside. Now she had to almost stoop to avoid banging her head on the low oak beams as Sarika gestured towards a couch, where Grimes sat, pulling out a notebook and pencil. Sarika took a chair opposite.

'I told the police everything I know. Is there news? Have you found who sent the photograph?' Sarika asked nervously.

'I'm afraid not, not yet,' smiled Grimes. 'I know you've spoken to the police, but as you work at Porton Down, at the Chemical Defence Experimental Establishment on… sensitive issues, this is also a matter of national security, and I just need to follow up on a few things.'

'I'm worried for my parents. It's been over a week now, and they are also concerned. They are like prisoners in their own home.'

'They're being well looked-after,' Grimes assured her. 'And they'll continue to be protected until we've sorted this whole thing out.'

Sarika creased her forehead, unconvinced. 'But how long will that take? Have the police got any further in their investigations?'

Grimes sat back on the couch. 'Owing to the nature of your work,' she explained, 'the police have passed the investigation on to us. Maybe you could tell me a little bit more about what you do at Porton Down.'

Sarika looked uncomfortable, her hands wringing in her lap. 'I cannot do that,' she insisted. 'We have all signed documents that preclude us from talking about our work. It is classified, as I'm sure you must know.'

Grimes sighed inwardly, but her face expressed empathy, concern. 'I do understand, of course. But we can only conclude at this early stage that your parents have been singled out as… targets, in order to pressure you into taking some sort of action. You've received no demands, no instructions? No message? Are you being blackmailed?'

Sarika shook her head. 'No, as I told the police. There was nothing else with the photograph and nothing since. But that was terrifying enough in itself.'

'And what do your parents do?'

'They're retired. They go to the cinema, they have dinners with friends, they go to community meetings, my father watches cricket on the television… they live a quiet life of no consequence.'

'Exactly,' said Grimes. 'They themselves are not a threat in any way, yet they have, for some reason, become targets. We can only assume it's because someone wants you to do something – or stop what you're doing – at work. So, what are you working on?'

Again Sarika looked uncomfortable. She had explained as much as she could to the police previously, now here she was being asked the same questions all over again. It didn't feel right.

'I am sorry. As I said, I cannot tell you, except in the most general terms. As I'm sure you know, in the laboratories at Porton Down we investigate various diseases – bacteria, viruses, pathogens and so on so that we can understand them, develop resistance or antidotes to them. It is a scientific establishment.'

'And yet it comes under the auspices of the Ministry of Defence, yes?'

'You must know this also,' said Sarika.

'What have you been doing since receiving the photograph?' Grimes asked.

'Nothing. I've been on compassionate leave. I have been to see my parents, and anyway…'

'What?'

'I have been taken off the project I was working on.'

'Which was?'

Sarika lost her temper. 'How many times do I have to tell you? I cannot talk about my work! Now, if you have nothing useful to say please leave!' She stood and held open the lounge door.

This time Grimes sighed audibly. She put her notebook away, stood, and said, 'We know what you were working on. I just needed confirmation, but since you won't give it I can't help you any further. The security detail watching over your parents will be removed. Thank you for your time.' She walked out of the lounge and headed down the short hallway.

Sarika looked at her in horror as she opened the front door. 'Wait. Wait! Don't leave!' Her voice faltered, and she almost whispered, 'All right, I'll tell you.'

Grimes smiled, but when she turned to re-enter the cottage her face was serious again. She resumed her seat.

Sarika sat also, once more wringing her hands. She seemed reluctant to speak, her eyes darting this way and that, her heart racing.

'We'll keep an eye on your parents. And now that you've been withdrawn from the project they're probably safe anyway,' Grimes assured her. 'Now, tell me, what were you working on?'

'It was a project called Eirene-3.' She felt her eyes stinging; she knew she shouldn't be talking openly about the work, but this was an intelligence officer after all. Surely that was acceptable?

'Spelt?' grimes asked, poising her pencil above her open notebook.

Sarika told her. 'But it's pronounced "Eye-reeny."'

'And why the number?'

'It just refers to the phase of the project. We had completed phases one and two.'

'And what is it? What is Eirene?

'Eirene was the Greek goddess of peace,' explained Sarika. 'That's what the project is all about, peace.'

Grimes creased her forehead. 'Peace? How? In what way?'

'We developed – accidentally, as a by-product of something else we were working on – a compound which, when applied, results in the recipient becoming quiet, compliant. All aggression is suppressed, and the recipient will be obedient.'

'How is it to be used?'

'I can't tell you.'

Grimes quickly stood again. 'Then our conversation is over. I will have the security removed from outside your parents' house immediately.'

'No wait!' Sarika cried. 'I really cannot tell you because I don't know! We are rarely told what the end use of any of our projects is, we can only guess. We just carry out our orders! I beg you to believe me!'

Once again Grimes sat, but more tentatively. 'So what's your guess?'

Sarika sighed, looked away, then back at Grimes. 'We developed the compound first as a solid, then as a liquid, and when we were ready they were trialled extensively using the population of a small village. And before you ask, no, I don't know where it is, but I receive reports from there regularly. Anyway, as requested we recently successfully developed the compound into an aerosol, a gas… so many parts per million of the Eirene-3 agent. It's complicated. But as soon as we successfully turned the agent into gaseous form we were asked to run clinical trials as soon as possible. There was pressure to get this done urgently. I resisted, because it is taking shortcuts, ignoring correct developmental protocols. It needs to be tested in the laboratory first, on animals.' She shook her head vehemently. 'It is not the way science works or should be done.'

'And has it been tested on humans?'

There was silence. Sarika looked at the carpet, wrung her hands further, licked her dry lips. She finally looked back again at Grimes.

'Only in liquid and solid forms while I was working on it, not the gas. But I was told by one of my colleagues – privately – that they started clinical trials as soon as I was placed on leave.'

'And?' Grimes asked. 'What happened?'

More silence. Then Sarika said, 'It was only a small group, nowhere near what's required for proper data collection or analysis.'

Grimes spread her hands and raised her eyebrows, her body language urging Sarika to continue.

'Of just ten volunteers who were subjected to the Eirene-3 gas, two have fallen into comas. They might not live.'

49

Century House

Symes had the handset to his ear as he listened intently. With his other hand he clicked his fingers to attract Riley's attention across their desks. Riley raised an eyebrow.

'That's very interesting,' Symes said. 'Thanks. Keep in touch.' He replaced the handset in its cradle.

'What?' asked Riley.

'That was Defence. One of my… sources,' he smiled. 'He had a call from the factory in Hertfordshire where they assemble intermediate range ballistic missiles, the IRBMs. Apparently one of them left on a transporter in the dead of night. Guess where it's headed…'

Riley shrugged. 'Cumberland? Where we have – or had – a launch bunker? Forget what the place is called…'

Symes's tight smile remained in place, but not his usual dimplefest. 'You'd think so, wouldn't you? But no. It's headed for our "facility" as Stone likes to call it.'

Riley's jaw dropped. 'What? You're joking!'

'Wish I were old bean. The gatehouse security guard had instructions to telephone the village when the missile was on its way. He also then alerted his contact in the MoD, who just called me.'

Riley couldn't believe what he was hearing. 'But it doesn't make sense Symes. There's no launch facility there. In fact, the Blue Streak missile itself isn't viable and was cancelled, if you remember. It's part of a developing satellite launch programme now with our European friends, as far as I know. And anyway, what would they do with it in the village? And how are they going to hide something that size there? It would stick out like a proverbial sore thumb. Unless…'

Symes watched Riley, guessed that his thoughts were tumbling as he stared out of the window considering all possibilities. Symes did the same, gazing at the top of his desk as though the answer was written there for him on his blotter. It wasn't. Riley swivelled back from the window and sat upright.

'Or *do* we have a launch bunker there? Symes, I don't suppose you have any of your Etonian or Cambridge chums in the Royal Engineers?'

Symes chuckled. 'Of course old boy. Why?'

'Because if there is a silo there it must have been constructed by the military, and as I'm sure you must know – with your public school education and your myriad of contacts – it's the Royal Engineers who build bridges, prepare groundwork, construct roads, and, I'm guessing, dig holes. Big holes. If they did build a missile silo at the village they'll have records, surely? It's probably classified of course, but I'm sure you're resourceful.'

Symes nodded and made a note on a jotter. Riley continued. 'I seem to remember the village was started in the 1920s or 30s but looks much older. Given that the IRBM programme dates back to, er…'

'The 50s,' Symes added.

'Fifties, yes, then we're looking for construction sometime in the last seventeen years or so.'

Symes nodded again, scribbled some more notes, then looked up. 'The thing that doesn't make sense though is why we'd put a silo there. The east coast is closer to the Soviets, and to my knowledge that's where our launch sites were supposed to be. Strategically placed as it were, distance to target and all that. Unless we're expecting trouble from the Irish!' he laughed, and Riley smiled.

'I doubt we need worry about the Irish,' he chortled. 'Very well, if I can leave the engineers research with you, I'll see what I can dig up from Defence – if they'll play ball – and maybe Five has something of interest.'

'Ah yes, the remarkable Miss Tench,' Symes smirked. Riley feigned shock at the very thought and spread his hands.

'And,' Riley said, ignoring Symes's comment, 'we need to do some deep thinking about why the hell they'd want a missile in the village. It's big, distinctive; surely someone must know why it's going there? If we were allowed into Monitoring we'd probably see it arrive…'

They both picked up their phones and began dialling.

*

An hour or so later and they were once again staring out of the window at the low clouds. Their various telephone calls had netted them quite a bit of information, which they had shared, but which, as Riley had noted, required some further deep thought. Hence the silence, and the staring.

'We're missing something,' said Riley to the clouds outside his window. Symes looked across at him.

'What?'

Riley returned his gaze. 'If I knew that we wouldn't be missing it, would we? All that private education investment wasted. Tsk, tsk.' He shook his head in mock disbelief. But he swung his legs off the window ledge and pulled his chair up to his desk.

'A redundant missile – but most likely functional – has been taken to the village. Presumably it also went unfuelled, for safety's sake,' Riley said. 'Which means the fuel will be taken there separately by tanker. That's something we might be able to check on.'

Symes scribbled some more on his jotter. After a moment's reflection they then both started talking at once.

'And what about…' 'But there's also the…'

'Sorry Symes. You first.'

'I was just going to say that we don't know if the missile had a payload. Or indeed what sort of payload it would be.'

Riley slammed his hand on the desk. 'Exactly! Just what I was going to say.'

Symes continued. 'So, what would it be? A warhead? Nuclear?'

Riley scoffed. 'Nuclear? Why? And where would it be targeted?'

Symes referred to his notes. 'It could actually reach Moscow from there, or basically everywhere in Europe. Wouldn't make it to the United States though.'

'Well we're hardly likely to target them are we? They're allies.' Riley stopped and chewed his lip as he thought some more, then said, 'What if it's non-nuclear? What else could it be?'

At that moment Riley's phone rang. He picked up the handset.

'Riley.'

A female voice spoke to him. 'It's Reception here. We have a Miss Tench to see you. She doesn't have an appointment but she insists it's urgent.'

50

The Lonely Pheasant Pub, upstairs function room

Riley stood in the doorway and looked around the musty room with its thin carpet, the same old-fashioned pattern as the one in the bar downstairs.

He sniffed, and a waft of stale beer and cigarette smoke greeted his nostrils, but he saw the stack of chairs in a corner along with some tables and decided it would do.

He busied himself drawing the curtains across the windows and pulled the cords that activated the wall-mounted heaters, which reluctantly glowed orange as they battled against the chill of the room.

Riley heard footsteps on the stairs and turned to see Symes walk in.

'Ah, perfect timing. You can help me put out some chairs and a table or two.'

As they worked they didn't notice Anastasia Walker enter until she said, 'Well, well! Very domesticated. I could do with men like you at my place. Occasionally,' she added.

Riley smiled, shoved the last chair in place beside the table, and walked over to greet her.

'Anastasia. Glad you could make it.' He seemed genuine, and Walker relaxed slightly, although she was still wary of this late-announced and very secret meeting.

'I hope this is worth my while,' she sniffed, looking round at the faded wallpaper and the tobacco-stained ornate plaster ceiling. 'We have perfectly good meeting rooms at work you know.'

'Obviously we do,' said Riley, gesturing for her to take a seat. 'But I chose this salubrious location precisely because it's not our workplace, it's off the record as it were, and the chances of anyone else knowing that we're meeting here are virtually nil. I'm sure you appreciate that security is paramount.'

Walker seemed satisfied with the explanation and took a seat at the table. Symes sat opposite. Riley remained standing, ready to greet the rest of the group, but he placed his hands on the back of a chair, leaned forward and said, 'Before everyone else arrives I just want to say that we… well, we have a chance this evening to head off a most appalling situation. However, it will, quite possibly, be the end of our careers, and I just want to make that clear. If either of you wish to maintain your positions within the organisation, along with your generous pensions, then now would be a good time to leave.'

Despite the heaters warming up, the room seemed to grow colder. Walker glanced at Symes, who for once wasn't smiling, then back to Riley.

'I hope you know what you're doing,' she said. 'I was rather looking forward to another ten years or so.'

Before Riley could respond the door opened tentatively and two young people looked in, unsure whether to enter. Riley turned to them.

'Ah! Tommy and Chris, isn't it? Come in, come in, don't be shy.'

Tommy held the door open and Chris slowly walked in, nervously looking at the faces before her. Tommy, with a deal more confidence than he really felt, joined her.

'So,' he said, spreading his arms wide. 'We finally get to meet the powers that be. A pleasure, I'm sure.' He gave a slight bow and made a mock doffing of his cap, even though he wasn't wearing one. Chris elbowed him gently, a caution to behave.

'How did you get here?' Symes asked.

Tommy gestured over his shoulder towards the door. 'Charles dropped us off. Said it would be safer. And I know you're going to ask; yes he did take the long way round and made sure we weren't followed.'

Symes gestured for them to sit. Riley introduced himself and Walker, and said, 'We're now waiting on just one more person, then we can begin.'

Chris shuffled in her seat. 'You do know I'm a journalist, right? And as such I'm rarely off duty. I'll be taking notes.'

Riley creased his forehead and looked to Symes. Walker sat upright and smouldered. Symes smiled grimly and slowly shook his head.

'Did you not listen to anything I said at the garage young lady?' he asked her. 'When I spoke to you both – and Charles was a witness – I clearly pointed out that you were in breach of national security regulations. Do you seriously want to end up in prison?'

Riley butted in. 'The thing is, and it will become clear later I hope, you can't use any of what you hear this evening. Not yet. But we hope there will come a time – soon, with luck – when we will actually *want* you to put on your journalist's hat and report to the world some of what we've uncovered. Until then, if you mention a word of anything that's transpired – or is about to become evident this evening – you will, as Symes quite rightly said, be unable to report anything again.'

Chris bristled and seemed ready to get up and leave as she clutched her satchel and tightened her scarf.

'Go if you wish,' Riley said, extending his hands, 'But if you stay – and help us – you might find yourself as a chief political editor much sooner than you ever imagined.'

She held his eyes, but saw that he meant it. The alternative, which Symes had already emphasised, was not an option. She replaced her bag on the floor beside her and hesitantly loosened her scarf again. Tommy, next to her, relaxed his shoulders; he'd been ready to walk out in solidarity with her.

Riley was about to sit but the door opened once more and Judith Tench walked in. Like Walker, she did a double-take at the room before recovering her composure, then smiled at the group around the table.

Riley beckoned her to a seat and did the introductions.

'Sorry I'm a bit late,' Tench said. 'I've just come from a briefing. Apparently MI5 have got two Russian operatives in… custody, shall we say. They're the same ones, I believe, who chased you Tommy and stole George Brown's notebook from you. And from what I've heard, this meeting couldn't have come soon enough.'

This news was greeted with silence, and a general air of incredulity. Riley locked eyes with Tench for a second, then took the remaining seat and looked around at the group.

'Right. Good. Thank you, Judith. We'll get to the Russians in due course. Before we start though, some rules and clarifications.'

The focus on Riley was total.

'Nothing that is said or heard in this room is to be repeated to anyone else outside this group, is that understood?'

There was nodded agreement, some of it – in Chris's case in particular – reluctant. In fact she slowly shook her head.

'Good. Secondly, I want you to treat everyone outside this gathering as a potential threat, and therefore not to be trusted. Except,' he added, looking at Tommy and Chris, 'for Charles. You can trust him with your life. And I mean that.

'What I want to achieve this evening is… well, we need to piece together everything we know, what we think, and even what we fear, based on the evidence we've gathered. It's a bit of a jigsaw, but the more pieces we can slot together the clearer the picture will be, and – hopefully – what we can do about it. What is clear is that we have knowledge of something that is a serious and very real potential threat.'

Chris sighed and drummed her fingers on the table. Riley noticed but continued regardless.

'I'm going to hand over to Anastasia here to fill you in on the background. Anastasia?'

Since they'd discussed the meeting previously, Walker was expecting this and had prepared. She had brought no files or notes – didn't need to – and she began without hesitation.

'Almost three years ago the intelligence forces of this country established a "retirement village" for ex-intelligence staff on an isolated stretch of coast in North Wales. The land, which had previously been purchased by the Ministry of Defence, had already been developed into a hillside community of cottages, chalets, and more substantial buildings to be used as a training ground. The buildings were subsequently added to and enhanced for security purposes.

'An on-site central control centre was established, remote cameras installed, microphones and so on. Here in London at our headquarters a dedicated monitoring team was also established to remotely maintain surveillance on activities in the facility. If you like, we watched the watchers. Any questions so far?'

'Who authorised this?' Chris asked.

'The secretary of state for defence at the time,' Walker replied. 'The Right Honourable Peter Thorneycroft.'

'Why the cameras and the microphones?'

Walker looked at Riley, who nodded almost imperceptibly.

'Because as I said, the facility was for ex-members of the intelligence community. It was for their own safety and security – so we were told at the time. The surveillance measures would detect intruders and so on.'

Judith Tench pounded her hand on the table. Everyone jumped, then turned to look at her. 'Wait a minute!' she demanded. 'Thorneycroft?' She looked at Walker. 'Who was prime minister?'

'Alec Douglas-Home. Although he was in that position for less than a year. He took over from Macmillan due to…'

'Ill health, yes I remember.' Tench's face grew red. 'The bastard! Douglas-Home must have known about the village then, so why did he pretend he didn't when I told him about it?'

There was no answer, because no-one around the table had one. Only conjecture.

'Maybe,' Riley proposed, 'because he's testing you. To see how much you know. And how much you'll tell him. He'll be wanting to get back into power next election remember, so any advantage he can get will help him.'

Tench fumed, then something dawned on her. 'In which case maybe it was him behind the attack at my flat. He knew I was onto Unity!'

'Which reminds me, did you ever find him, the man who attacked you?' asked Symes.

Tench lowered her eyes. 'Let's just say… he was found, but in no state to tell us anything. It seems he didn't seek medical help quickly enough. Sepsis, apparently. Sorry Walker. Please carry on.'

Riley butted in: 'Yes, we're getting a little off-track. Anastasia…'

Walker continued. 'Initially the retirement village was just that. However, Defence took an interest, since they had jurisdiction over the land, and they hijacked it for their own purposes.'

'Which were?' asked Chris.

Walker was tiring of having a journalist at the table and sighed. 'Please just let me finish. I suggest you save any questions until the end.'

Walker paused to gather her thoughts, then continued. 'Defence also had – and still does have – jurisdiction over the research facility known as the Chemical Defence Experimental Establishment in Wiltshire. They realised that in the retirement village they had a collection of people, all of whom had signed the official secrets act, that could be used for "experimental purposes." They began using the village residents as a testing ground, for psychological interventions, trialling drugs, that sort of thing.'

Chris couldn't contain herself. 'Was this officially sanctioned by government?'

'By the MoD yes, so the secretary for defence must also have known,' Walker said. 'But the work of the establishment at Porton Down is ultra top secret, so they have their own rules and regulations. They operate in isolation, for obvious reasons. Anyway, that wasn't the only change in the environment of the village. Our own intelligence services also realised that this charming, yet totally secure quaint Italianate community, was perfect for holding captured operatives, some apprehended here on our own shores, others on the continent, and some further afield. It became much more than a retirement home.'

She paused to let this sink in, although most around the table knew it already.

'Now we come to the crux of the matter: Unity. Porton Down was working on creating a type of nerve agent, to be used in times of war. Something invisible, undetectable, yet effective in disabling an enemy, rendering them unconscious but without any lasting effects.'

Now even those in the room who knew this were transfixed, especially Tench, and Tommy and Chris, who were becoming increasingly uncomfortable with what they were hearing. Walker carried on.

'Our understanding is that the research went well, but during it they stumbled across a benign version of the agent, a sort of mood stabiliser, something that could make an angry person calm, or an uncooperative one acquiescent. Or an enemy peaceful without killing or even injuring them. They were given the go-ahead to develop it in pill and liquid form, under the codename Eirene. It was trialled on the usual lab animals – rats, mice, monkeys – but then they were ready for clinical trials, and needed a cohort, a group of real people on whom it could be tested. And the retirement village was the perfect place.'

Chris couldn't keep quiet. 'And you knew about this? You knew they were carrying out unauthorised tests on human beings and did nothing about it? Using them as guinea pigs? Unbelievable!'

Riley cleared his throat. 'Anastasia, if I may? Thanks. The thing is,' he said, looking straight at Chris, 'we knew about the retirement village, and we knew how its use was… changing, but apart from the rendition of operatives from overseas – which is not something we condone by the way – we saw nothing to get alarmed about. Anastasia and I, and Symes, were kept in the loop by our director general, a man named

Stone, with a brief to simply keep an eye on the place and report back on a more or less regular basis. Generally there was little to report, and the Eirene agent seemed to be doing its job. The agent was delivered to the residents individually as tablets or liquids. It was just medication as far as we knew, and it worked; the residents, even those who were recalcitrant, became calm, compliant, cooperative. Probably not too dissimilar to how ordinary retirement homes operate actually.'

Walker took over the discourse again. 'But that's when things started to go wrong. Defence, MI5, GCHQ – the Government Communications Headquarters – MI6 and our own department within it, are duty-bound to keep their ministers, including the foreign secretary, briefed on issues of consequence to national security. So of course he knew of the retirement village and what it was being used for.'

'This is George Brown we're talking about now?' Chris asked.

'The same,' Walker confirmed. 'And it seems Brown has been taking great interest in Unity.' She pointed at Chris and Tommy; 'As you know, he'd written about it in his notebook. Also, we learned from seeing his chauffeur's report after the incident in Trafalgar Square that Brown had ranted about teaching the youth of today a lesson, a lesson in obedience, compliance… and, he actually used the word: Unity.'

'So,' said Riley, taking over again, 'our concern is that he is interfering with the Unity programme, possibly for his own, or his government's means.'

Chris was stunned as she tried to take this in. 'But why?'

'The village really did start out as a retirement facility,' Riley said, 'but its collection of residents was too big a temptation to experiment with a microcosm of society. And if the residents there could be rendered compliant, then just imagine, just for a moment, a whole nation without industrial unrest, without crime or violence. A harmony across the land. Imagine also how willing such a population might be to vote for whoever they were told to vote. Imagine having all the peace you could dream of, but no freedom of choice.'

Riley could feel anger welling up from deep within him. It was something he'd managed thus far to contain, but now that the story was being told out loud, strung together for the first time in a succinct way, it unsettled him more than he expected. And he was one of the storytellers.

Tommy laughed and pushed himself back so that his chair rested on just its two back legs. 'You're kidding right?' he scoffed, rocking the chair back and forth. 'How would you get every person in the country, well, everyone of voting age, to take your magic potion, or pills or whatever? It'd never happen!'

Now it was Judith Tench who spoke up again.

'Unless of course they didn't know they were taking it.'

All eyes turned in her direction.

'I think I've got some bad news for you.'

51

54, Broadway, London

Olivia Wilson held the Browning 9mm HP semi-automatic pistol out in front of her with both hands, the left cupped under the right. She sighted along the barrel at the soldier, held her breath and squeezed the trigger three times in quick succession.

She slowly exhaled, then inhaled the satisfying tang of the cordite, an aroma she would happily have worn as a perfume on her wrists or her neck had Chanel had the presence of mind to make it. She'd mused once that *Chanel No. 9mm* had a more appealing ring to it than Chanel No. 5.

She lowered the gun, calmed her breathing, waited till her heartbeat had settled again, counted to three in her head, then whipped the firearm up and let off three more rounds.

Through her military-grade earmuffs the shots sounded more like dull thuds, but she knew that had she fired without them her ears would be ringing. She flicked the safety on and gently, almost reverently, lowered the Browning onto the table in front of her. She knew it still had seven rounds in the clip, and she would use those, with pleasure, in a moment.

For now, she just wanted to check her grouping. She slid the earmuffs down around her neck and wound the handle to her left, which brought the target via a pulley system from the far end of the dimly-lit basement range right up to her firing position, like a piece of washing on a line.

'Let's see how dead you are,' she muttered to herself as the target torso of a helmeted soldier with rifle approached her. She was the only one in the practice range this morning, so she could talk to herself as much as she liked, and she liked to do that a lot. It kept her sane, she rationalised.

All six bullet holes, she saw with a tight smile, were neatly grouped in the chest area. Had it been a shooting competition she would have won gold.

'Thanks Dad,' she whispered, and stepped out of the booth to get a new target to attach to the pulley.

The Browning HP – for Hi-Power – had been her father's, and was standard issue for those in the SOE, the Special Operations Executive. It was he who had taught her all about shooting, along with archery and fencing, but it was the firearm she enjoyed the most. And it was a direct link with her father.

As she fixed the new target to the clips her mind drifted back to those times he would take her and her brother into the woods beside their home in the Yorkshire countryside. He'd find a tree stump or fallen log and set up tin cans for them to aim at. Sometimes he would pin a bulls-eye target to a tree trunk so they could practice their accuracy. Breathe in, hold, sight, clear the mind, see not the target, only the part of the target you want to hit, squeeze the trigger.

Olivia was always better than her brother, and made sure he knew it. He was just over two years her junior and she took delight in teasing him. At least that's what she called it. He saw it as bullying, and always succumbed.

When she turned fifteen her father told her there was nothing more he could teach her. Three years later, after he'd died, Olivia was the one who inherited the Browning. Her brother got just the archery equipment, and bitterly resented it. On one occasion he let her know how unfair it was.

'Wait here,' she'd said, and left his room. When she returned she was holding the firearm. She cocked the slide and held it to his head, breaking every firearm handling rule she'd ever learned.

'I can show you what unfair looks like.'

But that was thirty years ago, and now, here in the basement firing range, her mind returned very much to the moment.

She adjusted the pristine target on its clips and held it out in front of her. 'You bastard,' she said, and wound the pulley handle in reverse. The target – she didn't see it as a charging soldier, a 'Commie' or a foreign invader, she saw only Stone with his pale skin, bald head, rimless glasses and piercing unblinking eyes – fluttered its way ghost-like down the range to the wall at the end. It came to rest against the huge neat stack of old telephone directories, three-deep, which were in place to bring the rounds to a stop after they'd penetrated the targets. Crude maybe, but effective.

As she was about to replace the earmuffs on her head she heard and felt a low rumbling, and remembered that the District Line train ran not far from here. She didn't mind; she needed to be able to shoot accurately regardless of the conditions or distractions around her, and this dingy range beneath the old security intelligence headquarters was ideal.

Six more shots, and she knew even at this distance and without reeling in 'Stone' that his torso would, internally, have been a Bolognese of blood, bone and viscera. The thirteenth and last round in the clip – the significance of the number did not escape her – she saved for his head, and a third eye bloomed in the centre of Stone's brow.

This time when she reeled in the target she unclipped it and rolled it up. She would take it home and stick it on her kitchen wall. It was all the trophy she needed, at least for the moment. In the absence of a live target, and with her barred from Monitoring for a few hours more, she would just have to kill time instead.

*

The cigarette smoke hung in the air like a fog, the soldier coming at her out of the murk. Wilson took a new cigarette from the packet and lit it with the remains of the old one, then stubbed that out. She leaned back once more against the kitchen counter and faced the target on the wall, where she'd taped it after getting home. She drew deeply on the menthol.

Above the target was the kitchen clock, which she glanced at for the tenth time since getting back to her flat from the range. She still had a couple of hours before she would be 'allowed' back in Monitoring, to check on how Operation Big Ben was going. Despite venting her anger at the shooting range it still infuriated her that Stone had banned her from watching her charge for almost a full day. Hence the chain smoking.

What she couldn't fathom was what Stone was keeping from her. And why he'd been so keen to learn whether the subject had mentioned any word or phrase repeatedly, without ever telling her what it might be.

Rummaging in a cupboard below the sink she found some old newspapers and spread them out on the kitchen table. She then took the custom-made case with the Browning in it, opened it and laid the firearm on the paper. From another cupboard came a small wooden box full of rags, brushes, cleaning fluid, cotton balls and tips, and a small oiler. With everything on the table she sat down, stubbed out her cigarette and began cleaning the gun.

It was a ritual that always calmed her. The firearm was in superb condition for its age, initially thanks to her father's meticulousness, but in recent years due to her own loving care and attention.

She began by doing as her father had taught her: even though you might know the chamber and magazine are empty of ammunition you always, always check. She began by removing the magazine clip, locking the slide back and sighting down the barrel. Clear. Then she removed the slide-stop, the spring and the barrel and laid the parts out on the newspaper. The cleaning and lubricating could now begin.

As she worked, which she did on autopilot, her mind wandered back to the village. She was mentally transported there, and could almost smell the plants, the sea air, and feel the warmth of the sun. Around her the village's residents strolled with their sun umbrellas, bid her good day, and seemed at peace.

Which of course they were thanks to the drugs she'd been using as supplied by Porton Down. The testing had been extremely successful overall, but she'd been frustrated that she wasn't allowed to use the medication on her charge, the recalcitrant Number Six. Was it because Stone wanted him undamaged? That he planned to employ him again sometime in the future? Her lack of insight disturbed her, and she realised she was cleaning the gun far more forcefully than was needed.

Glancing at the clock again she now worked out where her Operation Big Ben would be up to, and realised that the prisoner would soon be 'back in London.' Except of course, as with so much of what she oversaw in the village, it was simply a ruse, and he would still be in the village.

Her plan was for Six and his accomplice Nadia to 'arrive' in their crate at what looked for all the world to be the plush London offices of one of his superiors. There he would encounter real people whom he knew, using their real names. They had been given acting lessons so that they would be believable, that they were glad to see him return, and he would, hopefully, be at ease in their company.

He would of course tell them all about the village and how he'd been held captive there, and, she fervently hoped, he would explain why he had resigned. Then she could report the satisfactory outcome to Stone.

The ruse would be totally believable, totally convincing. She had even had the idea of using a hidden tape recorder to play traffic noises and the chimes of Big Ben, to add authenticity to the experience. All of this action would take place in an interior office. She could hardly wait to get back to Monitoring, and she could only hope that whatever it was Stone needed to achieve in the village would have been accomplished.

She looked at the clock again. One hour to go. She carefully reassembled the Browning, took some .9mm ammunition from a box and fully loaded the magazine, which she locked into place with a satisfying click. She flicked on the safety.

The Browning was ready once again.

52

Chemical Defence Experimental Establishment
(CDEE)
Porton Down

It was the same four motorcyclists, two in front
and two behind the same Land Rovers, only this time
the convoy was arriving at the Chemical Defence
Experimental Establishment at Porton Down.

Here the security checks were far more stringent
than at the aerospace factory; two gatehouse guards –
soldiers – torches in hand, inspected the saddlebags of
all the motorcycles, and went over the Land Rovers in
minute detail. A third guard, a sergeant, stood to one
side watching the inspection process, and gave updates
on a walkie-talkie to someone within the establishment.
All the guards were armed.

'Right, one last thing,' the sergeant in charge of
the security detail said to the outriders as well as the
drivers and passengers of the Land Rovers. 'If you hear
the siren sound while you're inside you are to follow
the instructions you are given. Do not argue, do not
deviate from those instructions. If they give you gas
masks to put on, put them on. If they tell you to
evacuate the building, evacuate the building. If they tell
you to strip naked and stand under a shower that's what
you do. Do you understand?'

They did, and nodded. But the sergeant wasn't
having any of it. He shouted, 'I said, do you
understand?'

This time they all stood more to attention. Three
of them said 'Yes sir!' but the sergeant still wasn't
finished. 'Here,' he said, holding out a clipboard and
pen. 'Sign this. It says you acknowledge that you have

been given the appropriate safety briefing. No signatures, no entry.'

Names were scribbled with varying degrees of enthusiasm; the riders and drivers weren't used to being treated like schoolboys, and resented being shouted at, but they had also been told that, as with the missile, their cargo would be of vital importance and of relevance to national security. They were to collect it, secure it, transport it and deliver it with the utmost care, and they were not to ask any questions.

Finally the group was waved on, and they drove towards a lone figure waiting for them outside the main building. They could see his slight form silhouetted against the glare of the security arc lights, his breath condensing in the cold night air.

Once the motorbikes' and Land Rovers' engines were switched off, the lead vehicle's driver marched up to the waiting figure, saluted, gave his name and rank, and handed over his order papers. The director took them, put on his glasses and studied the documents, holding them at an angle under the lights. They were of course in order, and he handed them back.

'Thank you,' he said. 'Sorry about the fuss at the main gate, but we can't be too careful. There are things here, which, if they accidentally got out, as it were, could cause a great deal of trouble.' By which he meant countless deaths, although that remained unsaid. The driver nodded as though he completely understood what he was being told. He didn't.

The director said, 'Follow me,' and the driver indicated the others to do the same. 'No, sorry, just you. Security. As I said, can't be too careful.'

While the others leaned against the Land Rovers and smoked, the director led the driver through a side door, where they found themselves in a large and well-lit garage area. There were two ambulances, and various fire engines, along with portable fire-fighting equipment. Ominously, a row of full hazard suits hung on one wall, each numbered. They looked like monsters staring out into the room, monsters with trunks attached to air filters.

'Yes I know, scary the first time you see them isn't it? Especially in the early hours of the morning,' said the director. 'Hopefully we'll never have to use them. But anyway, here's your cargo.'

He led the driver over to a four-wheeled trolley, on which was a steel cradle. Held securely on webbing in the middle of the cradle was a metal box. The director flipped open a couple of catches and opened the lid to reveal a shiny stainless-steel cylinder about four feet long and twelve inches in diameter. It had fins at one end, a conical tip at the other, and was nestled securely in firm rubbery material moulded to its shape. It bore no markings. At one end there was a valve or spigot, and a split-pin such as those found on hand grenades. Attached to it was a red and white bordered label with the word 'WARNING!', and, 'ONCE REMOVED CYLINDER IS ARMED.'

The director patted the canister. 'It's perfectly safe, as it is. But if you should have any… unforeseen circumstances on your journey and the cargo is damaged, you must not touch it, is that clear? Report directly to me immediately with your location and the condition of the cargo.' The director handed him a card, then went to a crate underneath the gas suits, and took out some gas masks, each with a filter canister attached by a hose. He walked back to the driver.

'Here, just in case. If you do have any issues, put these on immediately before you assess any damage. Do not under any circumstances allow members of the public near the cylinder, is that clear?'

'Very clear, sir,' the driver gulped. 'Er, can I ask what we should do if we are exposed to the, er, contents sir?'

The director smiled, although without any humour. 'Oh I shouldn't worry. You won't feel a thing.'

53

The Lonely Pheasant Pub, upstairs function room

Tench had their undivided attention. 'It seems the Russians have been onto Unity for a while, though God knows how they found out. We're working on that. Meanwhile the pair are being kept in a safe house in Middlesex, under twenty-four-hour guard.

'And they've been interrogated?' This was Symes.

'Do you torture them?' This was Chris, who was now angrily perched on the edge of her seat and looked ready to pounce on someone.

Tench shook her head. 'We prefer "interviewed" rather than interrogated. It's more civilized. We're not thugs.'

'And?' Riley asked, voicing the question for all of them.

'They're two Soviet nationals, one male, one female. The male came into Britain just a few months ago and doesn't speak much English, but the woman came here as a teenager and speaks it perfectly. So good in fact she's been passing herself off as one of ours, even carrying a very realistic but forged identity card.

'We first heard about them after George Brown's chauffeur – the one who Anastasia just mentioned – was paid a visit by the woman, calling herself Lillian Grimes. With your Charles's help and a contact in our service they found that the car the pair were driving was registered to a minor diplomat at the Soviet Embassy. So we put a tail on the vehicle.'

'So how did they find out about me and the notebook?' Tommy asked. 'I've still got a few bruises from meeting them.'

Tench smiled. 'You were lucky. The man's a nasty piece of work by all accounts. But we're not sure how they knew you had the notebook. They'd staked out the Virgil Street garage, we know that much, but we suspect they've got an informant, in Westminster, Whitehall, your service Riley or ours. Or, God forbid, in all of them.'

Symes shuffled in his seat and said, 'That doesn't sound good. What else have you got from them?'

'Ironically enough, a notebook,' Tench chuckled. 'The pair were followed to the home in Amesbury of one of the scientists who works at Porton Down, a Dr. Sarika Khatri. Grimes or whatever her name is fooled Khatri into believing she was from the intelligence service. Khatri, unwisely and against protocol, told her about the work she'd been doing on the nerve agent project, Eirene, the basis for Unity.'

Riley asked, 'Did they have time to report back to their handlers, or superiors, or whoever's managing them?'

'No,' said Tench, 'we don't think so. We had two teams on them, and as soon as they left Khatri's house one of those went in to speak to her. She of course didn't want to speak to them and thought *they* were the ones pretending to be from MI5 but they managed to convince her. The other team followed their car. They were, however, spotted, and the Russians tried every evasion technique in the book but thanks to a narrow country lane, a tight corner and some fresh manure on the road they ended up in a ditch. There was no radio in the car, so no, they hadn't had a chance to report what they'd discovered.'

'Which was?' asked Walker.

Tench clasped her hands in front of her and looked uncomfortable. 'Well, this is where it gets interesting…'

She told them the details of Sarika Khatri's work at Porton Down, how she'd been urged to speed up the Eirene research, and how her parents had been targeted to leverage her cooperation.

'Anastasia has already explained the basis of the project – how they'd discovered a compound that could render a subject or subjects compliant, how it had been taken through its solid and liquid stages and trialled on residents in the village – and finally to a gaseous state, an aerosol. But we now know that Eirene had been urgently moved to a clinical trial, to test the gas.'

Tench then told them how, of the ten human guinea pigs subjected to the aerosol, two had fallen into comas. There was silence once again in the musty room as everyone absorbed the information.

'Two out of ten? In a coma which they might never recover from?' Walker voiced it for all of them. 'A twenty percent failure rate? No pharmaceutical company would release anything like that onto the market so surely Porton Down's boffins wouldn't allow its release for military use either. It's not only unethical, it's downright dangerous.'

'So are bullets,' shrugged Riley, 'and we use those. Defence might have decided that the collateral damage associated with the Eirene gas is acceptable in a theatre of war.'

'This is ridiculous!' Chris exploded, standing up and leaning on the table with her fists, her knuckles white against the scarred wooden top.

'You all sit here, rambling on about nerve gasses, Russian agents, a secret village with a population of ex-spies… seriously? You expect me to believe any of this?' She pushed her chair back and began pacing the floor, gesturing angrily as she fumed.

'And George Brown wants to somehow use this Eirene stuff?' She turned and glared at them. 'He's an alcoholic no-hoper, not a criminal mastermind. No, the whole thing's preposterous.' She slumped back into her chair and folded her arms, refusing to meet anyone's eyes.

There was a collective breathing out as Riley and the others realised she'd finished her rant. Then Symes broke the silence.

'You don't want to hear about the missile then?'

54

Century House, Sub-basement 2

Stone watched the main screen from Sub-2's observation lounge. McCauley stood beside him. Towering above the village a giant mobile crane was very slowly and very carefully lowering the ribbed cylinder that was the missile down into its launch tube deep inside one of the main buildings.

Other cameras showed the village deserted.

Stone had only then just noticed. 'Where is everyone?'

McCauley cleared his throat and said, 'Asleep. Well, drugged actually, but out of it for the duration. They're all fine and being monitored by the hospital's medical staff on a regular basis. The only ones witness to what's happening are the skeleton crew in village control, a few essential security personnel around the village, and of course the defence contractors in charge of the installation of the missile. All trusted, all signed-up. It's really all going very well.'

Stone grunted. 'I won't be satisfied until it's in place and fully concealed. How are we doing for time?'

McCauley checked his watch as well as the clock on the wall behind them. 'Good. Slightly ahead of schedule actually.'

'And what of our man's journey to… London? Where is he now?'

McCauley picked up a nearby cordless telephone, the one directly connected to Number Two. It was answered immediately.

'Ah, McCauley in Monitoring here. Mr. Stone would like an update on our captive.'

He listened for a few seconds, then said, 'Good. I'll pass that on. Oh, and Major Wilson will be back on duty within a couple of hours. She'll be watching the arrival of the escapees. Just thought you'd like to know.'

He listened to what was said on the other end of the line but decided not to repeat it to Stone.

He replaced the phone. 'Three hours until Six "arrives in London." The cast, as it were, are already in place and the reception venue is ready. At this point our man believes he is arriving somewhere in England and will be transported to HQ here in the city. Quite the ruse I must say!'

Stone however found it difficult to be positive. There was too much at stake, too much to go wrong. He worried that Wilson was initiating increasingly complex ploys, and he was beginning to doubt whether the efforts were worth it. He had half a mind to order the use of some Eirene gas on the subject, to make him fully compliant, but then there was that issue he'd been told about, that irritating twenty percent chance it would render him unconscious. Or worse. And then they'd learn nothing.

'The Number Two in place at the moment,' said Stone, not taking his eyes from the big screen, 'how's he been? What's your view?'

McCauley flattened his tie against his shirt, then ran a finger under his collar. He wasn't used to being asked for an opinion by the chief.

'Best one so far I'd say.' He flicked a switch and brought up a view of the inside of the main dome. The bearded and scarved Two sat in the globe chair watching the same feed of the missile installation as they were. He was like a statue, unmoving, except for an occasional blink of the eyes.

'I think he's got the measure of Number Six. I'm not sure if you're aware – and this was Major Wilson's idea I believe – but he organised an art competition for the village people, which went very well. Six won a prize for a sculpture, but he then went on to use the materials to escape with the girl Nadia. We anticipated he would, of course.'

If Stone thought this cause for celebration he didn't show it. He glared at McCauley. 'He's tried more than a few times to escape, and who can blame him? One of these days he'll succeed, but I want him broken well before then. I'll be making it very clear to Major Wilson that it's time we put maximum pressure on him, by whatever means she sees fit.'

McCauley almost bowed. 'Yes of course, and we'll monitor his every move. As always.'

Stone returned his attention to the main screen. 'Show me the exterior view again.'

McCauley brought it up. The missile was nowhere to be seen, and already the crane was manoeuvring a hatch into place on the roof, covering completely the launch tube below.

'Good. Satisfactory.' Stone looked at his watch, turned and left the room.

McCauley let out a long breath, having not realised he'd been holding it for the last few seconds. He looked down at the rows of empty seats and screens, their operators still away and enjoying their unexpected day's leave.

Once more he looked at the village, the crane now slowly swinging back and away behind the main buildings.

At least, he thought, when the payload arrives it will be far simpler to install. But first the missile installation crew needed to complete their work and depart. Then, after his own monitoring crew had returned in the early evening it would be time to enjoy the fun and games – as he thought of it – of watching Number Six emerge from his crate after having travelled sixteen hours from what he believed was 'Lithuania.'

He chuckled, knowing that in reality the crate containing Six and his fellow escapee Nadia had been driven around various local back country roads, loaded onto a small coaster at a port for a period to simulate crossing the North Sea, then driven some more replicating the final leg of the journey to London. But it would, of course, end up back at the village.

'Yes, much better than anything I've seen on the television!' he muttered gleefully to himself.

*

At 1900 hours Olivia Wilson joined the throng of people in the corridor heading for Sub-basement 2. Having enjoyed their surprise day off the monitoring staff were now heading back to work, not really sure why they'd been given a holiday, but also not questioning it. Wilson however was consumed with curiosity.

She pushed her way through the doors and into the observation lounge, looking immediately at the main screen for any clue as to what had been going on. She saw nothing unusual. The village residents seemed to be acting normally, the little white taxis with their striped canvas tops plied the cobbled roads, and the sun shone brightly across the pastel-hued buildings. Apart from some workmen repairing a roof there was nothing out of place.

McCauley entered the lounge, a spring in his step and a smile on his face. 'Ah, Major Wilson, there you are.'

'Yes, here I am,' she seethed. 'So, what's been happening? Have you been here all this time?'

'Me? No, sir. The place has been off-limits for most of the day. Like you I was *persona non grata*.'

She didn't believe him. When someone is asked a question about their actions or whereabouts and they immediately answer with 'Me?' it's nearly always a stalling technique while they gather their thoughts. She knew this; lie detection 101.

'Really,' she fumed, her sarcasm falling on deaf ears. 'Of course.' But she let it drop; McCauley wasn't about to admit to anything.

'So where are we with our escapees?'

McCauley brought her up to date with the progress of the mock journey, taking delight in the whole theatrical nature of it all. But despite his fawning enthusiasm it sounded like it had all gone to plan. They would know within the hour, as the crate was soon to arrive at the 'London offices.' The key players, two of them known personally to the escapee, were in place and aware of their duties.

It was showtime.

55

The Lonely Pheasant Pub, upstairs function room

Chris slumped further back into her seat. 'What missile?' she asked, not really wanting to hear yet more mastermind villain antics. She had watched only one James Bond film and had vowed never to watch another. Yet here she was hearing about *Goldfinger*-scale schemes from real spies. Her patience was running out at the same rate that her frustration level was rising at not being able to report anything.

Riley explained about the transporting of the intermediate range ballistic missile to the village, how he and Symes had learned from MoD engineering records that a launch silo had been created there a few years before, and that the weapon would almost certainly now be in place.

'So… what?' Chris asked. 'Is it a nuclear thing? Where's it aimed?' She was beginning to take more interest now.

Walker answered. 'We don't know. Yet. And no, we don't think it has a nuclear warhead.'

'It hasn't.' This was Tench. 'It's almost certainly to be armed with the Eirene-3 aerosol – gas – if it isn't already.'

Everyone turned to look at her. 'Are you certain?' Symes asked.

'As certain as I can be. The two Soviet agents haven't talked much, but the notebook the woman had with her tells us all we need to know. Add to that the information that Dr Khatri gave us, confirming that she'd been ordered to fast-track the gas trials, *and* her parents were being targeted to leverage her cooperation, well, it just adds up. The gas is effective even in a concentration of just few parts per million, so a little goes a long way.'

'Far enough to put people in a coma, or kill them.' Chris stated flatly. 'Surely this is illegal?'

'That's why we're here,' Riley pointed out. 'We – all of us round this table – believe things have gone too far. Unity is out of control.'

'Then if you just let me report it we can stop it!' Chris said, banging a fist on the table. 'Surely if we go public with all of this it can't go ahead…'

'And then all of us end up in prison,' Tench said, 'or worse. We'd all be guilty of treason, of compromising national security, and God knows what other misdemeanours. No, we have to stop it in the same way it's being handled: covertly, stealthily, effectively. We need to stop it in its tracks.'

Riley could see Chris was about to explode. 'Judith's right. If we can sabotage Unity in some way, cause it to stall – or better still be cancelled completely – then that has to be the best outcome. We need – and I know this sounds incredible – to stop the missile, render it useless somehow, get our man out of the village and… shut the place down.'

Even as he said it he felt his confidence drain away, although he tried not to show it. But now that he'd voiced it, it all sounded too much, too complex, too ambitious. How could this disparate and desperate group fight effectively against an operation that had the backing of government, seemingly unlimited funding, as well as the foreign secretary, and likely Stone and Olivia Wilson in league. It was hopeless, surely.

'And what? All those behind it get to walk away? To retreat, regroup, and do something like this all over again?' Chris asked incredulously. 'They can't be allowed to get off scot-free.'

'They won't,' said Walker, sensing Riley's despair. 'That's partly where you'll come in. Once we've surreptitiously terminated Unity, we're the ones who can retreat and regroup and you can expose the whole bloody business. Well, most of it anyway.'

Symes added, 'We have someone on the inside, at the retirement village, as we speak. He was urgently installed very recently, so we must move quickly. In everyday life he's a diplomat with an exemplary career in the civil service and he has a very persuasive nature. His name is Barnaby Carrington-Hall, and he's extremely well-connected in Westminster. From a political standpoint we're confident he can help ensure that the village is either returned to its original function as a retirement facility, or closed down altogether, while at the same time those behind the hijacking of it – in government, the MoD, even Foreign Secretary George Brown – can be brought to account. As an assistant political editor you can blow the lid off Unity. This might even bring down Harold Wilson's government.'

Chris could finally see the enormity of the story, and, selfishly perhaps, how it could positively impact her career.

'So, what do *we* do?' she asked, waving a thumb at Tommy and herself.

Now it was Riley's turn. 'For the moment we don't want you to do anything that publicises what's going on – it's too soon. Just absorb what you've heard here this evening and be patient. Your time will come. But you, Tommy, might be able to do something for us. With Carrington-Hall in the village right now he might need some help.'

'And how would I be able to do that?'

'Well,' smiled Riley, 'you've always wanted to know where the "departed" go, haven't you? How do you fancy a ride in an ambulance?'

56

Century House, Sub-basement 2

Olivia Wilson held her breath as the large crate, now manoeuvred into an upright position in the mocked-up London office, was prised open. She watched intently as the action took place on the large central screen, McCauley standing equally enthralled beside her in the central monitoring section.

Their quarry emerged, along with Nadia, the so-called 'resistance' member, both of them looking remarkably well given their 16-hour confinement. Nadia was led away as arranged, ostensibly to freshen up, while 'the Colonel' welcomed Number Six back.

'This is it,' whispered Wilson. McCauley nodded, but said nothing.

'This is where we get the information we want.'

But they didn't.

Wilson watched with a rising sense of horror and disbelief as the escapee paced around having failed to convince the Colonel of the existence of the village. The Colonel, contrary to instructions, wasn't amiable or relaxed, and, as Wilson reported later, far too insistent on asking why the man had resigned. After almost a full day confined in a wooden crate, she knew this was the last thing he would want to talk about, and she had instructed that it was not a question to be pressed too soon, yet here it was happening before her eyes.

'I don't believe it!' she whispered. McCauley again thought it prudent to say nothing.

'I do NOT believe it!' Wilson repeated, but now shouting it. The surveillance staff at their monitors heard her, even through their headphones, and turned in her direction. What they saw was a woman with a red face, a scowl, tightened fists and glaring eyes. She was shaking with rage.

'No! NO!' she yelled, as on screen she witnessed Number Six find the hidden tape recorder that had been playing background sounds of London traffic, and the chimes of Big Ben. The final straw had been when he had realised that the number of chimes – eight – didn't tally with the European time difference. He was supposed to have travelled across a time zone, and now having found the tape recorder he knew for certain he'd been duped.

Wilson's heart sank as she watched him walk out a door and back into the village, which, he now realised, he'd never really left. He looked crestfallen, yet still resolved.

Her yell was blood-curdling, and mournful. The surveillance team looked quickly back to their monitors and concentrated on their jobs. McCauley backed away and quietly moved off to what he thought was a safe distance, hoping to disappear behind his control desk in the gloom at the edge of the room.

It was not to be. One of the telephones lit up as he sat down. He listened for a moment, then stood and took the cordless handset over to where Wilson was standing, now slightly bowed over, hands clenched, still staring at the main screen.

McCauley approached hesitantly. 'Er, Major Wilson? It's for you. Mr. Stone.'

She robotically took the phone from him, held it to her ear. 'Sir.' She said it as a statement, not a question, more than a degree of defeat in her voice.

'I'd like a report from you on how it went. My office. One hour.'

He cut the connection.

*

253

As ordered, Olivia Wilson arrived at Stone's office exactly one hour later. Her journey upstairs hadn't been direct though, by any means. She had left the building and gone to a nearby pub where she downed two large brandies, one after the other, the first quickly, the second more slowly. Ostensibly it was to calm her nerves, but the failure of her Big Ben plan had hit her hard, and she was driven to the alcohol. In a few gulps her five-years of being dry had been wiped, and she knew her next support meeting would be one of admittance.

But that was the least of her worries right now, and by God the liquor tasted good. It was just the antidote she needed.

However, she was still shaking slightly. The tape-recorded sound effects had been her own idea, a last-minute addition, hence the recorder's placement in a cupboard. Had it been installed properly by people from the audio-visual team it would have been fully concealed and undetectable.

She thought of ordering another drink but instead drained the dregs in her glass, sucking in and savouring the last drops.

But the fault lay firmly with her, there was no denying it. She could not blame anyone else, except that nobody else had questioned her orders to have Big Ben chiming eight o'clock – nobody else had realised the significance of the different time zones. Such a small detail, but now with huge ramifications. She was surrounded by imbeciles.

She fully expected that Stone would dismiss her and find someone else to take over the control of the village trial. Her joy at overseeing one of the most fascinating experiments in psychological manipulation had evaporated in less than a quarter of an hour.

She also now fully expected the captive to never reveal his information, and to wear them all down into submission. Is that why he was there? Had that been his aim all along? If so, he was winning. But maybe not. Maybe there was one last push, one final ploy that would break him.

And now here she was entering Stone's office. He didn't welcome her, nor did he invite her to sit, so she remained standing, but not at ease.

He finished what he was doing – scribbling notes in a file, as always – and looked at her. He squinted at her, took in her blotchy face, the slightly glazed look in her eyes, and was… was she slightly swaying as she stood there?

'I gather it didn't go well.'

Wilson swallowed. 'No sir,' she croaked, then cleared her throat and tried again. 'No sir, it didn't.'

Stone swivelled in his chair and looked out of a window. She feared he was thinking about asking her what she would try next, but he suddenly swung back, stood and slammed a hand on his desk.

'A disaster! A damned disaster Major Wilson!' he shouted. She had never heard him raise his voice before. She flinched, blinked, looked down and away from his angry face distorted in rage. But he wasn't done.

'I have been very patient with your… your grand theatrical approach to breaking our man. You convinced me that playing with him, toying with him, was the way to finding out what he knows, yet here we are, after God knows how many attempts and still, STILL we know nothing.'

Stone left his desk and paced at the other end of the room.

Wilson could feel tears welling; she hadn't had a dressing down like this since she first joined the army. 'I'm sorry sir,' she whispered.

Stone stopped and glared at her. 'What? What did you say?'

From somewhere she found more strength for her voice. 'I said I'm sorry. Sir.'

'Sorry. So you're sorry are you? The so-called psych "expert" …' – his voice dripped with sarcasm – 'says she's sorry. Well it's NOT GOOD ENOUGH!' he yelled.

She flinched again.

He moved towards her and she genuinely feared he might strike her, but he stopped, his face inches away from hers. She tried holding her breath so he wouldn't smell the alcohol. Fortunately, after glowering at her up close for what seemed an age, but was actually only about two seconds, he moved away again to continue pacing. Quietly Wilson let her breath out and began breathing normally. Well, as normally as her flight mechanism would let her – her heart was racing and her temples pounding.

'You know I must report to my superior. Yes, I too have one, the chain of command doesn't stop in this office Major Wilson. And I must report failure. *Your* failure Major – I will make that quite clear. But let me tell you…' and here he strode up to her once again, this time waving a finger at her, 'you have one final chance, just one, to set this right, or it's back to the army for you, stripped of your rank, if not a dishonourable discharge.

'Do you have a plan? Can you break him this time? Can you save your career, and, more importantly, save me from further embarrassment and ridicule? Can you?'

The relief washed through her like a tide coming ashore. She raised her chin, looked slightly above Stone's head, and said with authority, 'Yes sir. I will break him. I am confident.'

'How?'

Wilson's mind went blank, but only for a second. Then she remembered what Carrington-Hall, the new Number Two, had wanted to try.

'Regression therapy sir. We'll take him right back to his childhood and guide him through his life. There will be a degree of subtle hypnosis, and we will bring him afresh back to the present, to his resignation. He will see no reason to withhold information any longer. I will guarantee it.'

Stone sneered. 'You will, Major Wilson. And I'll be putting Riley, Symes and Walker back on observational duties to make sure you do. Is that clear?'

Wilson nodded and looked down, partly with a sense of defeat and partly to hide her resentment at once again being put under a magnifying glass.

Stone turned away from her and waved a hand.

'You have one week. Get out.'

57

Foreign Secretary George Brown's limousine

Daniel Forbes waited until Stone had joined George Brown inside the car, then gently closed the rear door of the Jaguar. He made his way round the vehicle – now dent- and scratch-free, with a new driver's window and no hint of any of the damage from Trafalgar Square – and slid into the front seat.

'Where to sir?' he asked the foreign secretary.

'Take us somewhere quiet, Daniel, somewhere a bit out of the way where Mr. Stone and I can have a chat without being seen or overheard. There's a good chap.'

'Yes sir,' said Daniel as he started the car. This was new, he thought to himself; not going to a particular destination, not to a meeting, nor home. But it was no surprise; when he'd checked his schedule he'd seen that Brown's secretary had pencilled in this trip over a week ago, but she hadn't added a destination. Now he knew why: Brown and Stone, the director general of a department within MI6, he understood, wanted to have a private off-the-record conversation.

Before he engaged first gear he reached down and felt under his seat. The tape recorder was still there, where he'd hidden it earlier.

As he drove, his mind wandered back to a few days ago when he'd gone to the garage in Virgil Street to collect the newly repaired vehicle. It had been away a while, so he was pleased to have got the call from Charles to say that it was finally ready.

'Took your time,' he teased Charles when he arrived. 'Not as young as you were I guess, eh Charles!'

Charles flicked an oily cloth at him. 'Cheeky bugger,' he smiled. 'No, it wasn't me. The panel shop took their time. It only took me half an hour to fit the new window this morning, so don't go blaming me young man.'

Daniel patted the gleaming car. 'George Brown'll be glad to have it back too,' he said. 'I've been driving him round in an old Rover and he's not been too happy about it. Plus he's got a meeting with your boss next week and wants me to take them somewhere, so at least they'll be in some comfort.'

Charles raised an eyebrow. 'My boss? You mean Mr. Symes?'

'No, bloke called Stone. From MI6 apparently. All passengers have to be identified on the schedule before I drive them anywhere; it's a security thing. Isn't he the top man?'

Charles nodded. 'That he is.' Charles wouldn't go into any more detail, but he mentally filed the meeting away. Mr. Symes might be interested.

Daniel peered into the rear of the car. 'That was all a bit weird about Brown losing his notebook,' he said. 'And the Russian woman coming to my place, pretending to be MI5. I knew she didn't seem right.'

'Well,' said Charles, 'it was quick of you to get the registration number, but don't ever go telling me fibs about getting into scrapes in your Mini again. I can smell a lie from a mile away.'

Daniel reddened and kicked one of the car's tyres in mild embarrassment.

The next day he'd received a visit from Symes. This time Daniel spent a lot longer examining the ID card, and quizzed Symes about Charles, asking him things that wouldn't be easily known. Symes passed the test and congratulated Daniel on his diligence.

'I wish there were more like you,' he'd said, 'but you did talk slightly out of turn when you picked up the car, didn't you?'

'What d'you mean?'

Symes smiled his usual charming smile. 'Oh don't worry. I'm glad you did, otherwise we wouldn't have known that your boss and my boss were going to have a private meeting, and although they must do so quite regularly, this one is intriguing. And very timely. So, we've got a job for you.' And then he'd brought out the miniature tape recorder. He'd shown it to Daniel and demonstrated how it worked.

'Simple, isn't it? And excellent quality. What we'd like you to do is try and record whatever Brown and Stone talk about. Simple.'

But Daniel wasn't so easily recruited. 'Why? And why do you want to secretly record them? Whose side are you on?'

'Oh, very much the right side,' Symes purred, 'you can be sure of that. Don't worry, we're not in cahoots with the Soviets or anything like that. But there is something going on, and we need to nip it in the bud, so to speak. All we're doing is gathering intelligence, which, let's face it, is what we do for a living.'

Daniel had been reluctant. 'Yeah, that's as maybe, but you're spying on your own people. That don't seem right.'

'All right, here's the deal. I'll leave the tape recorder with you. Talk to Charles again, ask him to verify that we're not subverting our organisation, or spying for the Russians. If he doesn't convince you, you can turn the job down.'

Symes turned to leave, but then stopped and looked back. 'But if you do, we'll find another driver, and you'll get a surprise day off. You could use it to visit the labour exchange. Cheerio.'

So here he was, on duty as usual. Charles had convinced him that Symes was genuine and that there was nothing to worry about. Other than getting caught, of course, and that was something Daniel was determined not to do.

He drove to a royal park on the edge of the city where he knew there was usually plenty of space for vehicles to park, especially on quiet days. This was a quiet day, and when he arrived he was pleased to find a spot well away from any other cars or even buildings. In fact, the view through the windscreen was one of rolling grassland and trees. Ideal for a clandestine meeting. He applied the handbrake and switched off the engine.

'Will this do sir?' he asked, looking in his rear-view mirror.

'Perfect Daniel, thank you. Please, go and stretch your legs for half an hour.' This was not-so-subtle code for 'leave us alone so we can talk.'

'Of course sir,' Daniel nodded, and exited the vehicle. Before he closed his door he leaned in and said, 'I'll just move my seat forward sir, give you a bit more leg room,' at which point he bent down, quickly switched on the recorder, and slid the seat slightly forward.

Daniel strolled a short distance from the car, but kept the vehicle and his passengers in sight. He sat on a bench enjoying the sunshine on his face, and wondered what Brown and Stone were talking about. Brown had been looking tired of late, and Stone – whom he'd never met before – had said nothing when he picked him up, but Daniel thought he looked stern, maybe annoyed or worried, or a combination of the two. Whatever, he hadn't engaged in pleasantries.

Brown didn't waste any time after Daniel had strolled out of earshot.

'Have you broken your operative yet?'

Stone hesitated slightly before answering. 'No, no we haven't. The last attempt ended in failure again I'm afraid.'

Brown gave a slight growl of disgust. 'Does he remain a threat?'

'Not while we have him incarcerated, no. But he is a thorn in our side and his every move is monitored. I've given my people a last chance to fix things once and for all. A week from now he will either have told us what we want to know or… he'll have been neutralised.'

Brown looked out of the side window. 'I don't want to know what that entails. All right, I'll assume he's not a threat and that we can proceed.'

Stone nodded confidently, although inside he wasn't so sure.

Brown turned back. 'So, we need to light the touch paper, and stand well clear. It's time.'

Stone sighed and pinched the bridge of his nose with a thumb and forefinger. 'George, why must you always talk in metaphors? You mean you want to launch the missile.'

Brown looked at him. 'Yes. It needs to be given a proper field trial. Time to test it and gauge just how effective this Eirene gas is in a real situation. Defence Secretary Healey says the MoD is very interested to get results from outside of a laboratory, and I personally want to see how effective it is.'

Stone frowned and turned to him. 'It's not as simple as that George! You're talking about launching a bloody missile for heaven's sake, not a bonfire night firework! And the gas…' His voice trailed off.

'What about it?' Brown grumped.

'The testing was never properly completed – partly because you insisted the timetable be brought forward. I had to arrange for the lead scientist to be, well, *coerced* into pushing the testing through, but that didn't work. She contacted the police and next thing MI5 were onto it.'

'Did they link anything to you?'

'No. I'm not an amateur George. The scientist was put on leave and the testing continued under a new lead. But there was only time to trial it on a limited cohort, and the results were, well, concerning.'

'In what way?'

Stone told him about the gas putting two out of the ten human guinea pigs into comas.

Brown waved a hand dismissively. 'Pfft. A minor detail. What of the others, the ones who didn't react?'

Stone sighed again and slumped back in his seat. He would have to confess. 'They were like lambs. Peaceful, compliant, just as expected. They would do whatever was asked of them, as we hoped. On the battlefield an enemy, exposed to Eirene, would surrender when told to, put down their weapons when ordered. But we're not at war George. We're not actively engaged in any battles, other than covert ones, and yes, I can see how Eirene could be useful in that context too in certain circumstances. But it needs further development and testing! It's just not ready!'

Brown shook his head. 'Yet you say the gas is now installed in the missile?'

Stone clenched his fists. 'Against my every instinct. But yes, it is.'

'Good. So Unity is ready. Then we'll test it.'

'And what will the target be George? Has the MoD suggested somewhere? It can't be behind the Iron Curtain, we wouldn't be able to monitor the results, so it will have to be somewhere in Europe. The thing is there are no major conflicts at the moment, and the missile's range wouldn't reach Vietnam, which would perhaps be the most logical target. But if we brought the Americans into it and let them use Eirene in their combat zone, we'd lose our hold on all the research we've done, and the advantage we have with Unity as a strategic weapon. A British weapon need I add. If it's to be tested, the missile needs a precise and measurable target, the guidance system needs to be programmed…'

'No, Stone. There's a target closer than Vietnam, and closer than anywhere in Europe. Much closer. I've received an intelligence report that another anti-war protest is planned, in London again, but this time the numbers will be much greater. The last one turned into a riot. This one has the same potential but with considerably bigger impact. We're talking about an angry mob of young people, with disregard for society, a grudge against the government, and hatred in their veins. They must be stopped!'

Stone couldn't believe what he was hearing. His mouth opened and closed as he tried to think of something to counter the madness of what Brown was saying.

'George! Is this some sort of petty revenge on your part? You can't be serious!'

'I've never been more serious, Stone. The protest is in eight days. I'll send you a copy of the intelligence report, but start things rolling with the MoD now. The missile's in your backyard, so I'm counting on you to coordinate the launch. Don't let me down. You've done that too often recently.'

Stone was too shaken to argue, but Brown wasn't finished.

'And I never did get my notebook back.' He fumed. 'With all the resources of the police, MI5, and your lot, it's still missing, and is most likely in Moscow being analysed page by page and word by word. One of which is Unity remember.' He looked sourly at the seatback in front of him, then his eyes dropped to the floor. He knew the book couldn't be there, but he bent forward to look anyway.

58

RAF Northolt

As usual, the hangar doors slid open on approach and Charles drove the hearse inside the cavernous interior, the doors closing behind him and shutting off the bright daylight. This time there was no body in the casket, only Tommy sitting up front beside Charles.

To keep up appearances they were both wearing black funeral attire, although Tommy, given free rein for his wardrobe choice, had been to a second-hand store and bought a white tuxedo ruffle shirt with matching frilly cuffs, and an embroidered black military topcoat, something a bandsman might wear. To the casual observer watching the hearse go by he still looked the part, but what stepped out of the hearse after it had come to a halt in the hangar was part circus ringmaster and part virtuoso, although his white footwear belied both of those roles. He was himself, and from what he'd heard of the village community's rules, he would be just the catalyst Riley and the others needed: a rebel, a maverick.

Since the meeting in The Lonely Pheasant, Tommy's life had been a whirlwind of activity, largely driven by Riley and Symes. Chris had reluctantly done what she was told and gone about her business at the newspaper, but inside she was champing at the bit to break the story – the story of a lifetime. She would have to wait.

Tommy meanwhile had been 'inducted' into the workings of the village. Riley had shown him a map of the community, and photographs of the grounds and key buildings. He also showed him file photographs of the man they aimed to rescue, Number Six, and of the incumbent Number Two, Carrington-Hall. There was a wealth of other detail too, all of which he absorbed.

These pressure-cooker sessions had been done away from Century House, since Riley didn't want Stone, Wilson or anyone else in the organisation to see Tommy before he was inserted into the village.

'I still don't know what I'm supposed to do,' Tommy had said at the end of his first session.

Symes and Riley had exchanged glances. It was Riley who spoke.

'Nor do we, unfortunately. You're going to have to ad-lib. Your file says you used to have a talent for amateur dramatics, so treat the whole thing as a production and just play along.'

Tommy had folded his arms and smirked. 'And that presumably includes sitting there without complaint while they inject me with mind-bending drugs, or torture me with electro-shock therapy. That's not something I can ad-lib my way through, man!'

Another exchange of glances. This time it was Symes: 'We're hoping it won't come to that. We've concocted a plausible story as to why you've been sent there – not too far from the truth actually. You worked for our department's garage, stole a car, got caught and thrown in jail, then stole the foreign secretary's notebook and showed it to a newspaper journalist. As punishment, you need some "re-education," hence you're being sent to the village. We've already filed the application and it's been approved, so they'll be expecting you. In fact, they've already assigned you a number.'

'Which is?'

'Forty-eight,' said Riley.

'My lucky number!' smiled Tommy.

'Really?'

Tommy said, 'We'll see.'

Riley moved on. 'Number Two, Carrington-Hall, knows to expect someone, but because all communications to and from the village are closely monitored we've been unable to tell him who or when. He was aware before he took up his position that we'd be attempting to infiltrate the community, so hopefully you'll get a chance to introduce yourself. But you'll have to do it out of range of any cameras or microphones. I suspect he'll recognise you anyway, even though you've never met.'

And now here was Tommy, finally getting to witness what happened to the departed, as he'd called them, those that he and Charles 'extracted.'

The ambulance was waiting, the back doors open. Don, the usual driver, came over to Charles and Tommy.

'Blimey! We've got a live one this time! Or is 'e a bloomin' ghost?'

Charles was disinclined to get into too much detail. 'He's on an assignment; need-to-know, and you don't need to know.'

Don shrugged. He knew he wouldn't learn anything more, but he wondered why this clean-shaven young man with red hair and sideburns was going to the village. They have their reasons I guess, he thought.

He turned to Charles. 'So, is he going in the pod? Do I knock him out?'

'No,' Charles shook his head. 'He can ride up front with you until you get close to the village, then strap him in.' Charles put an avuncular hand on Tommy's shoulder. 'Just pretend you're unconscious son, you'll be all right. From what Mr. Symes tells me you know what to expect.'

'Right,' said Don, closing the back doors of the ambulance. 'Let's be off.' Then he paused and turned back to Charles. 'I've been doin' lots of overtime recently Chas. Had to drive a bloomin' busload of people up there recently, strange lot too. Some soldier types, some ordinary geezers, and definitely some boffins. Weird lot. Oh well, never a dull moment! Come on young feller.' He opened the driver's door and climbed in.

Tommy started to walk round to the passenger side, then turned and smiled at Charles. He made a circle with his thumb and forefinger, put it briefly to his right eye and said, 'Be seeing you.'

*

Behind the service station on the West End Road which ran along the perimeter of the air base, Derek poured coffee from his thermos into a mug. Wayne, his fellow plane-spotter, sat on his camp stool beside him. They'd been there only a few minutes.

Wayne spotted movement at one of the buildings in the distance, a hangar, and raised his camera with its 400mm telephoto lens to his eye.

''Ello, 'ello. What do we have 'ere Derek?'

Derek stopped pouring and squinted where his friend was pointing the camera. 'What?'

Wayne shot off three or four images then turned to Derek.

'The hearse, and the ambulance. Pity that reporter bloke ain't here to see it. He could have followed them on his motorbike and found out where they're going.'

59

Judith Tench's flat

The right-hand spool of the tape recorder was full. The left-hand one let go the last bit of tape which flicked through the guides, then flapped round and round as the full spool spun without restraint.

Symes leaned forward and pressed the stop button on the miniature machine. There was silence in the room, as he, Riley and Tench absorbed what they had just heard.

Tench was first to break the silence. 'Unbelievable. The foreign secretary wants to use the Eirene gas on Londoners? This makes him nothing less than a terrorist.'

'A terrorist with accomplices,' added Riley. 'The secretary for defence, our own Stone, and God knows who else.'

'Shall I bring him in for questioning?' asked Symes.

Riley and Tench looked at him. Tench furrowed her brow. 'Who?'

'God.'

Riley sighed and passed a hand across his forehead. 'Symes, this is no time for levity. Grow up. This is serious. If Eirene's used on our own citizens – illegally and without their knowledge, remember – it could harm twenty percent of the people subjected to it. So to release it over London, well…'

He paused as he did the maths in his head, but Tench was already there.

'It could put over one and a half million people in comas… or worse.'

Symes turned a mild shade of red. 'Sorry. You're right, and I know; it's worse than we feared.'

'On the other hand,' said Tench, 'we now have more than enough evidence. That driver, Daniel, was it? He deserves a medal.'

Symes nodded. 'He certainly deserves a bonus. He almost got caught. Says he was walking back to the car and saw Brown bend down, possibly to double-check the floor where his briefcase had fallen. If he'd looked under the seat he'd have found the recorder, but Daniel opened the door and distracted him. Seems they had actually finished talking and he was instructed to drive them back to their offices. It was a close thing. But I think we've got all we need.'

'I'll bring Walker up to date when I relieve her in Sub-2 later,' said Riley. He saw Tench raise an eyebrow.

'Yes, forgot to tell you, Stone has put us all back on observation duty. Said something about Major Wilson playing her end game and that he wanted to keep close tabs on it. Finally we'll be able to get a close-up view again of what's going on in the village.'

But Tench still looked worried. 'The thing I don't understand is why use a sledgehammer to break a nut? Why use something as big as a missile to quell a riot? I mean, surely the missile will kill or injure people when it falls from the sky. Why not just spray the gas from a helicopter or a plane?'

'Good point,' said Riley. 'I can only guess that Brown has, well, flipped his lid. That he wants to make a show of this and demonstrate not only the nation's power but his own. It's megalomania.'

Symes chipped in. 'Actually, I've learned from a contact in Defence that the missile is designed to fly at high altitude, and once over its target release a canister of the gas. This flies unpowered on a falling trajectory releasing the gas as it goes. A parachute at the rear will open and it will fall gently to the ground or onto a rooftop. It will raise questions but has no identifying markings. The missile meanwhile continues over and beyond the target to crash to the ground elsewhere. Hopefully in this case somewhere off the coast.'

'Except we can't let it come to that,' added Riley. 'As we just heard, Stone is now a key player. Obviously he has been all along, but now he's essentially in charge of the missile.'

Tench nodded. 'He has to be stopped, but what about your Major Wilson? How much does she know? Surely she must be in on it?

'Not according to the reports Walker's seen. In our absence Wilson's been reporting directly to Stone but copying in Anastasia, as instructed. There's no mention of a missile, although there were a few acerbic comments about her being excluded – along with the monitoring staff I might add – for almost a whole day while something happened in the village.'

'And I think we can assume that was the missile being installed,' Symes said to Tench. 'The date and times correspond with when it left the aerospace factory.'

A ringing telephone interrupted their talk. Tench went to answer, then came back into the lounge. 'Speak of the devil. It's for you, Riley. Anastasia Walker.'

He went to the phone and listened, grunted a few times, then hung up. He came back into the room looking worried.

'Yes, Walker, phoning from Sub-2. We have a problem. Your chum Barnaby has locked himself and our operative away in one of the village's underground chambers… for a whole week. Totally out of touch even with village control and with no communication with Monitoring either.'

'Why?' Tench and Symes both asked at the same time.

'A last-ditch attempt at breaking Number Six using regression therapy. Our Number Two has said it's a case of "till death us do part," and that only one of them will come out alive.'

60

Century House, Sub-basement 2

'Is this what you planned?' asked Walker incredulously, after she'd called Riley out of Wilson's hearing.

'Actually no,' admitted Wilson. She turned to watch the main monitor, which showed the activity in a subterranean chamber beneath the village's green domed building: Number Two guiding a 'young' Number Six through all his life stages, from schoolboy to intelligence officer. The round room was sparsely furnished with various simple props representing those ages and stages – a playpen, see-saw, rocking horse, blackboard, and so forth. To one side, and reached by some steps, was a compact 'apartment' complete with fully stocked kitchen, some furniture, even a waste disposal system. Ominously, there were bars across the front, access being via a sliding grille.

'It was Number Two's idea. Regression therapy,' Wilson said. 'By taking him back to his beginnings and leading him through his growing up – boyhood, schooling, wartime experiences, career in intelligence, right up to when he resigned – he might just tell us why he quit.'

'And it's seriously going to take a whole week?'

'That again was Carrington-Hall's choice. I would have done it in a day, maybe two, but we disagreed. He was very insistent.' She folded her arms and her reflection frowned back at her from the observation lounge window.

Anastasia Walker hadn't finished. 'But this "decree absolute" business, as Number Two calls it, that only one of them will leave the room alive. That's a bit extreme isn't it? To put it mildly.'

'Yes,' growled Wilson. 'Again, not an outcome I would have aimed for. If Six dies, then we'll never get the information we wanted and Stone certainly won't be happy.'

Walker increased the pressure. 'But it's murder, Major! He's proposing *murder*! He's a diplomat for God's sake, not an assassin. Six on the other hand has been a field operative – the best I might add – for years; he knows more than a thing or two about aggression, conflict, about how to handle himself. There can be only one outcome if push comes to shove.'

Wilson seemed unmoved, although after she'd returned to her observation role Walker had detected signs that she wasn't her usual confident self: a constant massaging of the neck with her hand, fingernails digging into her palms, and – the most obvious symptom of all – she was smoking, something Walker knew Wilson did but had never seen her do on duty. She was smoking now.

Wilson whipped round and stubbed out her cigarette with more force than necessary, squashing it into a smudge of ash, tobacco and filter. 'There's a contingency,' she said, glancing back at the window. 'As you can see, the only other one with them is the little butler, who's job at the moment is to support Number Two in his therapy tactics. He's been instructed to, let's say, "manage" the situation if required.'

Walker waited, but no further information was forthcoming. She resolved to bring it up again later though, or get Riley to when he took over the next shift.

The lounge door opened and Supervisor Holland stepped in brandishing a manila folder. He held it out for Olivia Wilson.

'Sorry to interrupt Major, this came for you. It's the file on the latest resident. He's just arrived.' She took it from him without a word. Holland glanced at Walker with an almost imperceptible nod and left. Walker knew what he meant; she had questioned him about Wilson's behaviour earlier and he'd confirmed what she thought: that she was showing signs of strain, and uncertainty, both wrapped up as barely concealed anger. She was losing control.

'Who is it?' Walker asked, even though she knew the answer. Wilson flicked open the file and scanned the few pages inside, along with what looked like a passport photo of the subject. It showed a young and cheeky face topped with curly hair, although being in black and white she couldn't tell what colour. He had strong cheekbones.

'Hmph,' grunted Wilson, tossing the file on the control desk. 'The last thing we need is another new resident. And with Two locked away for a week it's absolutely not good timing.' She picked up the red phone, and on the monitor showing the village control room they saw the supervisor pick up the call.

Walker listened as Wilson instructed him. 'This new arrival,' she said, 'go easy on him for the moment. With Two *hors de combat* you can keep an eye on him, but don't undertake any remedial work on…' – she checked the file again – 'Number 48 until we know the outcome of the regression therapy. I want your full focus on Two and Six. Is that clear?'

Walker had to stifle her sigh of relief; it meant that Tommy would be less likely to be subjected to re-education programming, or any other serious 'interventions.' It might give him some breathing space to begin his disruption. She moved to the desk and pretended to browse through the file but her mind wandered back to the last meeting she, Riley and

Symes had had with Tommy before he was taken to the village.

'Like I said before, what am I supposed to do?' Tommy had asked. Riley looked at Symes and said, 'Your turn.'

Symes had pulled up a chair, swivelled it backwards and sat on it. 'We don't have enough time to formulate a proper plan unfortunately. But as Riley pointed out, you have form as an actor, so that's what you'll have to do: act. The performance of your life.'

Tommy smirked. 'Going to be a tough audience.'

'It is, but you'll manage I'm sure. As you know now, the village is all about compliance, obedience. What those in charge can't stand is any behaviour that displays non-conformity, or disruption, as we've witnessed with the recalcitrant Number Six. That's perceived as failure on their part. So, the more you can disrupt and disturb the order of things, the more unsettled the hierarchy will become.'

Tommy nodded slowly, and cocked his head sideways, raised his eyebrows, indicating for Symes to continue.

'Yes, and the more unpopular you'll be. The best we can hope for is that you gain access to the missile silo and get a chance to damage the controls, or guidance system if you can find it. Don't even think about doing anything to the missile itself; if it's fuelled it's hazardous. There will be computers, plenty of them, which *are* easily damaged. And we'll need you to report directly to us.'

'You got a miniature radio for me then? A transmitter?' he scoffed.

'Actually we do have those available, but the problem is you'll be searched when you arrive, so that's not an option. However, luckily for us the community surveillance equipment is so total that we'll be able to hear your report or even see you give it if it's safe to do so, simply by commandeering one of the microphones or cameras in Monitoring.'

'That, however,' interjected Riley, 'means we'll have to receive your reports when Olivia Wilson's not on duty, and – slightly trickier – we'll need the agreement of one of the supervisors, probably Holland or McCauley. But leave that to us.'

They'd spread out a map of the community for Tommy and shown him where the best microphones and cameras were to use, and suggested one in particular on the edge of the grounds, one of the cameras hidden inside a statue.

Tommy laughed, but not with much humour. 'Sure man, I just roll on up to this sculpture and start chatting away to it. Easy. Happens all the time!'

Symes smiled an equally humourless smile. 'Obviously you'll do it when nobody else is around or can overhear you. But yes, you will have to be careful. So before you go we'll sort things out in Monitoring and let you know what times you'll be able to report.'

That was two days previously, and now here was Anastasia Walker wondering when she'd get a chance to reach an arrangement with Supervisor Holland. Unfortunately Wilson had arrived before she could broach the subject and had been here all shift.

She closed Tommy's file and put it on the control desk just as Riley arrived. He quickly glanced at her but she shook her head slightly: no opportunity yet.

Walker brought him up to date with what had been happening, wished him luck, and left. Wilson, still watching the main monitor as Two guided Six through his adolescence either failed to notice the shift change or was uninterested.

Riley tried small talk but Wilson was unresponsive, her attention fully on the screen. In the main monitoring section he saw Holland replaced by McCauley, and decided to take the opportunity.

He took Tommy's file and headed into the main room. If Wilson saw them she would assume Riley was discussing the new arrival.

However, first Riley needed to know that McCauley would comply. He proffered the file, but instead of referring to it said, 'McCauley, a discreet word if I may.'

'Of course. All ears.'

'Major Wilson. How has she been recently?' He saw McCauley raise his eyebrows, so Riley continued. 'In the sense of being fully in control. I only ask because Mr. Stone likes to keep tabs on things, and he's always keen on a second opinion, as it were.'

'Oh right! Of course. Naturally. Well, if I may speak candidly?'

Riley pointed to the open file in McCauley's hands. 'Without question. But let's just, for appearance's sake, look like we're discussing the new resident.'

McCauley relished the opportunity to indulge in a bit of deception, looked at the file and nodded. 'Right, yes. Well…'

And he told Riley all about Wilson's rage at her Big Ben project falling at the last hurdle, how her anger had manifested itself, and how all those in monitoring had been cowering in fear for a few moments.

'Since then she's seemed somewhat… distant,' he added. 'And certainly more irritable.'

Riley decided to go for it. 'That's what we thought. Thank you for confirming it. It's possible we will have to replace the Major, but for now Mr. Stone has given her an opportunity to redeem herself. But tell me – and please don't bother denying it because I checked the roster – a couple of weeks ago you were on duty during a period when the rest of Monitoring, including Major Wilson, were excluded from being here. What was that all about?'

And now McCauley's confidence faltered. He'd been told by Stone not to discuss anything he'd witnessed of the missile installation with anyone, emphasis on *anyone*. Riley could see he would need some gentle persuasion.

'The thing is McCauley, we believe there is someone in the organisation – very possibly here in Monitoring – who is passing information to the Soviets. An investigation is underway and everyone on this floor is subject to it, including yourself. One of the things that's being reviewed is who friends, family and, well, lovers might be, so we can do background checks on them. The examination will be total and thorough. Actually quite… *invasive*. And it will of course include all the supervisors here.'

He let the lie hang in the air. He knew he was taking a gamble; there was no investigation, not yet, but he had a feeling that McCauley might, in his personal life, have certain liaisons that might pose a security risk. It was pure guesswork of course. But it worked.

McCauley passed a hand across his brow and looked at the floor. 'I see. Right. Understood.' He looked directly at Riley. 'I'm not working for the Russians and I'm not passing information to anybody. But seemingly it's permissible to pass information to you…'

'Not only permissible. It's essential.'

McCauley told Riley everything he'd seen. When he'd finished, Riley decided the time was ripe to recruit him, which he did with ease. McCauley agreed to commandeer one of the village's cameras – the one they'd told Tommy to use – and that he would personally oversee that the feed came straight into the observation lounge for Riley, Symes, or Walker to view. Nobody else in Monitoring would be aware of it.

Riley had secured their communication line with Tommy.

61

Century House, Major Wilson's office

Olivia Wilson sat at her desk and contemplated the large sheets of newsprint paper she'd taped to a wall. They were full of diagrams and scribbles, circles, arrows and boxes. Some words were underlined in triple. It looked, she thought as she drew deeply on her cigarette, something like a work of abstract modern art.

But then she shook her head at her own lack of focus and stubbed out the remains of her smoke.

She stood and went to the charts, studied them up close, followed lines of thought, until finally her eyes settled on three words roughly yet urgently circled: *Judge, Jury, Execution?*

This was her final tactic, the last ploy. It was based on Number Six emerging from the subterranean chamber alive, having survived his regression therapy intact, and either having given them the information they wanted, or not. It didn't matter to her one way or the other now, she was almost beyond caring. And it assumed Number Two was dead, or at least incapacitated. That didn't matter either; she had no need of a subordinate in the village any more. The on-site controller could manage technicalities, but she would need someone to act for her… who, she wondered?

She returned to her desk and lit another cigarette, looked once again at the charts. Then she closed her eyes and leaned her head against her seat back, letting her mind wander to the village, its buildings, grounds, its subterranean chamber where Six and Two were approaching the end. The end of what? The regression therapy, sure, but the end of a life? Two lives?

Unlikely; if the butler did as instructed, Number Two's 'death' would be… temporary. And she had every confidence in Six surviving intact.

She cleared the thought from her head; it was clouding the issue. But then another cloud appeared on her mental horizon: Number 48.

The new arrival was proving disruptive, and the village controller had reported that he refused to wear the community uniform, was often 'at large' in the village grounds despite the attempts at security, and had apparently sabotaged the little taxis by putting sugar in their petrol tanks. He had set fire to a wooden folly in the grounds, and had been discovered exploring part of the subterranean area which he'd somehow managed to discover and access.

But he had been caught, and was now being held securely. Wilson had been tempted to order the use of drugs on him, or to put him through re-education, but with Six and Two's confinement about to reach a conclusion she didn't need the distraction. Holding 48 securely would be enough for the moment.

She opened her eyes and looked again at the charts. On the extreme right was a circle around the number Six, and an arrow pointing to another circle. In it was the number One. That's what he'll want, she thought, when he emerges. She had told the village controller to ask Six what he wished after he emerged victorious, and she knew he would want to meet Number One. She would oblige, but only in a manner of speaking.

She closed her eyes again and visualised the scenario: the now 'free' captive, victorious, vindicated, his struggle to regain and retain his freedom and individuality rewarded in its totality. He would be given back his original clothing, so that he could be 'himself.'

She decided at that moment that he would no longer be a number and would be addressed as 'sir.'

But she wanted to subject him to an intense review of his incarceration, a sort of 'passing out' parade, except all within the confines of the chamber. She had already engaged the most extras she had ever used for this last piece of drama, including the 'delegates' she had arranged to be placed in the village, who she foresaw acting akin to a jury. They would represent all the various sectors of society and would listen to the summation of the captive's actions and his resolve.

And while they were at it they could pass judgement on the upstart, Number 48. He would get his comeuppance, along with Number Two since he had failed, assuming he lived. If not, so be it.

She took a moment to congratulate herself on her supreme organisational skills. The 'extras' had been chosen weeks before, had been put on stand-by for short-notice deployment. They were new army recruits who had been put at her disposal, with the Ministry of Defence's blessing, and as such they would follow orders. They were in place, even if they didn't know where that place was. And they would be drugged, just as the village's residents were, to be compliant, malleable. They would not be soldiers; they would be puppets.

But where there's a jury, she'd realised, there must be a judge, hence the word scribbled on the charts. Or at least, in this case, a sort of master of ceremonies. She had someone in mind, but her thoughts were interrupted by her desk phone ringing. She picked up.

'Wilson.' She listened as the village controller gave her an update on the regression therapy. Forty-eight hours to go, and Six was gaining the upper hand. Still no confession, no reason for resigning.

'Maintain observation. Report on time.' She cut the connection and drew again on her cigarette. She thought for a moment, then reached a decision.

She picked up the phone again, pushed the button for an outside line, and dialled a number that was well known to her.

A woman's voice answered politely, giving the name of the organisation she worked for.

'It's Olivia Wilson here. My brother is in your care. I need to speak with him.'

62

Judith Tench's flat

'Well that's not helpful.' Tench topped up their Earl Grey tea and pushed the cups back across the kitchen table to Riley and Symes.

Riley shrugged. 'Unfortunately it was always on the cards. He was going to get caught sooner or later, but seemingly the 'do not harm' order that Major Wilson gave remains in place. However, we have lost our inside informant, at least for the time being.'

'What was his last report?' Tench asked.

Symes chipped in: 'That there had been more transport activity; a busload of people, which he saw arrive. It had blacked-out windows and it seems the inside was sealed off from the driver. We suspect the passengers are not supposed to know where they are, so they're a bit of a mystery. Tommy says he saw a number of large wicker baskets unloaded too, the sort he said that you might see in a theatre props department, holding costumes and suchlike. He didn't get a chance to see what was in them before he was captured though.'

'So something's imminent,' said Riley. 'A "cast of thousands." And add that to what Charles told us about the ambulance driver having also taken what he called "soldier types" to the village, it looks like the balloon's about to go up.'

'Well, not a balloon,' said Tench, 'a missile.'

'Agreed,' chipped in Symes. 'But I also agree with Riley: there's something else going on. All right, let's narrow it down; we know the missile is to be launched with its cargo of Eirene gas on Saturday, two days away.'

'And we know,' added Riley, 'that Carrington-Hall and Six are locked away until just before then, in fact about the same time as the launch must be scheduled. What does that mean I wonder?'

They fell silent as they contemplated the timing. Tench spoke first: 'Well, if Six emerges victorious maybe he'll be able to stop the launch. That's if he even knows about it.'

Riley nodded. 'And if he doesn't – know about it, or stop it – then it's all over. The missile launches and…' his voice trailed off; silence took over again as they contemplated the consequences. The outcome didn't bear thinking about, and yet that's exactly what had to be done.

Riley slapped the table. 'We need to be in Monitoring for when Six – or Two – wins the battle of the minds, and we need to be able to see whatever coverage there might be of the launch site, the silo, or control room. McCauley says there's another blackout of staff scheduled for that time – just as there was when the missile was installed. He says only he and Stone will be present.'

'We can't let that happen,' Symes said. 'We need to somehow force Stone to call off the launch. Could McCauley do that?'

Riley chuckled. 'McCauley? No. He's not the "man of action" we need. Although…'

They both looked at him and waited, but Riley was vague. 'Maybe he could be of use. But you know what? I have a feeling that we've missed a potential ally who might be of use.'

'Who?' Tench and Symes both asked together.

'Major Olivia Wilson.'

Silence again, this time as Tench and Symes absorbed the bombshell.

'I thought you'd said she was becoming, what was the word you used? *Unhinged?*' Tench said.

Riley nodded. 'Yes, and increasingly at odds with Stone. They are both on the cusp of individual personal achievements: she's about to witness the culmination of all her efforts to break Six while Stone is under orders to oversee the launch of the missile. And from the recording we recently heard, Stone is not a fully compliant accessory in this, while Wilson is also not in control. Put the two together and we've got a perfect firestorm, and if we can get in there to dampen the flames then maybe, just maybe, we'll be able to do something.'

'I've got another idea,' Tench added. 'George Brown. If you've got Stone and Wilson together in the same room, and we can isolate Brown and confront him at about the same time, we get the treble.'

Riley patted her hand. 'And how, my dear, would we do that?'

Tench rapidly pulled her hand away. 'Oh don't be such a misogynist. Really. I am MI5 you know, and George Brown is a terrorist. It's time I alerted our lot to the threat.'

63

Century House, Sub-basement 2

Olivia Wilson chewed a fingernail as she watched the final moments tick away in the village's subterranean chamber, 'home' to numbers Six and Two for the past week. McCauley stood beside her.

'Looks rather like they've, er, swapped places,' McCauley said tentatively.

Wilson snorted. 'They have. Six has the upper hand now; Two is in decline.'

On the large main screen it was now Carrington-Hall who was being manipulated. The prisoner had come through the regression therapy without revealing a thing that wasn't already known about him. As the final hours ticked away, Number Two's confidence had waned with every sweep of the second hand on the large wall clock.

He'd had one last stab at re-establishing a connection with his adversary: he poured them both a drink and engaged in convivial banter about the chamber's 'apartment,' which, he disclosed in an off-guard moment, was detachable.

There then followed a bizarre sequence in the remaining few minutes during which Carrington-Hall was quickly reduced by his cellmate to a snivelling wreck of a man, a mere husk of his former self-assured, diplomatic self.

His buoyancy crumbled, he crawled, begged for pity, stumbled into the apartment and shakily topped up his glass, took a final drink. Within seconds he had collapsed to the floor of the accommodation. Six bent over and checked for a pulse, seemingly finding none. Two's eyes stared sightlessly at the ceiling.

Time was up. The chamber's steel doors hummed open, and the village's controller entered. He locked the apartment grille, said that the body would be needed 'for evidence,' than asked Number Six what he desired.

As he replied, 'Number One,' Olivia Wilson whispered the same words in synch with him, then punched her right fist into her left hand. 'Yes! Exactly as I predicted!' she shouted. 'Exactly!'

Her face, reflected in the observation window, smiled broadly back at her, the first time it had done so since the operation had begun.

'Congratulations,' said a smooth voice behind them. McCauley and Wilson both jumped and turned. They hadn't heard anyone come in, but there he was: Stone, a tight smirk on his face, but with eyes that lived up to his name; they were as cold as granite.

'Sir! I… I didn't know you were coming…' stammered Wilson, her exuberance draining away along with the blood from her face.

Stone's eyes bored into McCauley. 'I believe you have duties.' McCauley bowed slightly and said, 'Yes of course, as you instructed sir,' and left the lounge in some haste, making a point of avoiding Wilson's eye.

'Well, congratulations,' scoffed Stone, obviously not meaning it. 'You've excelled yourself.'

Wilson said nothing. Her face reddened, her spine turning into an iron rod, her neck as stiff as concrete.

Stone walked to the observation window where the main screen showed Six reclaiming his own clothes, as Wilson had dictated. As with many newly-released caged animals, the former captive showed hesitancy, uncertain whether this was yet another ruse, or whether he was genuinely on the edge of freedom.

'And it's not over yet,' Stone said, almost to himself. He turned to Wilson with a raised eyebrow. 'I gather from your last report that you have one last set-piece, a finale.'

Wilson felt it was now or never if she were to claw back any degree of authority, confidence, or what was left of her career. She stood more upright, feet shoulder-width apart, hands behind her back.

'Yes sir. He is now to be judged and given the choice between remaining in the village as its leader, or the freedom to go. He hasn't revealed anything about why he resigned and I believe he's not likely to do so to anyone else.'

She moved to the observation window, but something caught her eye, distracting her from the screen. Below, in the gloom of Monitoring's main floor, the operators were packing up their bags and satchels and beginning to file out as McCauley looked on. Within a few moments the whole space had been vacated.

'Where…?' Wilson's voice trailed off as she realised that something was happening to which she wasn't a party.

'They're leaving, on my orders,' said Stone, turning away from the window and taking three paces back into the lounge. He stopped and turned. 'And you will too.'

Wilson felt the ground almost sway beneath her.

'But sir, I haven't finished! We're about to have a last go at breaking Six, giving him a real taste of freedom, giving him a final chance to tell us why he resigned because… because it doesn't matter anymore! It's…'

Stone held up a hand. 'It's over, Major Wilson. At least for you.'

Suddenly the door opened, and Riley and Symes burst in. Stone looked aghast.

'You two? What are you doing here? Never mind, I don't care, but Monitoring is off-limits for the next couple of hours. Get out!'

When they failed to move, he yelled. 'NOW! I said get out!'

'No, they're staying.'

It was Wilson. They all turned to her, only to find they were looking down the barrel of a .9mm Browning HP pistol which she held expertly in a two-handed and very confident grip.

She waggled the gun slightly. 'Shuffle together. No sudden moves.' They did. 'Now, the three of you, through the door, and stay tightly together. Go.'

They did as they were instructed and without question. The calm on Wilson's face, the self-assurance in her demeanour, the focus in her eyes, was evidence enough that she was in total control. The gun in her hands was unwavering, rock steady.

They filed out of the door, until all four of them were through and standing above the rows of tiered monitor screens, Wilson maintaining a safe distance behind her three captives. Quentin McCauley turned from watching the main screen.

Wilson didn't wait for him to react. 'McCauley, sit at the desk nearest to you and face the front. Riley, lock the main door. Don't even think of opening it.' He did as he was told, without deviation.

'Now,' she said to them when Riley had rejoined the group, 'do the same, the desks nearest where he's sitting. All of you sit, face the front and place both hands on the monitor in front of you. You as well McCauley. If you take even a single finger off it you'll find out how good a shot I am. Do it.'

Once again they obeyed. Now Wilson moved to stand two rows behind them as they sat in the front row, their torsos clearly outlined against the glow of the huge main screen; perfect targets should any of them make a move. She was reminded of a row of tin ducks at a fairground shooting range, a sideshow where she had never failed to win the main prize of a huge teddy bear or panda after slaughtering the entire flock. Her brother never won a prize, and she never gave him any of hers. If he couldn't shoot as well as she could, then tough.

She forced herself back to the present. On the screen the surveillance cameras showed that the village controller had led the prisoner and the butler – who, it seemed, had now swapped allegiance to his new master – down a sloping passage towards a rugged door at the bottom. It swung open and she watched as they entered a huge cavern with smooth floor. Within were troops of soldiers in helmets, overalls, and with machine guns slung over their shoulders. A medical team in scrubs was setting up off to one side, and in the centre on a dais was an elaborate chair, a throne. Beyond it, she saw, were three tiers of robed and hooded figures, each wearing masks in a nod to the comedy and tragedy symbols of the theatre: one side happy, one side sad, one side black, one side white. It was surreal, even though she had requested some of the more theatrical touches herself. But soldiers she had definitely not asked for. Or the technicians manning the bank of computers on a raised platform at the back of the chamber.

'What's this?' she asked in disbelief. 'What the hell is this? Stone! Talk!'

Stone lifted a hand off the monitor in front of him and started to turn towards her. The screen in front of him exploded in a shower of glass, smoke issuing from the monitor's innards and sparks intermittently flickering and jumping on to the desk in front of him. The noise of the shot in the room deafened them all.

'The next one goes through your head,' Wilson announced calmly when silence had resumed. 'Hands back where they were. Talk.' Stone didn't argue. His fingers gripped the sides of the blackened monitor, his knuckles white.

But it was Riley who spoke. 'Major Wilson. You don't seriously propose to shoot all four of us do you? How many rounds does that thing hold?'

Wilson swivelled the gun in his direction. 'Shut up Riley. More than enough to kill you all twice over. Three times actually. Stone! I said *talk*.' The Browning's aim settled back on Stone's silhouetted bald head, and this time he talked without moving.

'The chamber you see on the screen is a launch control room. There's a missile over on the left, ready for launch, you can see the vapours from it.'

Wilson's forehead creased. 'What missile?'

And so Stone told her about the Eirene project. And Unity.

For just a moment Wilson's Browning dropped slightly as she processed what she was hearing. She even sat at the desk nearest her while she listened, her hands resting on the monitor in front of her, but with the Browning still aimed in the direction of her targets. Not that any of her captives noticed – they didn't dare turn round.

On the screen there was chaos. The launch chamber doubled as the quasi-courtroom Wilson had envisaged, only her plan had been to establish it in the same chamber as Two and Six had just completed their battle of wits.

'Why is my "finale" being held here?'

Again it was Stone who spoke. 'Because it conflicts with the timing of the launch. I thought it prudent to combine the two events. Up to a point. I really do admire your work you know Major, you've been very inventive, very… creative in your attempts to break our subject. And this final evaluation… this critical summary of what we've seen over recent months is commendable. I wouldn't have missed it for the world. I can recommend you for a promotion, you know. In fact, I will.'

Wilson, again for a moment, allowed herself a sense of satisfaction, but she knew deep down that this was Stone trying to win her round, attempting to sweet-talk her, catch her off guard. Well he wouldn't.

'Shut up. You…' But she was interrupted by the banging of a gavel.

They all watched the screen as a 'judge' dressed in fine orange robes and with the full requisite white wig, called the assembly to order. He was erudite, in control, and yet, Riley thought, slightly… manic?

The judge explained that they were there to solve an issue of democracy, and revolt. He invited Number Six to take the throne, which, surprisingly, he did. The judge gave an award-winning and masterful performance as he addressed the chamber and the robed and hooded delegates behind him, a performance delivered as though his life depended on it.

As he spoke, McCauley, Riley, Symes and Stone heard a sniff behind them. Then another. They all wanted to turn to see what was happening, but couldn't risk it.

Wilson uncupped one hand from under the butt of the Browning and wiped away a tear from her cheek, then another on the other side with the back of her hand. Her brother was performing flawlessly.

Outside Monitoring, in the corridor, Anastasia Walker very gently punched in the access code and slowly tried the door handle. As she expected, it was locked.

'No good,' she whispered to the man and woman who were with her. They both held firearms, but now returned them to their shoulder holsters.

Walker pressed the earphone tighter into her ear and listened, but shook her head. 'Nothing apart from whatever's happening on the screen,' she reported. 'And that sounds like something out of a courtroom drama.'

She listened again, to try and hear anything that Riley's hidden microphone might pick up. 'Wilson appears to have gone quiet…'

The man, D'Amelio, said quietly, 'What next? The only other option is the fire door, but it opens outwards and there's no handle this side…'

'Then that's not an option,' Walker replied irritably.

Caitlin Trainor, crouching next to him, spoke in her soft Irish accent: 'What about the ceiling panels? Is there a void up there we can access?'

Walker chewed her lip. 'Maybe. We'd need to look at the building's plans and I have no idea where they are, or even if we have them. And we don't have time.' She sighed. 'All we know at this stage is that Wilson's got Stone, Riley, Symes and McCauley captive. She's army trained and an expert shot; she won't make any mistakes. She must also know there's no way out of this for her whatever happens. But we can't risk four lives. We've got to *do something*.'

She went back to listening, but could only hear the judge on the main screen, now once again eloquently addressing the assembly and then… who was that? Someone, a male, talking very hip, talking in… what was the word? Jive, that was it. At one point whoever it was started singing a song: *Dem bones, dem bones, dem, dry bones…* then it dawned on her that it was Tommy, engaged in what sounded like a random banter contest with the judge who was getting more and more irritated with the rebellious Number 48.

D'Amelio spoke up again. 'It's a sloping floor in there isn't it? So when maintenance have to change light bulbs, they're unlikely to use a ladder. They're more likely to access the ceiling lights from above, so there *must* be a void.'

'Wait! Lights,' whispered Walker with urgency. 'Maybe that's it. What if we cut off all power to the room – screens, lighting, everything – they'd be plunged into darkness.'

Trainor shook her head. 'But ma'am, that wouldn't solve the problem; Wilson would still be armed even if the others could take cover. And sure wouldn't there be emergency lighting?'

'As far as I know the fire door is the only one with an emergency light, just a box with "Fire Exit" glowing green above it.'

'But with her military background that might still be enough for Wilson to pick them off,' D'Amelio cautioned.

Walker chewed her lip again, then said, 'Not if we were quick enough. You're field operatives, don't we have explosives? Couldn't we blow this door off its hinges at the same time as we cut the power?'

D'Amelio and Trainor looked at each other and smiled. 'Now you're talking,' Trainor said. She grabbed D'Amelio by the arm. 'Come on, let's go!'

*

Stone's arms were tiring, dropping slightly as he tried to maintain his hold on the shattered monitor in front of him. The others were wearying also, holding such unnatural positions for so long. Necks were stiffening, shoulders aching.

Riley used the cover of the noise on the screen – as Tommy raced around the launch chamber creating momentary havoc before he was caught again – to whisper to Symes beside him: 'We need to be ready. Anastasia will almost certainly try something with a field team. When it kicks off we'll have to move quickly.'

'Don't I know it old boy,' said Symes, flexing his fingers on the monitor to encourage circulation.

'Quiet!' Wilson shouted, 'or I'll put a bullet through someone.'

Symes shut up.

*

Outside, Walker nodded her head and whispered to herself. 'Good man Riley. You know we're coming.' She had just been able to make out what Riley had whispered to Symes.

She checked her watch. They'd been under Olivia Wilson's watchful eye for at least half an hour, and Walker knew that before long Wilson would have to make a move.

'Come on!' she whispered. 'Where the hell are you D'Amelio?'

Then her attention was caught by something; in her earpiece she heard a command given, not by Wilson, but on screen, in the launch chamber. 'Resuscitate!'

What followed was a miracle. Not in the biblical sense, she realised, but a miracle of science. After listening for a while to the activity in the chamber it dawned on her that it was Number Two, Carrington-Hall, who had been resuscitated, brought 'back from the dead.' And judging by his laughter and joviality he was very happy about it.

But his jubilation did not last long. His mood changed when he realised he had lost his status. She heard him address the assembly, expressing regret that he himself had resisted against the village autocracy for so little time, and finally – acknowledging that Number Six had emerged victorious – he relinquished his position as Number Two. He was taken away.

Walker jumped as she felt a tap on her shoulder. She turned to find D'Amelio and Trainor kneeling beside her. They had a tray full of bars of C4 plastic explosives, cables, detonators and a battery. They had also found time to visit the armoury: both now carried general support M60-20 machine guns slung over their shoulders.

D'Amelio winked. 'Did somebody order room service?'

*

Wilson was thinking hard about how to bring the situation to a conclusion, but her mind was torn as she was mesmerised by her brother's amazing performance in the chamber on the main screen. She had taken him from the care home, exercising her authority as his legal guardian, and promising to return him 'in a few days.'

She had gently persuaded him to take part in her last piece of grand theatre, told him all about the village, its community, its hierarchy, and about her failure to break the man who quit his job as an intelligence officer.

She said her brother could now play the role of a lifetime, and that if he did well she would arrange for his release from the mental hospital. And yet she had, out of his hearing, promised the charge nurse to return him there.

Looking at the sitting ducks in front of her, and knowing that she was as trapped as they were, he might, she realised with genuine regret, have to find his own way back.

She shook her head to clear it, her attention once more on the screen. Her brother's address to the assembly was coming to a close. He offered Number Six a choice: freedom, or the opportunity to 'lead' the village community. The delegates were quiet, the soldiers scattered around the room's perimeter on alert. Tommy and Carrington-Hall had been secured and transported to an even deeper chamber further underground. She had no particular plans for them. They could rot there for all she cared.

And then she saw her brother invite the former prisoner to step onto a platform similar to those which had taken Carrington-Hall and Tommy down below. He was finally to meet 'Number One.'

He cautiously stepped onto the elevator plate, which wasted no time descending through the floor, taking him to his destiny.

With her brother's role complete, Wilson stood, looked at her charges and, still holding the Browning steady and ready, walked slowly round in front to face them, her back to the main screens.

They could now see that her face was blotchy, her eyes red. They realised she'd been crying, but why?

Riley took the opportunity to speak, partly to try and engage Wilson, but mainly so that Anastasia through her earpiece would get a clearer picture of what she and her team would face when they burst in, as he knew they surely must.

'Major Wilson. There is no way this situation can end well. You stand there in front of the four of us, with your gun pointed at us with, what did you hint at? Twelve rounds? Enough to kill us all three times over? And where would that get you? A life sentence? Four life sentences?'

'Shut up Riley. Stand up all of you, let go of the monitors, put your hands on your heads.'

They did as they were told. There was no option.

'Now, line up here where I'm standing, in front of the screen facing towards the room.' She moved aside, always keeping a safe distance, out of range of any attempt to strike her with fist, arm or leg. They did as instructed. She backed up one level of the steps, then two, and stopped.

Riley tried again. 'Major, lining us up to shoot us? Really? Do you…'

The gunshot was deafening. Riley fell backwards and tumbled to the floor.

The others turned in horror, their hands now dropping from their heads.

Wilson's face was a mask of anger, hate, fury. 'I SAID HANDS ON…'

But she never finished her sentence. The lights went out. All the monitor screens died. The main screen went dark. Everyone froze in place. The only light now was a faint green glow from the fire exit sign, but it was enough.

Wilson stepped one pace forward, lined up her gun on Stone's forehead. 'You. You're to blame for all of this, Stone.' She squeezed the trigger.

But the gunshot was lost in a much larger explosion that sent debris, smoke and dust flying into the room as the wads of C4 explosive blew the main door and its frame to pieces.

Shadowy figures darted in through the hole in the wall where the door had been and disappeared into the murk to the left. Dashing to the other side, Anastasia Walker shone a bright torch through the smoke, picking out Wilson at the front, three crumpled figures behind her, one still standing.

Wilson brought up the Browning, aimed for the torch and squeezed the trigger again, but if any shot was fired it was drowned out by multiple bursts of machine gun fire.

Lying in a pool of sticky blood on the floor, Riley's consciousness slipped away. His last thought before darkness overtook him was, 'That's an awful lot of guns.'

*

High above North Wales a missile flew across the sky, gaining height rapidly as it turned and headed towards its target.

64

Grove Park Cemetery, London

Black was the order of the day, as it is with most funerals. The few mourners stood around the grave as the minister went through his routine, ashes to ashes, dust to dust, so forth. Autumn leaves skittled across the ground, blown by a cold wind, some falling into the open grave as the casket was lowered in.

An elderly couple to one side consoled each other, with other family members adding support around them.

Unusually, in the background, the hearse was still there, parked on the road that ran through the cemetery. A tall older man in formal funeral attire, with top hat now held respectfully in front of him, stood beside it.

His younger assistant, similarly dressed, came round from the passenger side and stood beside him.

'Go on,' said Charles. 'Pay your respects.' And he gently pushed his assistant towards the group gathered around the grave. Tommy didn't resist.

He came up and stood beside Symes, who glanced briefly at him, then turned his attention back to the ceremony before him. 'Number 48,' he said. 'Good of you to come.'

'Least I could do.'

'You've done more than enough Tommy. There was nothing you could have done about this though.' He bent, picked up a handful of dirt, and cast it into the grave, just as others were doing. Except in his case it was a very casual toss, without much emotion or respect.

Riley edged up to them, his arm in a sling. 'Thanks for coming,' he said to Tommy.

'I'm here on duty, man.'

'Yes, but you didn't have to actually come graveside,' whispered Riley, gesticulating at the mound of earth and wincing as the pain reminded him how close he'd come to death himself. 'But he'd have appreciated it, even though you never met him.'

The minister finished his service. Everyone said 'amen', and that was it. The gathering began to drift away in ones, twos and threes, the cemetery gravediggers respectfully waiting until the opportune moment to move in with their shovels.

Riley, Symes and Tommy stayed where they were for a bit longer.

'So what actually happened?' Tommy asked.

Riley and Symes looked at each other. Riley said, 'I'll let Symes tell you that; I was out of it for a while.' He walked slowly away.

Symes put an arm round Tommy's shoulders and led him just far enough away that the gravediggers could begin their work unhindered.

'You did everything right young man,' he said. 'You've made us proud.'

'Yeah, well… thanks. But…' he gesticulated towards the grave, now being filled in.

'Ah yes,' said Symes. 'Poor old McCauley. I think you already know what the situation was in our Monitoring section when Major Wilson took over, as it were. But she wasn't actually in control, not of herself anyway. We're fairly certain she was emotionally disturbed, though she fell back on her military training and kept us all tightly reined in. When she shot Riley we believe she deliberately aimed for his shoulder – no mean feat, but she was an expert shot. I don't believe she ever intended to kill him. But Stone? That was

304

different. She was definitely about to dispatch him, but just as she fired, two things happened: The power went off and the lights went out. McCauley dived either in front of Stone or to push him clear; we'll never know. Either way he took three bullets full in the back, actually saved Stone's life. At exactly the same time the C4 explosives did their job: they blew the bloody doors off, the rescue team came in and the rest, as they say, is history.'

Anastasia Walker had quietly joined them. Tommy nodded to her.

'It was chaos,' she added. 'I held my torch out at arm's length and Wilson fired at it. Given the smoke, the noise, and as I say, chaos, she shot very well. The torch flew out of my hand in pieces, but,' and here she waggled her right hand at him, 'I am intact. In fact, intact enough to shake your hand.' Which she did. Tommy blushed.

'Neither of you seems too upset though,' Tommy said. 'Didn't you work with this guy?' he said, waving a hand towards the rapidly-filling grave.

'We did,' said Walker. 'But we also knew that someone inside our organisation was leaking information to the Soviets, and it turns out it was McCauley. He was – however reluctantly – recruited by them. They had a hold over him. But it seems his recruitment was quite recent and before he died in hospital he said he hadn't told them much. We hope that's true.

'Deathbed confession,' said Tommy. 'What did they have on him?'

Anastasia furrowed her brow and looked towards where the gravediggers were busy with their shovels. 'That's something he's taken to the grave I'm afraid.'

65

Judith Tench's flat

Riley stretched his legs out and very gently massaged his shoulder with his fingers. The doctors had said he was healing nicely and would regain full use of his arm and shoulder, although they said it was likely his squash and tennis days were over. Luckily, he'd told them, he didn't play either.

Judith Tench came into the lounge, headed to the cocktail cabinet, and poured them both a generous glass of whiskey. She handed Riley's to him and sat beside him on the couch.

'So,' she said, 'one more funeral to go. Here's to the departed.' She clinked her glass against his.

'Yes,' he sighed. 'One more. And with full military honours. I don't get it, I really don't. I mean she shot me!' Even his voice sounded wounded.

Tench chuckled. 'And let you live. Could have been worse.'

They both took sips and drifted away into their own thoughts for a while. The fire crackled in its grate, grey clouds scudded across the leaden sky outside the windows, the trees in Tench's garden – bare gnarled fingers – reached up as though in search of sun and warmth.

'What's the latest on our George?' Riley asked.

'Tired and emotional George Brown?' Tench laughed. 'Well, as you know, we picked him up the morning of the supposed missile attack on London. Thanks to his driver, Daniel Forbes, working with us, we knew exactly when he was being collected and where he was going, so we didn't even have to follow him. We just waited at his weekend retreat on the Thames in Middlesex and met him there. Much to his surprise.'

Riley nodded. 'Yes, so I heard, but what now?'

Tench put her glass down and turned to him. 'He's working for us.'

Riley's eyebrows shot up. 'For you? For MI5? You're joking.'

'I never joke in my work Mr. Riley,' said Tench, paraphrasing a line from her favourite Bond film. 'No seriously, in return for, let's say, a "degree of immunity" he's keeping us in the loop on all cabinet affairs, his foreign secretary portfolio, and how his diplomatic endeavours are going with our friends and others overseas. Even the so-called plot against Harold Wilson, although we're still not so sure about that. He's proving useful.'

'You pay him?'

'We keep him in drink.'

Riley chortled, then frowned. 'And have you seen Carrington-Hall's report yet?'

Tench smiled. 'I have, and so shall you.' She got up and went to an elegant rosewood davenport, lowered the lid and withdrew a file. She handed it to him.

'There. Consider it an early Christmas present. It's a copy, which of course I'm not supposed to have, so if you tell anyone I'll have to get my fruit knife. Anyway, read it – it's why I invited you over.'

'And here's me thinking it was for my witty conversation and charming company.'

He opened the file and began reading.

Report No. 112TS/Dept.5/1967/11
Author: Barnaby Carrington-Hall, DFC, GCMG
11 December, 1967

Preamble

I have been privileged to have served my country in numerous and various capacities in my career as a civil servant – and latterly senior diplomat – since the 1940s. But I have never witnessed anything quite so extraordinary as what I saw earlier this year when I was 'invited' to take part in what I was led to believe was the interrogation of a rogue secret intelligence service operative. It was felt that my diplomatic experience might succeed where others had failed.

I was, in short, seconded to a classified British joint intelligence 'retirement community' established on a coastal location in North Wales, where I was to be in command of the commune until such time as I had discovered why its latest resident (see above) had resigned from the service.

It was a place I had been to before, about a year previously when I was sent as an observer. My report at that time (ref. 015TS/Cas./1966/5) made it clear that I was concerned for the welfare of the so-called 'retirees'; that they were being held against their will, were being medicated beyond what might be called a 'reasonable level,' and that the

general operation of the place
(usually referred to as the
'facility,' or 'village') was
bordering on a dictatorship.

This year, when I was contacted
by a Major Olivia Wilson – who was
seconded at the time to the SIS – and
asked to return to the village - this
time in the capacity of its leader -
I was wary. But since my earlier
report had apparently been stamped,
filed, indexed and ignored, I decided
to undertake the assignment in the
faint hope that I would see positive
changes and commendable progress in
the running of the place. I saw no
such thing.

Report

The operative, who for security
purposes I have been told should
remain nameless, had resigned
suddenly from his job. He had
indicated it was on a matter of
principle, but I was told by Major
Wilson that in his anger he quit
without giving any further detail.

The security service therefore
was concerned that he carried
invaluable information in his head
and might offer it to a foreign
power, or be captured by such and
have the information forced out of
him.

Quite separately to this, and before I was allocated my turn in the village, I was contacted by an intelligence officer from the same organisation who told me that this charming innocent-looking retirement village was being used for 'experimental purposes;' that the residents had been given various medications, drugs, and therapies, and that they were being used in psychological experiments without their consent. I must say I wasn't surprised; it confirmed what I feared. He further indicated that the Ministry of Defence, which owns the land the village is on, were developing a new biological agent to be used in theatres of war, one that could render an enemy ineffective. In fact they would become docile, compliant, obedient, to the extent that…

Riley skimmed through the next few of pages, flicking them over in haste. He saw enough detail to confirm that Carrington-Hall had not been endeared to Wilson and that he had maintained his own modus operandi, which had caused friction between them.

Tench came over and topped up his glass.

'Are you speed-reading or have you lost interest?'

Riley took a sip of his whiskey. 'No, I just want to get to the bits I don't know about. Like any good novel, one wants to see what happened in the end!'

He went back to the report, picking up the narrative where Carrington-Hall and Tommy had been taken below the launch chamber in restraints.

… we were confined in glass or clear plastic cylinders. Our arms were held securely by metal straps, while around us staff or technicians in the same white robes as the so-called delegates above worked at control panels or similar. There was nothing we could do.

My fellow captive, Number 48, had tried in the chamber above to cause havoc, to disrupt as best he could, (as instructed, so I learned later), but now we could do nothing.

And then, out of nowhere, Number Six arrived along with my erstwhile support colleague the butler. I hoped they would free us immediately, but Six had other things on his mind: he wanted to meet the mysterious Number One, and was guided up a spiral staircase by the butler to do so.

I learned from the operative later that there was no Number One, just another figure in a gown wearing a monkey mask, and when that was removed Six came face to face with himself.

I know it sounds bizarre, but I have seen more unbelievable things in the village than that. I presume whoever was wearing the robe was also wearing a mask moulded from Number Six's face, and I assume this was yet another of Major Wilson's crazy concepts.

What followed was a melee. Six tried to achieve what Number 48 couldn't – to disrupt the technology and the systems to the point where the missile would be rendered either inoperative or ineffective. This, it transpired, had been his plan all along: to put a stop to the Unity project, which he'd uncovered by accident.

So it was time for him to fight back. He and the butler did an excellent job of incapacitating the technicians and soldiers with a combination of fire extinguishers and fisticuffs, finally freeing Number 48 and I in the process.

He later told me that he'd found the guidance system and had randomly altered it, and – this I thought rather dangerous – had started the missile launch sequence. You will have to ask him why he did that; he never told me.

Arming ourselves with the weapons we'd taken from the soldiers, we made our way back up to the launch chamber. Time was now against us; the missile was about to launch - we had to escape.

Six led the attack using a machine gun he'd taken from one of the soldiers. We followed, but it was a fierce firefight: four of us against far more of them, but it was one of their own weapons – a large machine gun on a rotating platform – that helped save the day. The machine gunner was knocked out of action but with his finger still on the trigger the gun kept firing, the platform swivelling round the room and taking down many of the soldiers.

The delegates, technical staff and others had now been given the order to evacuate. They fled, the firing finally stopped, and I led our band of mutineers to the supposed 'apartment' that Six and I had used in the regression therapy. It was on a transporter, as I knew of course, and had originally been backed into place, so in fact all we had to do was climb aboard and drive out.

The butler brought his driving skills into play and took us in the truck along a dark tunnel until eventually we crashed through the gate at the end and out into the light. And freedom.

Above us we saw multiple helicopters, used, I'm guessing, to evacuate the village's personnel.

Just as we joined a proper sealed road the missile streaked overhead, but where it was headed we of course didn't know. I later learned that it had altered course and crashed

harmlessly into the Irish Sea, so
Six's disruption worked.

Riley flipped through the few remaining pages but decided a further sip of whiskey was more in order, by way of celebration if nothing else. He closed the file and placed it on the seat cushion next to him.

'Well? What do you think?'

Riley shrugged, then winced. 'Ow!' he cried, as his shoulder reminded him that shrugging was off-limits for a while.

'I think, dear Judith, that we all got off lightly. Cheers.'

The doorbell chimed and Tench went to answer it. When she returned it was with Symes.

'Here, let me take your coat,' Judith said to him.

'No, it's all right thanks, I can't stay. Just thought I'd pop in as I was passing. I knew Riley was here.'

'How?' Riley asked.

Symes's dimples formed two craters in his cheeks. 'Need-to-know, old boy,' and winked.

'Did you have me followed here?'

Symes feigned shock. 'Me? No of course not. But didn't you see the hearse behind you?'

Riley laughed. 'Actually no. And anyway, why would it be there?'

'Well, you have resigned…'

Tench intervened. 'No, he hasn't; he's retired. That's not the same thing. Anyway, at least stay long enough for a drink.'

She poured him a glass and handed it to him.

'Let's have a toast,' Tench said.

'To whom or what?' asked Riley.

'Well,' smiled Tench, 'given that Christmas isn't far off, and given also the nature of Unity, how about "peace for all"?'

They laughed, clinked their glasses together, and drank.

EPILOGUE

Stone was relieved of his position as chief of his department and forced out of the intelligence community. Anastasia Walker replaced him as director general.

Symes, as expected, filled the vacancy left by Riley's retirement.

Chris Watkins was given copies of various reports into Unity but they were heavily redacted. She was restricted in how much she could report, and 'encouraged' to focus instead on the general reduction of biological weapons within the military. As a result she resigned as assistant political editor to write a book on Unity and the role of the British intelligence services in it. Publishers rejected it out of hand as being too absurd. It has never been published.

George Brown resigned as foreign secretary in 1968 after ongoing disagreements with Prime Minister Harold Wilson. He was given a seat in the House of Lords. There is no evidence that he was a terrorist or was plotting a coup against the prime minister.

Barnaby Carrington-Hall was appointed to lead a full independent inquiry into the Ministry of Defence's and the Security Intelligence Service's roles in Unity, the village, and the use of its residents for experimental purposes. On his recommendation the village was closed down. At Porton Down the development of the Eirene gas was allowed to continue, but only on the basis of medical research. The MoD's role in having oversight of the Eirene project was rescinded.

Tommy continued to work for Charles for a while and was offered a full-time job in security intelligence by Symes. However, he declined and later quit his mechanic's role, deciding instead to travel the world. His so-called 'criminal record' was wiped clean by Symes. Symes's offer of a job remained open.

Riley retired to a cottage in the country. Judith Tench, having resigned her cover position as senior policy advisor to Alec Douglas-Home, joined him there after a couple more years with MI5.

'Number Six' returned to his flat in London accompanied by the butler who had offered him his services. The former intelligence officer was given the opportunity to return to his role in the SIS but declined, saying his resignation still stood. After contributing to Carrington-Hall's independent inquiry he gave the butler the option of moving on, which he took. Six himself slipped quietly out of Britain, a free man. His whereabouts are unknown, although his Lotus sports car was last seen in Australia.

INFORMATION

Biological Warfare Experiments in Britain

These actually took place, with, in some cases, the public used as 'guinea pigs' without their consent or knowledge. The following paragraphs are courtesy of Wikipedia…

The Dorset Biological Warfare Experiments were a series of experiments conducted between 1953 and 1975 to determine the extent to which a single ship or aircraft could dispense biological warfare agents over the United Kingdom. …Tests, between 1971–1975, were known as the DICE trials. The tests were conducted by scientists from Porton Down, initially using zinc cadmium sulfide (ZnCds) as a simulated agent. Early results clearly showed that one aircraft flying along the coast while spraying its agent could contaminate a target over 100 miles away, over an area of 10,000 square miles. This method of biological warfare attack and the test program to study it was known as the Large Area Coverage (LAC) concept.

In the early 1960s, Porton Down was asked to expand the scope of their tests to determine if using a live bacteria instead of ZnCds would significantly alter the results. Scientists from Microbiological Research Establishment at Porton Down selected South Dorset as the site for this next phase of testing, with Bacillus subtilis (also known as Bacillus globigii or BG) selected as the test agent.

This bacteria was sprayed across South Dorset without the knowledge or consent of the inhabitants.

Meanwhile, the British government's website gov.uk has this to say on its Porton Down facility:

During the cold war period between 1953 and 1976, a number of aerial release trials were carried out to help the government understand how a biological attack might spread across the UK. Given the international situation at the time these trials were conducted in secret. The information obtained from these trials has been and still is vital to the defence of the UK from this type of attack. Two separate and independent reviews of the trials have both concluded that the trials did not have any adverse health effects on the UK population.

Today, any MoD biological experiments undertaken in a military context involving humans are covered by the policies of the Ministry of Defence Research Ethics Committee (MODREC).

Blue Streak Missile

The Blue Streak missile also existed, though never amounted to a practical strike option, and was cancelled before becoming fully operational.
Online encyclopaedia Wikipedia has this to say…

The de Havilland Propellers Blue Streak was a British intermediate range ballistic missile (IRBM), and later the first stage of the Europa satellite launch vehicle. Blue Streak was cancelled without entering full production.

The project was intended to maintain an independent British nuclear deterrent, replacing the V bomber fleet which would become obsolete by 1965. The operational requirement for the missile was issued in 1955 and the design was complete by 1957. During development, it became clear that the missile system was too expensive and too vulnerable to a surprise attack. The missile project was cancelled in 1960, with US-led Skybolt the preferred replacement.

Partly to avoid political embarrassment from the cancellation, the UK government proposed that the rocket be used as the first stage of a civilian satellite launcher called Black Prince. As the cost was thought to be too great for the UK alone, international collaboration was sought. This led to the formation of the European Launcher Development Organisation (ELDO), with Blue Streak used as the first stage of a carrier rocket named Europa.

Europa was tested at Woomera Test Range, Australia and later at Kourou in French Guiana. Following launch failures, the ELDO project was cancelled in 1972 and Blue Streak with it.

Section VII

Section VII was a top-secret British resistance movement created by the Security Intelligence Service during the Second World War in the event that the Nazis successfully invaded and occupied Britain.

Unusually it was MI6 rather than MI5 who initiated it, since MI6 had no real jurisdiction on British soil.

The movement recruited many young people – teenagers too young for military service – and trained them in such things as how to derail trains, how to create incendiary devices, how to sabotage factories (or even blow them up), sniping, and how to garrotte enemy occupiers.

All participants were required to sign the Official Secrets Act and were cautioned never to disclose anything about their training. Very few of them ever spoke of their experiences, and, as we know, their training was never required to be put into effect.

The Village

Yes it really does exist, though as a hotel rather than a retirement home for ex-intelligence personnel. It is called Portmeirion (**https://portmeirion.wales/**) and was used as a key location in 1966-1967 for the shooting of the 17-episode *The Prisoner* television series starring Patrick McGoohan as Number Six.

The grounds are open for day visitors also and it is well worth a visit.

If you have enjoyed reading *Unity*, you can look forward to my next novel, currently in progress. Called *The Liscannor Intercept*, it is set in 1970 and takes the Irish Troubles as its backdrop. It is a sequel to *Unity*.

Anastasia Walker and Rupert Symes are alerted to a consignment of guns, bombs, missiles and explosives making its way to Northern Ireland by sea. The IRA is desperate to receive it, but the ship carrying the menacing freight gets into mechanical difficulties off the coast of County Clare.

Agents Trainor and D'Amelio are dispatched to Ireland's West Coast where they're to rendezvous with a team of SAS soldiers. Their mission is two-fold: to intercept the IRA's attempt to reach the stricken boat, and to prevent the deadly weapons from ever reaching shore.

But not everyone in the little village of Liscannor can be trusted. Who are IRA sympathisers, and who are not? How can Trainor and D'Amelio stop the ruthless IRA faction? When D'Amelio is captured and tortured, their mission seems doomed…

And finally…

Please consider supporting the author via his 'GoFundMe' page: **https://gofund.me/d01cceac**

As stated at the start of this book, *Unity* is a work of fan fiction, and the author cannot make any profit from sales. Therefore, any and all donations would be welcome to both support the author and help complete and publish the *Unity* sequel, *The Liscannor Intercept*.

Visit the Unity website: **www.unitystory.com**

Printed in Great Britain
by Amazon

34566427R00185